Reading U

JO PLATT

Reading Upside Down

CANELO

First published in the United Kingdom in 2013 by Jo Platt

This edition published in the United Kingdom in 2020 by

Canelo Digital Publishing Limited
Third Floor, 20 Mortimer Street
London W1T 3JW
United Kingdom

A CIP catalogue record for this book is available from the British Library.

Print ISBN 978 1 78863 736 7
Ebook ISBN 978 1 911420 58 3

Look for more great books at www.canelo.co

Printed and bound in Great Britain by Clays Ltd, Elcograf S.p.A.

For my highly excitable friends in The Short Book Group.

And, of course, for the extremely calm neighbour I married.

Prologue

'Shall we go in?' His expression was unexpectedly solemn and, just for a moment, it occurred to me that he may be presenting me with an option.

I shook off the thought and squeezed his arm. 'I think we should, Dad. I'm rather integral to the plot, you know.'

The doors opened and I heard the collective rustle and creak of a hundred people turning in their seats. My attention was drawn immediately to a dark-haired, deathly pale young woman, in a rear pew, as she gasped and pressed a hand to her ridiculously large, ridiculously red, lips.

'Why isn't she smiling?' I thought. 'She's got the mouth for it.'

Chapter 1

'Hello-oh.' Celia always gave the greeting a sing-song air with the addition of an extra syllable.

'Hi, it's me,' I said, flatly, whilst mentally observing that my all-too-obvious misery was probably a plus point. After all, genuinely suicidal people were always outwardly positive to the last, weren't they? *It's always the ones you least expect*, and all that. I had a sudden mental image of myself leaping from the top of a multi-story car park, waving cheerily with both hands and shouting, 'I'm fine! Honestly, I am!' before landing untidily on the tarmac below.

'Ros!' My sister remained determinedly upbeat. 'This is a nice surprise. You're calling late. Been out? How's the book trade? Anything exciting happening in St Albans?'

'The guinea pig is dead.'

'What, *your* guinea pig? The one who came with the house? Mr Edmund?'

'Mr Edward,' I corrected.

'Oh dear, no.' She said this almost to herself and I detected a slight note of panic in her voice. I felt a rush of guilt.

'Oh, it's OK. I'm fine,' I said, somewhat unconvincingly.

'I'm so sorry, Ros,' said Celia, 'but he must have been getting on a bit. How old was he? Three or four? Doesn't that make him a geriatric? And he had such a lovely life with you, didn't he, bless him. I mean, what would have happened if you hadn't taken him on? Weren't they going to put him down?' She paused for a moment. 'Look, I know it's dreadful but you mustn't get too distressed about it. Do remember all the positives in your life right now: your lovely home, your great job, your friends at work, all the people who love you so very much… Ros?' I stared out of the bay window, forgetting the need to respond. 'Ros? Are you still there?'

'Yes, I am.'

'I'm just saying that you have got a lot of things going right for you at the moment and that guinea pig was one lucky rodent. Who knows what may have become of him if it hadn't been for you? He really landed on all four feet. Very lucky indeed. You should have called him Mr Lucky, really!' She laughed lightly.

'My neighbour ran over him with his lawn-mower.'

'What?'

'My neighbour,' I spoke slowly and deliberately, as if addressing a toddler, 'ran over him,' I paused and took a deep breath, 'with his Flymo,' another breath, 'and then he buried the bits and came round here this evening with a bunch of flowers and an apology.'

'How terrible.' Her voice shook slightly and I wondered whether she wanted to laugh, in spite of herself. I would have laughed myself, except that I knew it would have the potential to become maniacal, before terminating in the kind of abandoned weeping which was, thank goodness, increasingly infrequent these days and usually kept at bay until bedtime. I put my hand over the receiver to prevent Celia from hearing my shortened breaths, the prelude to tears.

'Actually, you know, I wonder if I could talk to you later, Ce,' I said after a moment. 'I have just remembered that I have to—'

'That's fine.' She rescued me from the unformed lie with an interruption. 'I've got to run myself, actually,' she said briskly, feigning ignorance of the distress at the other end of the line. 'But I will need to talk to you tomorrow about what we're going to do for Dad's birthday,' she continued, attempting to give me an alternative point of focus whilst, at the same time, preparing the ground for checking-up on me the next day. 'You'll arrange the cake, won't you? You know how hopeless I am at that sort of thing.' Now she was trying to make me feel needed, capable and superior. 'I'll call you tomorrow, Ros. It'll be quite early – hope you don't mind – but I'll be out with Ben at football, in a muddy ditch with no mobile reception, for most of the day.' This final statement was, I knew, code for: *I shall call you before dawn and, if you don't pick up, I will contact our parents and they will be banging down your front door by 7.30am.*

The latter had actually happened, one Sunday morning just a few months earlier, when I had decided to stay over at a friend's house after a dinner party and had forgotten both my mobile phone and, more crucially, a promise to call my mother. Fortunately, upon being unable to gain entry to my home, Mum had made a few phone calls, and she and Dad had tracked me down before embarking upon 'Stage 2' of my father's master plan. This, as he proudly explained to me later that day, had been 'to jemmy open

4

the kitchen window with my new jemmy. You know, the one I now keep in the car, just in case.'

My mother had at least had the decency to roll her eyes at this point and add, 'You know your father, Ros. And he was desperate to use his new jemmy.'

'Ros?' Celia was sounding anxious again. 'Ros? I keep losing you.'

'No, sorry, I can hear you.'

'Great. So we'll speak first thing then?'

'Yes. And I'm fine, Ce. Really. It's just a bit, you know...' I coughed to hide my inability to finish the sentence.

'I know you're fine. It's a nasty thing to happen to anyone. I'd be really upset if someone... Well, anyway, lots of love.' She was sing-song again and I recognised it as her way of keeping everything light. She didn't want me to feel that I was at all burdensome to her, even though I knew I absolutely must be at times – frequently, in fact.

'Me too.' I said and hung up.

I went into the kitchen and poured myself another glass of Cava, feeling dismayed at my own selfishness. Why on earth had I told Celia about Mr Edward? I had spoiled her evening and marred her enjoyment of whatever she had planned for the weekend ahead – plans she didn't want to talk about, in case she unintentionally made her hapless and hopeless, younger sister feel worse. And I had been so rude to my poor, apologetic, guinea pig-slaying neighbour. Clearly, I had some apologising of my own to do.

Chapter 2

The event which had so impaired my ability to manage my feelings of loss and abandonment over Mr Edward's death, involved a rodent of a less appealing kind and had occurred eighteen months and three days previously. It had been a day, as they say, to remember: perfect setting, perfect dress, perfect flowers, one hundred and eight guests – and one, total and utter, rat.

I still had the album, a rather morbid keepsake, the existence of which I kept secret, lest friends and family should see it as justification for calling in two healthcare professionals and having me sectioned. It contained just four photographs, which I had selected from the twenty or so the official photographer had taken that day.

The first featured my father and me, sitting together on a wrought iron bench, in my parents' garden. He had his arm around my shoulders and we were smiling broadly at each other. It was taken approximately ten minutes before we stepped into the waiting, open-topped vintage car – I had a shot of that too.

The third photograph in the somewhat masochistic collection, was unposed and captured bride and brides-maids standing together outside the church. Antonia had just informed us that she had peed a little on her dress in her haste to get out of the loo and we were all laughing helplessly. It was my favourite picture of the four, as well as my greatest torment, constituting, as it did, my most up-to-date piece of hard evidence that I had once been a contented, perhaps even a highly contented, person. I studied it often, trying, but invariably failing, to recapture the feeling, experiencing instead a mixture of pity and contempt for the eternally giggling, foolishly optimistic, three inch high photographic version of myself.

The final picture of the four I kept merely as a record of the moment *before* the moment of derailment. It was a poorly-centred back-shot of my father and myself, taken as the large, wooden internal doors of the church were opened and we prepared to walk down the aisle. What we didn't know, of course, was that on the other side of those doors, a heavily perspiring best man was waiting to inform us that, just moments earlier, The Rat had fled the building, it was presumed via the vestry window, and was now nowhere to be found.

–

I remember nothing of the rest of that day and little of the following weeks, which were spent at my parents' home in Hertfordshire. The days merged into an homogeneous, unfocused expanse. Twice-weekly sessions with a therapist, Tina Sharpe, did little to help the situation. She was blonde, beautiful and successful, with a three-storey home, two golden-haired children and a gorgeous husband. She spoke in soft, supposedly calming, tones about taking things slowly and letting the fog lift, whilst her family portraits screamed 'loser' at me from the walls. Eventually, a sense of time and reality reasserted itself, at which point I decided that London, and work, was preferable to Tina's in-your-face perfection and my parents' anxious concern. Thus, after two month's sick leave, skeletal in appearance, and still reliant upon anti-depressants to help me to get *onto* the commuter train each morning, rather than merely standing on the edge of the platform, weighing up the merits of throwing myself *under* it, I returned to work.

As soon as I was back at my desk, my boss, Alan Bullen, recognising my 'mental turmoil and emotional fragility', as he expressed it in his return-to-work pep talk, vowed to do everything he could to ease me back into things gently and to keep things as low-pressure as possible. He seemed to feel some degree of personal responsibility for both my condition and my rehabilitation. I wasn't sure whether he saw himself as some sort of father figure, despite being just ten years my senior, but, more than once, he expressed regret that he hadn't been able to prevent 'The Tragedy', as he called it.

We had worked together for three years and, although he and his wife, Anne, had dined with us on a number of occasions, I had never considered him to be a close friend. In truth, I had occasionally found Alan a little irritating, prone, as he was, to adopting a rather more personal and emotional approach to staff matters than I thought helpful. Following The Tragedy, however, I began to see value in his more paternal, or even maternal, way of dealing with people problems and, through my depressive haze, I was quietly, internally, unnoticeably, grateful to him. At the same time, I realised that, no matter how much pressure and responsibility he took from me, the real problem was being left unaddressed. Pressure, and being able to cope with pressure, were not the issue; caring was the

8

issue – and I, quite literally, could not care less – about anything. Whereas *before*, I was devastated at a forgotten email, a late start or a misspelt name, *afterwards* I struggled to remember why any of those things mattered at all.

The extent of the problem was perfectly, and, as it turned out, terminally, illustrated during a meeting, to which I had arrived late, with James Gaville, our somewhat charmless Chairman and CEO. The purpose of the meeting was to discuss the corporate insurance programme for the coming year and, although Alan was more than capable of representing our division all by himself, he had, as part of his '3Rs Initiative' (reintegrate, rehabilitate, rejuvenate Ros), asked me to attend also. The meeting was, I think, proceeding well when, in what I later recognised to be an uncharacteristic attempt at humour, Gaville teasingly commented that he found it curious that in some sections of a corporate brochure, for which I was ultimately responsible, he was listed as James T. Gaville, whilst, in others, he was listed as James Gaville – *no 'T', did I see?* He then expressed smiling dismay at this 'heinous lapse in continuity'.

I can recall little of the full exchange. Suffice to say that my side of it included letting Mr Gaville in on the fact that the vast majority of his employees believed that the 'T' actually stood for 'tosser' and so, if I were him, I would think that the more often it was omitted the better.

I wasn't actually fired, and Gaville was even gracious enough, albeit with a rather nervous look in his eye, to encourage me to stay. However, in the circumstances, I chose to accept the voluntary redundancy which Alan somehow wangled for me. I felt I had let him down horribly and this re-awakening of at least some sense of responsibility, only added to my misery. He was, of course, as I had latterly come to expect, understanding to the last and didn't seem to blame me in the least for the sorry sequence of events. Indeed, his parting words to me, as he popped me into a cab, following my farewell drinks, were, 'I'm so sorry Ros. Really. More than I can say.' And, as the cab departed and I turned to see him staring mournfully after me, I found myself wishing that I had recognised him for the kind, caring human being he was earlier in my career. And that, of course, just made me more miserable still.

Chapter 3

Although now unemployed and, I was pretty certain, unemployable, I was not, by any means, destitute. Thanks to a decent salary, and the deaths of grandparents and a maiden great-aunt some years earlier, I had a comfortable, two-bedroomed flat in Muswell Hill, which I had held onto, and rented out, during my period of co-habitation with The Rat. This accumulated rental income, coupled with savings, and an extremely generous redundancy payout, meant that I was under no immediate, or even medium-term, pressure to work at all.

And so began a period of determinedly *not* working. Just for good measure, I decided to throw 'not eating', 'not answering the phone' and 'barely washing' into the 'not doing' mix. After three weeks of 'Ros not', my parents, my sister and several long-suffering friends, instituted a calling-unexpectedly rota, which involved them turning up at my flat, unannounced, between the hours of 9am and 8pm and suggesting walks, cups of tea and shopping excursions. However, more often than not, the visits simply resulted in them cleaning the kitchen and bathroom and then sitting next to me, whilst I kept up to date with *This Morning*, *Loose Women* or *Eastenders*, depending upon the time of day. In the end, of course, it dawned upon me that if I was ever going to be able to watch television in peace again then, outwardly at least, I had to get my act together. I just wasn't sure how.

–

As it turned out, the 'how' came in the form of Tom Cline, a 6'3", pleasantly plump solicitor, and one of my oldest friends. I opened the front door at 7.15pm on the second Wednesday of the rota, to discover him leaning nonchalantly against the communal hall wall with a tired, and somewhat resigned, expression on his face.

'Oh my God. They've not got you in on this too?' I said.

''fraid so,' he sighed. 'So, do I get to come in, or what?'

I stood back and welcomed him in with a theatrical sweep of the arm. 'Can I get you a glass of wine or something?'

'What have you got?'

We went into the kitchen and I opened the fridge. I was aware that he was scanning the room, taking in the cluttered work surfaces and unwashed dishes. 'It's not the tidiest, I know.' I said.

'You're bloody right it's not,' he said sternly. 'And if you think I'm drinking that,' he gestured towards the bottles of both white and red wine lying in the fridge, above a variety of festering vegetables – uneaten gifts from the other poor souls manning the rota, 'you are sadly mistaken.'

I looked up at him, wondering if he was hoping for a riposte, a show of spirit. His turn to be mistaken.

'Fine,' I said, reaching in and taking out a bottle for myself.

'Stop,' he said in a concerned tone, placing a hand on my arm. 'I can't let you do that to yourself, Ros.' He exited into the hall before returning with his briefcase. Opening it up, he took out a bottle of Reisling, showing me the label with a proud smile, in the manner of a father presenting his firstborn for admiration. 'Ta da!' he grinned.

I returned the smile and then started to sob. Delaying only to pop his prized bottle in the freezer, Tom put his arms around me, enveloping me in an enormous hug, before leading me back down the hall, towards the living room.

Half an hour later, I had stopped blubbing and we were sitting together on the sofa, watching *Eastenders* on catch-up and drinking our first glass of wine.

'This can't go on, Ros,' he said.

'I've already realised that,' I sniffed.

'I mean, you look like shit and you're being a real pain in the arse to us all. Your family is worried sick and the rest of us are really missing out socially. I'm meant to be having dinner with Amy tonight, not sitting watching Phil Mitchell fall off the wagon. Again.' He looked me up and down. 'And, good God, Ros – you used to be quite fanciable. Now you look like the bag lady at Embankment who wears the big Hush Puppies.'

'Tea-cosy lady?'

He sipped his wine and turned back to the TV. 'She's the one.'

I looked down at my floral, mis-buttoned shirt and grey sweat pants and tried hard to care but really couldn't see what the big deal was. They were clean, apart from two small splashes of red wine and a little bit of something from yesterday's lunch. Besides, it wasn't as if I was about to hit the town. I glanced up at Tom's stern profile and considered attempting to lighten the mood by fetching the tea-cosy from the kitchen and putting it on my head. That would be funny, wouldn't it? But I wasn't sure and, on further reflection, thought it might actually make me cry again, and possibly Tom too, so gave it up as a bad idea.

'Ah yes, Amy the Cambridge-educated, Olympic fencer who goes like a train,' I said instead.

'Commonwealth fencer – never made the Olympics. Is Ian Beale still in Eastenders? Jesus.'

'Oh yeah, sorry… I forgot. Her high-flying medical career got in the way of stabbing people, didn't it?'

He looked surprised and turned to face me.

'Y'see,' he said, smiling. 'The charming you of old is still in there somewhere.' He picked up the remote, turned off the TV and put an arm around me. 'What happened was awful, Ros. Unequivocally awful. But you're barely thirty. Don't let this ruin a whole lifetime.' He squeezed my shoulder. 'We all hoped you were feeling better when you got back to work. But, you know, even after what happened there, you could be looking at this as a real opportunity to make a new start. You could—'

'Have you seen him?' I interrupted.

He sighed and sat back. 'You know I have.'

'But recently. Have you seen him recently?'

'I saw him last week. We met for a drink.'

'Oh.'

He offered no further information and I tried to leave it at that but, after a brief, half-hearted, internal struggle, I asked, 'Has he told you why yet?'

14

He rolled his eyes. 'No, he hasn't,' he said. 'And I've stopped asking,' he added, clearly irritated. 'Oh God, please don't cry again, Ros, otherwise I'll be reaching for the bloody anti-depressants myself.'

'I'm crying more because my medication has been cut,' I wailed, pressing my hands hard against my eyes.

'What fantastic timing!' he exclaimed angrily. 'Jesus, who *is* your GP? Has anybody actually seen any of his qualifications? He's probably one of those bloody fakers you read about in the papers, with a GCSE in metal work and a 50m swimming certificate.'

There now descended an unhappy silence, during which I dabbed at my eyes with some tired loo roll I had found in the pocket of my sweat pants and Tom rubbed the back of his neck, which I knew to be an indication of extreme discomfort. When he finally spoke, his tone was gentle again. 'I'm sorry, Ros. But it would just be nice to have you back, you know. From wherever it is you've gone.'

'I barely remember me,' I sobbed quietly, leaning against him and blowing my nose. 'I try, sometimes, to think how other Ros would have dealt with a situation, or what she would have said, but I just can't remember. Besides, when I think of what she did, of what happened to her, how can I do anything but despise her? How could she have been so stupid?' It was a genuine enquiry and I looked at Tom for an answer.

'You weren't stupid. Nobody saw it coming. Everyone thought you were the perfect couple...' He ground to an uncertain halt and topped up our glasses before continuing. 'Look,' he smiled, 'I don't know whether it makes things better or worse telling you this but he says he still loves you. Very much. He's devastated at the effect all this has had on you.'

'I know.' I laughed bitterly. 'He told Celia the same thing.'

'Ros,' Tom put a hand on my cheek and gently turned my face towards him, 'you know that I am one of the most cynical people going. But I do believe him. If there was another woman involved, I would have heard about it and I would have told you because, according to Amy, I have no tact, subtlety or ability to judge a situation. But there isn't anyone else and he hasn't told anyone why he legged it that day; just that he had to.'

'Oh for God's sake,' I said angrily.

'Maybe he's having some sort of drawn-out nervous breakdown,' he offered.

'Business is good from what I hear.'

'People crumble in different ways, you know, Ros. Not everyone who has mental health issues ends up bankrupt and in the nuthouse.'

'Don't they?'

'Oh for fuck's sake, I don't know,' he groaned, rubbing his forehead. 'I'm just trying to stop you blubbing all over me again. This shirt cost a bloody fortune and it's now got your snot all over it.' He pointed to a large stain on his right sleeve.

I smiled.

'There,' he said, 'and I barely heard the creak of facial muscles. Now,' he continued, reaching down and opening his briefcase, 'I have a business proposition for you.'

'Are you serious?' I said.

'Absolutely.' He took out a bundle of papers and clicked shut his case. 'Are you ready?'

'Do I look ready?'

He eyed me uncertainly. 'I tell you what,' he said after a brief pause, 'you deal with whatever that is dangling from your left nostril and we'll just crack on with it anyway.'

Chapter 4

Within just a few months of signing up to the deal proposed by Tom, my day to day life had changed considerably. I had re-let the flat in N10 and was myself renting a two-bedroom, one box room, slightly dilapidated, semi-detached house in St Albans, with a 250ft part-wilderness of a garden; home to at least one fox, a tumbledown shed and a guinea pig, Mr Edward. The latter had come with the house, as his previous owners were unable to take him abroad with them, and, although I never would have thought of buying a pet, I felt real affection for him and would spend more afternoons than necessary cleaning out his new hutch and run and then sitting with him on my lap, either in the kitchen, or on what approximated to a lawn, feeling not exactly happy, but far from miserable.

Tom's business proposition had consisted of an investment in his friend, and former colleague, Andrew O'Farrell's second-hand and antiquarian bookshop, *Chapters*, in St Albans. The business had taken off, or at least broken into a gentle jog, and Andrew was looking for a small investor to provide the cash he needed to comfortably acquire and re-fit larger premises. I fitted the bill, and, in addition to injecting capital, I was appointed to work three half-days and two full days each week 'co-managing' the shop. I represented not so much a sleeping partner then, as a semi-conscious one and during the first few weeks of my employment, when I crashed the till on a daily basis; failed to remember that the customer was always right; misplaced keys and, what is worse, failed to show the appropriate level of concern over any of these incidents, I was pretty sure that Andrew would have willingly paid me more than my weekly wage just to go away. But the agreement was very clear: I came with the cash.

Celia's husband, David, had reviewed the contract on my behalf and had also kept me abreast of my mother's repeated attempts to influence him as to inclusions and amendments which, he said, had more of an eye on my emotional well-being than on raking in the millions. I was not at all surprised by this and had no doubt whatsoever that if she could have inserted a clause to the effect that: '*The party of the first part will, moreover, wash her entire body, brush her hair and teeth and wear co-ordinating attire at all times*', she would have.

Gone therefore were the daily train journeys into the City, the contracts, the business lunches and the conferences. Gone also were the after-work drinks in dark pubs, heaving clubs and subterranean wine bars; all replaced by a stroll, or bike ride, into the centre of St Albans; shelves of aged books; chicken salad sandwiches, munched behind a cash register; cups of tea; and light, inconsequential conversations with my three new co-workers: Andrew, George and Joan.

For a short while, I continued, from time to time, to visit my old London haunts with ex-colleagues but on each occasion, with the exception of my one-to-one drinks with Alan, I was uncomfortably aware that we all faced the dilemma of whether or not to refer to The

Rat. He was the metaphorical elephant in the room and the effort of ignoring him as a topic of conversation was embarrassingly large. Added to that, the evening journey into, and out of, the capital began to seem a chore and on the odd occasion one of my City friends was unable to make it, I always felt guiltily relieved. The obvious consequence of all this was that I gradually saw less and less of them, until I no longer felt a need, either polite or emotional, to keep in touch at all.

Chapter 5

It was whilst sitting in my living room, sipping a glass of Cava and indulging in a session of quiet self-assessment, one Friday evening approximately eighteen months after my almost-wedding day, that I was surprised by the realisation that my situation could be described as 'significantly improved'. I genuinely liked my co-workers; St Albans suited my mood; I no longer thought about The Rat on a daily basis; and, most significantly, my friends and family were clearly worrying less about me, which I took as objective confirmation of an upturn.

What I failed to appreciate at that moment was that the continuous improvement in my outlook and circumstances had not, as yet, been threatened by any real challenges in terms of personal, financial or professional pressure of any kind – my family and friends had seen to that. The unanticipated death of a pet, therefore, although comparatively minor by normal life-event standards, for me would represent the first real test of my ability to cope with fresh emotional distress. And as undeniably inconsequential as the incident initially appeared, it would not be overstating the case to say that the untimely demise of Mr Edward was to prove to be a moment equal in significance to the flight of The Rat, in terms of its effect upon me and the course of my own personal history.

I didn't know any of that, of course, as I stood up, refastened my bathrobe and went to answer the door that tranquil evening in late April. At that moment, as I peered out of the window to see who was calling, I felt only annoyance that my quiet night in, with a bottle of fizz and a DVD of *Sense and Sensibility*, was under threat from a beardy bloke with a bouquet. He didn't look like Interflora and, in any case, I was certain the flowers weren't for me. I walked into the hallway and towards the front door, tutting as I struggled to keep my towelling turban in place.

On opening the door, my thoughts turned immediately to fish fingers and Robinson Crusoe. My visitor was fair, over 6' tall, wearing a grubby, grey Aran sweater, which looked like it had been knitted on scaffolding poles, and sporting the kind of beard which is usually held in place by garden wire over the ears. However, as soon as he uttered a tentative, 'Hello… good evening', his voice revealed him to be, not the salty sea dog I had assumed, but actually, quite probably, Home Counties born and well-bred. The overall effect of appearance and speech was wholly contradictory and rather unnerving. I took half a step back and closed the door a little.

'Hello,' he repeated, attempting a smile so insincere and tremulous that it served only to alarm me further. 'Are you Mrs,' he glanced at my left hand, resting on the door frame, 'or Ms Shaw? Have I got the right number?'

'Can I help you?' I asked, reluctant to divulge any personal information.

'Er… well, yes. Hello. Again. My name is Daniel McAdam. I'm your neighbour. Well, not really your neighbour. My garden backs onto your garden. Sort of…' He gestured towards the back of my house, attempted another smile, gave it up, quite reasonably, as a bad job and ground to a halt.

'I see,' I said, although, of course, I didn't see at all, not yet.

'I live in Clarendon Road…?' he ventured. Was that a question?

'OK…' I paused and, despite my discomfort, managed to reflect that this was another contradiction. They were all sizeable, apparently well-maintained, houses in Clarendon Road. Mind you, perhaps one of them was a clinic, or, better still, a half-way house. Bet the other residents loved that. I smiled inwardly. 'OK, well, it's nice to meet you, Mr McAdam, but I'm just about to put the children to bed so…'

'You have children?' He looked grief-stricken. 'Sylvia said she didn't think you did.'

'Sylvia?'

'My next door neighbour. She knows your landlord.'

I began to lose patience. 'OK, well, no, Sylvia's right, actually, I don't have children. What I meant was that I have my niece and nephew staying with me tonight and I was just going to put them to bed. So…'

'God, yes, I'm sorry, it's just a bit difficult.' He bit his lower lip and I was distracted by the thought that the sensation must be similar to chewing on a toothbrush. The beard was truly dreadful – he had to be in some sort of alcohol rehabilitation programme. Or maybe he was just rich and odd. I recalled the apparent tramp, into whom I had stumbled, whilst on an evening out in London, several years earlier. It was only when I had stopped to apologise for my clumsiness, that I had recognised the man as a rather famous, award-winning actor. Perhaps my neighbour was similarly monied and eccentric.

I became aware that he was talking again '…and so, I asked if anyone owned a guinea pig, or a dwarf rabbit, and Sylvia said, yes, she thought you did.'

'Oh, my guinea pig!' I finally understood. 'Has he escaped again? He is so naughty. Did he wander into your garden? I'm so sorry. God only knows how he gets out. Have you cornered him? I'll just pop some jeans on and come round and help.'

He stood, unmoving, on the doorstep. It was hard to identify his exact emotion, as approximately sixty per cent of his face was covered in hair, but I thought I saw extreme sadness, tinged, perhaps, with a hint of fear, in the blue eyes visible between brows and beard.

I looked at the bouquet and then back at those agonised, trawler-man eyes. 'Is he OK?'

He shook his head.

'What happened?' I asked. And then, as he explained about the lump in the grass, the unstoppable swing of the Flymo and expressed his extreme and profound regret, I closed the door gently, but firmly, in his face, and on his flowers, and returned to my bottle of Cava, carefully supporting my towelling turban as I went.

Chapter 6

'So let me get this straight, dear,' said Joan, as we sipped mugs of tea and readied the shop for opening the following Monday morning. 'This retarded young gentleman—'

'Er, Joan,' interjected Andrew, pausing from putting the newly-acquired Hardys on a shelf and turning to look at her from the top of his step stool, 'I'm not sure that's a term with which people are entirely comfortable these days.' His face remained impassive but I detected mild irritation in his tone. He looked as if he might be about to say more, but then seemed to think better of it and instead returned his attention to the books.

'Of course.' Joan smiled benignly, appearing thoroughly untroubled by his admonition. 'You must forgive me, Andrew, I am of a different generation, and I do forget the need to use a more up-to-date turn of phrase sometimes, but you are quite right. I will begin again.' She cleared her throat deliberately and slowed her speech to half its usual speed. 'This *mental*,' she said with emphasis and a beaming nod in Andrew's direction, 'mowed Mr Edward to death and then brought you flowers by way of an apology. Is that what happened, my darling?'

I glanced at Andrew to see if he would rise to the bait but, other than for a slight sagging of his shoulders, he showed no response.

'That's right,' I said, 'and I was incredibly rude to him. But Joan, I'm not sure that he was actually...' I hesitated, my mind drawing a blank as to the politically correct term, 'er... simple,' I continued, more quietly, in an attempt to prevent Andrew from hearing. A loud sigh from his direction told me I had failed.

'Aah, you mustn't be so hard on yourself, Rosalind, my darling,' said Joan, reaching out and squeezing my free hand. 'Who knows! The fact that he is a simpleton may mean that he didn't even realise that you were being rude. When I was a child, we had an *idiot savant* living across the street and he—'

'Jesus Christ,' muttered Andrew, putting down the pile of Hardys, dismounting and going into the small kitchen area at the back of the shop,

'—and he,' continued Joan, seemingly unaware of his despairing exit, 'encountered terrible prejudice but remained blissfully ignorant of all the unpleasantness. Had a very happy life, I believe.' She looked into the middle distance. 'Yes... Michael Baines; drooled rather a lot but his pencil sketches were simply marvellous.'

'Were they? That's lovely but I'm not sure that my man is quite in the same category as Michael Baines,' I said, finishing my tea and following Andrew into the kitchen. 'He just looked a bit strange, and dressed rather oddly, as if he might suffer from... mild to moderate learning difficulties,' I concluded, smiling at Andrew, who was leaning against a cupboard, arms folded, eyes fixed on the ceiling, desperately searching, I assumed, for his happy place.

I thought, not for the first time, that the relationship between Andrew and Joan was a rather fascinating one. It seemed to me that, quite often, he would choose to be where Joan was not, taking himself upstairs, whenever, for example, she recounted an anecdote from her youth – which invariably involved herself, alcohol and outdoor nudity. From the moment she had greeted me on my first day, with a long embrace and the words: 'You poor darling, Rosalind. Men can be such shits, can't they, dear?' I realised that Joan was what is commonly termed 'a loose cannon', although she preferred the classification 'free spirit' and used this frequently with reference to herself. She was a sixty-two-year-old, unmarried, am-dram enthusiast, working flexible hours in the shop to supplement her pension and living alone, save for the 'obligatory mad bat's cat', as Andrew put it.

Personally, I had my suspicions that Joan wasn't quite the mad bat that Andrew took her for and actually derived considerable amusement from her ability to force him from a room, as if by telekinesis. But, however they felt about one another, it was clear that she loved her job and he couldn't deny that, from a business point of view, she was a real asset, being extremely popular with customers. More than one stopped by for a chat with her and left with a book or two, seemingly unconsciously purchased whilst under the influence of 'Joany'.

She now joined us in the kitchen, with her empty tea mug and a determination not to let the conversation drop.

'So dear,' she said, starting to wash her mug, 'What next?'

I looked across at her. 'What do you mean?'

'Well,' she placed the mug on the draining board and dried her hands, 'have you thought about how you might begin to comfort yourself over the loss of Mr Edward?'

'Er...' I glanced at Andrew, expecting to see him pulling out handfuls of hair but instead he was looking at me with something approaching interest. 'Er... well, I guess I could get another guinea pig... in time.' I paused, hoping that this would satisfy her. No such luck.

'I was thinking, my darling, that maybe it was time to move on from rodents. I was thinking more along the lines of—' She was interrupted by the sound of the shop door opening and the tinkling of the bell which hung over it. 'Ooh, customer!' she beamed and was gone. I sighed, feeling relieved, and looked at Andrew.

'Saved by the bell,' he said, with just a hint of a smile. 'Mind you,' he continued, turning and heading out of the kitchen, 'it's something to think about, isn't it?'

I was a little surprised by this comment but then, despite spending much of my week with him for over six months, I felt I hardly really knew Andrew at all. Outwardly, he was a serious, highly intelligent, utterly work-focused, quietly-spoken Irishman – and not, as I had acknowledged to myself very early on, at all unattractive – thanks to his green eyes, thick, dark hair and, of course, that accent. On first acquaintance, I immediately thought of at least two single girlfriends to whom I could introduce him; however, it didn't take long for me to realise that he was as firmly off the market as I was myself.

From Tom, I had learned that Andrew had moved from a small town in Galway, to London, almost seventeen years earlier, in order to attend university, and had decided to stay on in the UK after completing his studies. This brief, and rather dull, history was supplemented, and given a little colour, by the fourth member of the bookshop staff, Georgina, or George, as she preferred to be known. She told me that the real reason that Andrew had decided not to return to Ireland was that, towards the end of his degree course, he had fallen madly in love, and had remained in that blissful state for a good seven or eight years, until his partner died in tragic, but frustratingly vague, circumstances. The recounting of this woeful history had concluded with the fact that Andrew had not been in a serious relationship since. I had expressed surprise to George that she had been able to elicit this level of personal information from him but she explained it away with the comment that he was 'more communicative after a Guinness or two.'

Perhaps because I appeared too emotionally crippled by my own unfortunate, recent past to be interested in anyone else's, or perhaps because I had never bought him a Guinness, Andrew had confided nothing more personal to me than a deep love of James Joyce and Ted Hughes. In my experience, and company, a Guinness-less Andrew appeared disinterested, and was steadfastly unforthcoming, when shop-floor conversations turned towards anything more personal than pricing the Shakespeare, or relocating his precious first editions. I did admire him for almost always managing to disguise his frustration at finding himself working with three women so apparently unlikely to take either him, or his business, seriously. However, with the exception of myself, with whom he was lumbered whether he liked it or not, he had hand-picked his staff – so it was hard to feel too sorry for him when he occasionally appeared pained, as if the trivial nature of our conversations may be about to cause his intellectual ears to bleed.

–

When George turned up at the shop later that morning, Joan must have lost no time in updating her regarding Mr Edward's untimely demise. I returned from a four-minute excursion to put an advert, regarding the vacant hutch, in the local newsagents, to hear her concluding her précis with the phrase: 'drooled constantly but produced absolutely marvellous pencil drawings.' Fortunately, Andrew was nowhere to be seen.

'Oh, Ros,' said George, turning in her chair as I entered, 'Joan has just been telling me about poor Mr Edward. Gosh and poor you too. It must have been the most awful shock.' She looked at me with genuine concern and a sympathetic smile and it occurred to me, not for the first time, that she was what I might once have aspired to become.

George was a very attractive, perfectly attired and accessorised, mother to Lottie, aged six. Her husband, Mike, worked in the City and, even before I had seen her home, I knew from her account of his working day that she didn't need her 'little job' as she called it. She worked school hours, two days a week, and, when she wasn't looking after her child and opening her home to everyone else's, she jogged, played tennis, re-upholstered furniture, volunteered at school, frequented coffee shops and hosted and attended dinner parties. She was a former accountant and her gentle, frivolous chit-chat belied, but couldn't entirely hide, a sharp intellectual and emotional intelligence, which was revealed in her occasional references to more serious topics and in her sensitivity towards those around her. Yes, George had a lifestyle and grace which I coveted and, just occasionally, it felt painful to like her such a lot – but I couldn't help it.

'Well… I was a bit glum over the weekend,' I smiled, 'but I'm feeling much better about it now. Actually, you don't want the hutch do you George? Would Lottie like a pet?'

'She would absolutely love one,' she sighed, disentangling her multiple bracelets from a pale blue cashmere cardigan draped across her lap. 'But Mike would do his nut. He's heard too many tales about Naughty Nev to agree to a guinea pig or a rabbit… or anything really,' she concluded quietly, still smiling up at me.

'Naughty Nev?' I asked.

'Yes, he was a house rabbit. I got him just after I started my first proper job,' she sighed. 'Poor Neville. He was lovely but he could pooh for England and just would *not* do it in his litter tray – anywhere but, actually. Plus, he chomped through any electrical cable he could find. In fact,' her smile faded, 'it literally was the death of him. He chewed through the fridge cable.'

Joan shook her head. 'My goodness. What a lot of distressing pet stories today. But you know,' she continued, nudging George, 'I knew a bit of a naughty Neville too – my great uncle Neville. He was, well, I suppose these days you would have to call him a sex addict. He was forever licking his lips and rubbing his inner thighs.' She stood up to demonstrate. 'Like this. All the time. Even during mass.'

George spluttered as the tea she was drinking went down the wrong way and, as Joan continued her tale of family dysfunction, we failed to notice that Andrew had joined us.

'Hello, George,' he said. 'What are you doing here?'

She greeted him with a smile and held up the cardigan. 'Forgot this, on Friday,' she said, standing up. 'But, actually, I do have another reason for being here.' She delved into her Mulberry sack and took out three silver envelopes. 'These are for you,' she said, handing one to each of us. Joan was the first to open hers.

'Oh, how wonderful,' she gasped, placing a hand across her chest. 'A birthday party!'

'Gosh, so Mike is going to be forty,' I said, looking at my invitation, 'I don't think I would have guessed that.'

'No, he's wearing well, isn't he?' said George, reapplying some lip balm from her bag. 'Better than me at any rate and he's four years older.'

Andrew mumbled something, making us all turn and look at him. He coloured slightly and said, 'Sorry, I was just talking to myself – wondering if I am free that evening.'

'Well, if you should discover that you have a prior engagement, I jolly well hope you sort it out,' said George, walking over to him and punching him lightly on the arm. 'You've got months and months to rearrange things and I'm getting the Guinness in especially for you, so it would be very rude of you not to come. Joany and Ros will be there, won't you girls?' she said, turning back to us.

'With bells on,' said Joan.

I looked at Andrew and wondered if he shared my concern that this might prove to be the literal truth. 'Yes, thank you, George,' I said. 'I would love to come.'

'And…' said George with a wink, walking towards the door, 'the three of you can bring whomsoever you choose. So,' she added, exiting, 'dig out those little black books and get dialling.'

Joan headed back to the till and began to chatter about dresses, whilst Andrew and I remained where we were, both, I suspected, feeling similarly awkward.

'Well,' I sighed, 'other than digging up Mr Edward and setting-to with a tube of superglue, I'm not sure I have any immediate ideas about whom to bring as an escort.' Andrew responded only with a grim smile. 'So,' I asked, 'who are you going to take?'

'I could bring Sandra, I suppose,' he said.

'Gay Sandra?' I asked.

'Yes, she is gay,' he said, fixing me with a stare, 'but I have noticed, you know, that gay people can still enjoy parties, in spite of their disability.'

I started to deny any prejudice but, to my surprise, he suddenly laughed. 'I'm joking, Ros,' he said, heading back upstairs.

'OK,' I said, a little disconcerted by this sudden burst of jollity. 'Well, you know, if you've got any gay male friends who enjoy parties, give them my number. Hey, but no one who plucks their eyebrows more than I do, please,' I added loudly, as he disappeared from view.

Andrew's head re-appeared at the top of the staircase. 'Fortunately,' he said, 'I love a challenge.'

Chapter 7

It was 7pm by the time I turned the corner into Clarendon Road and began to attempt to determine which of the homes might back onto my own. The houses were too big, and the gardens too long, for me to have any chance of spotting my small semi and it took several minutes of walking up and down the middle section of the road before I felt confident enough to knock on a door.

The first house I chose had a sweeping gravel drive, large bay windows either side of the front door and mock tudor beams. As I drew nearer, I couldn't see any signs of it being a hostel or a clinic and a peek through one of the windows revealed it to be furnished in a style of which my mother would have approved: several pieces of apparently antique furniture; a brass standard lamp with cream shade; a large, ornate mirror, above the pale marble fireplace; and a variety of landscape paintings, in a mixture of wooden and gilt frames, on the walls. I wondered if perhaps Daniel McAdam lived with his parents. That would be more likely than my clinic hypothesis.

'Can I help you?' said a clipped, female voice behind me. The front door had opened without me noticing and I turned to find myself being addressed by a middle-aged woman with greying hair, which was cut into a bob almost as severe as her tone.

'Oh I'm sorry,' I said, blushing, 'I was just trying to see if there was anyone home and—'

'May I suggest that ringing the doorbell is a more effective method of determining that than peering into drawing rooms,' she snapped.

Her features settled into an expression of concrete disapproval and, realising that I had little hope of ingratiating myself, I checked my watch and decided to cut to the chase. 'Right, well, I'm in a bit of a hurry, I'm afraid.' She opened her mouth to say something further but I didn't pause for breath. 'Does Mr McAdam live here?'

'No,' she said, her eyes narrowing, 'he does not.' She was clearly desperate to know who I was, and why I needed to speak to Mr McAdam, whilst at the same time realising that it was not her place to ask. I smiled pleasantly, enjoying her anguish and making no attempt to fill the lengthening silence between us. When she could bear it no longer, she said, 'He lives next door. Number 21,' before shutting the door with considerably more force than was necessary.

I extended my thanks to the glossy, black surface of the door and then trudged back down the drive and through the wooden gates, before turning left into the adjacent drive, this one paved with small, neat, oblong grey bricks, laid in an attractive, geometric pattern.

The house which faced me was a variation on its neighbour; slightly smaller, and lacking the beams, but otherwise largely the same. This time, there was no need even to contemplate knocking as a woman, whom I guessed to be about my own age, emerged from the house, dragging behind her a small suitcase on wheels and carrying a key fob, which she now pointed in the direction of a silver Mini convertible which was sitting on the drive.

She looked up at me, shaking her shining blonde hair from the delicate features of her lightly-tanned face.

'Hi.' She flashed me a dazzling smile, whilst opening the boot of the Mini and placing the suitcase inside.

'Hello,' I replied, wishing that I had thought to floss before leaving the house, 'I'm looking for Daniel McAdam. Do I have the right address?'

'You do,' she said. 'But he has a client meeting over dinner and won't be home for a while. You know how these things drag on. Thank God it wasn't partners or I'd be stuck there myself.' She blinded me with another smile before continuing. 'Perhaps there's something I can help you with? But, er,' she glanced at her watch, 'it will have to be quick, I'm afraid, as I'm already running a little late.'

I wondered at any possible connection between this woman and Daniel McAdam. Had she just implied that he was holding down some sort of paid employment? And that she was his girlfriend? How could that be? I found myself rapidly reassessing my recollection of his appearance, whilst, at the same time, appraising hers. She was wearing a fitted white shirt, open at the neck, and slim black trousers, the latter perfectly presenting for admiration a bottom of such pertness as could be achieved, I reflected, only by means of at least three visits to the gym a week. Her ensemble was completed by a heavy, silver bangle and a pair of perfectly plain, perfectly black pumps, on perfectly petite feet. She oozed casual sophistication from head to toe.

I felt suddenly self-conscious regarding my own appearance and glanced down uncertainly at the grey cardigan, white t-shirt, jeans, at least a size too big, and ancient Jesus sandals, which were remarkably comfortable but which now, suddenly, made me feel like one of the ugly sisters about to engage Cinderella in conversation.

'I'm running a little late,' repeated Cinders, now with just a hint of tension in her voice.

'Oh, I'm sorry,' I said, whilst experiencing a rising sense of disquiet that my three-minute, doorstep assessment of Mr McAdam's role in society and general intelligence levels may not, perhaps, have been entirely accurate. 'I'll pop back another time. I just wanted a quick word with him. He came to see me on Friday evening and I'm afraid he didn't catch me at a good moment.'

She closed the boot and looked at me in puzzlement. 'He came to see you?' she asked, looking me up and down, her gaze lingering disconcertingly on my feet.

'Yes, he, er, well, I'm Ros. I live behind you and Mr McAdam.'

'Oh God, you're the hamster woman!' she exclaimed, with what seemed to be a mixture of relief and horror. 'Sorry, I thought you'd be a lot older.' I experienced momentary discomfort but refused to allow myself to analyse this statement. 'Yes, Daniel told me you were quite distraught,' she said, opening the door of the car, reaching inside and taking out a small, pink, make-up case. 'He was so upset, you know.' She took a slim, silver compact from the case and began applying powder to the tip of her nose and forehead, before setting-to with a lip liner. 'I hope,' she said, indistinctly, as she attempted to continue the conversation and line her lips at the same time, ''at oor not eer oo,' she put the lip pencil and compact back in the bag and zipped it shut, 'that you're not here to have another go at him.'

'Oh no, absolutely not,' I said, reddening and shaking my head. 'I actually came to apologise for over-reacting. I hope I didn't—' I was interrupted by a black Audi turning slowly into the drive and pulling-up alongside the Mini.

'He's early,' she said, before walking over to greet the new arrival.

The door of the Audi opened and out stepped son of Captain Birdseye, although today, the heavy-knit Aran and baggy cords had been replaced by a smart, dark grey suit, white shirt and fuchsia pink tie. He was as immaculately attired as Cinderella and, in spite of the beard, I began to feel like the Buttons of the piece.

'You're early, darling,' she said, kissing him lightly on what I supposed would have been his cheek, under normal circumstances.

'Craig cancelled,' he said, closing the car door and encircling her waist with an arm, 'so I thought I'd come home and catch you before the off.'

'Oh, how lovely but I am just leaving,' she said. 'Still, at least we'll get a goodbye smooch, eh?' She laughed lightly and moved onto her tip-toes. Quickly deciding that I didn't wish to witness that particular event, I mumbled something about returning another time and attempted an inconspicuous exit.

I failed.

'Who's that?' I heard him ask, as I hurried towards the gate. I speeded up even more, losing a Jesus sandal in the process. I turned to retrieve it but he got there first.

'Here you go – oh it's you, Ms Shaw,' he said, handing me the giant piece of footwear with a smile.

'Ros, please,' I said, relieving him of the sandal. 'God, these things are so old – they've got bigger with time and won't stay on any more. I only wear them for gardening, really.'

'Oh right, well, I wear ugly things for gardening too,' he said, 'as you witnessed on Friday evening.'

I looked at my sandals. 'Ugly' seemed a bit harsh.

The sound of an engine starting interrupted the conversation. Cinderella drove slowly towards us, leaning out of the window as she did so. 'I'm sorry, Daniel, I've got to go. Miranda was expecting me at around eight and I'm already going to be late.'

He crouched down and kissed her. 'Have fun,' he smiled. 'See you Wednesday.'

'Yes. I'll pop home first to pick up some fresh clothes and then I should be with you around nine-ish.'

'Great.' He tapped the top of the car and she pulled out of the drive. I felt a desperate urge to get this over with and be gone.

'Look,' I said, 'I—'

'How about a cup of tea?' He walked back to his car and retrieved a briefcase from the back seat. I hesitated. 'Or are your niece and nephew still with you?' he asked, closing the car door and returning to where I stood.

I looked up at him, uncertain whether this was sincerity or sarcasm, and it occurred to me how rapidly the dynamics of the situation had changed. I had arrived with the intention of apologising for my incivility to a possibly alcoholic, possibly educationally sub-normal, neighbour and now, instead, I found myself being invited in for a pity-cuppa by a confident, well-dressed man who classed my footwear as 'ugly' and, almost certainly, had me

39

down as a lonely fantasist, who invented overnight guests because her only real friend in the world was a guinea pig.

'No,' I said, opting for a minimal information approach to the crisis.

'Tea then?' he looked at me questioningly, before adding, 'It was such a terrible thing, a little hospitality is the least I can do. Oh hi, Sylvia!' he said, raising a hand and looking over my shoulder.

I turned my head to see the neighbour whom I had encountered earlier. She was standing at the entrance to the drive with two small Daschunds, straining at the end of a double lead.

'Good evening, Daniel,' she said, without a smile. 'I see that the young woman eventually tracked you down.'

'Yes, she did. Thank you, Sylvia. Did you knock on the wrong door, Ros?' he asked, looking at me. I opened my mouth to reply but she got there first.

'I can assure you, she didn't knock *at all*, Daniel. I discovered her leering through my drawing room window,' she said crossly.

'You know, tea sounds great,' I said quietly.

'OK,' he smiled. 'Bye, Sylvia. And thanks for pointing my friend in the right direction.'

'My pleasure,' she lied, 'but if you could acquaint her with doorbells and knockers in the near future, it would be much appreciated.'

'Sorry about that,' I muttered, as we walked towards the house.

He laughed. 'It's OK. Her bark is much worse than her bite,' he said. 'She's just a bit fixated on burglary statistics. Anyway, come on in and I'll put the kettle on.'

I followed him through a black and white tiled hallway into a large, open-plan kitchen and living area, furnished in impeccable neutrals. The matte, grey tiled floor, was softened in the seating area by a large multi-coloured rug and the pale walls were intermittently interrupted by explosive oils and simple charcoals. French windows looked out onto the large garden, of which I had occasionally sought a glimpse through the tangle of untamed bushes and trees at the end of my lawn, and the tall hedge which surrounded his. There was nothing tangled or untamed about this green space – a large lawn, edged with neat borders and then a further section beyond, which a clipped hedge partially hid from view.

'Great garden,' I said.

'I love it,' he replied, edging past me and opening the doors. 'We could sit outside – it's not too cold, is it? Do you want tea?' he asked, returning to the kitchen. 'Or there's coffee or...' he peered into the fridge, '...fruit juice, lemonade, wine, beer...'

'A lemonade would be great, thanks,' I said.

'OK.' He stood up with a bottle and took two glasses from a cupboard on the wall.

'Look,' I said, awkwardly, deciding to make a second attempt at an apology, 'I came here this evening just to—' He handed me a glass of lemonade and gestured towards a wrought iron table and chairs outside on the patio.

'Thank you.' I said, walking out and sitting down. He pulled up a chair next to me. 'Right, so, I came here just to say sorry, really,' I continued, speeding up for fear of further interruption. 'You know, for being so rude on Friday evening, when all you were trying to do was apologise. And, as you may have guessed, I don't have a nephew and niece. Well, I do have a nephew, two, in fact, but neither of them were staying. I told you that I had guests because I just wanted to be left alone and I should apologise for that too. Anyway,' I continued, in the manner of a learner driver unable to locate the brake pedal, 'I was rude last week and now, what with your neighbour, these sandals and those fictitious relatives, I have compounded the situation. But, you know, I just wanted to clear it all up.'

I looked up from my glass, at which I had been staring fixedly. He was leaning forward with his elbows on the table, a hand pressed, as if in thought, against his mouth. I knew, without a doubt, that he was trying not to laugh. 'OK, well, thanks,' he said eventually. 'But you mustn't worry. I can assure you I have done things much worse than wearing ugly shoes.' Why did he have to keep calling them ugly? 'Oh and inventing a niece, Ros.'

His gentle use of my Christian name completed my growing sense of subjugation. I tried to smile, whilst reflecting, again, that this really hadn't gone at all according to plan. Any early sense of superiority had now completely evaporated and I was playing the role of needy, eccentric, badly-dressed misfit to perfection. I toyed with the idea of assuring him that I had perfect insight into the situation but decided that I had already said far too much. Instead, I comforted myself with the knowledge that I would never have to see, or speak to, him again. In a year's time, this encounter would be nothing more than an amusing dinner party anecdote.

'Thank you for your understanding,' I said, with as much dignity as I could muster. I desperately wanted to leave but thought any attempt to do so might prompt more kindly reassurances, with which I would be unable to cope. Instead, I opted for a change of tone and subject. 'So,' I asked lightly, 'how long have you lived in St Albans?'

'Three years,' he replied. 'I'm being sponsored, by the way.'

'You're being sponsored to live in St Albans?'

'No,' he laughed. 'I'm being sponsored,' he rubbed his chin, 'not to shave. It's for charity.'

'Oh, right, and you would like me to sponsor you?' I asked, uncertainly.

'No, no. It's just that I usually tell people about it as soon as I meet them, in case they think I'm a bit odd. Unfortunately, it wasn't really an appropriate topic of conversation last time I met you.' He twisted the end of his beard. 'I bet you've been wondering what on earth it's all about.'

'Oh no, not at all,' I said. 'I hadn't even really noticed you had a beard, to be honest.'

'Really?' he said, raising an eyebrow. 'Only you keep looking at my chin in an appalled manner.'

I began a denial and then slumped back in my chair and put a hand to my forehead, feeling suddenly exhausted. 'Oh God, do I?'

'Yes,' he smiled, 'you do.'

I looked at him grinning, pityingly, down at me and experienced sudden irritation that his long-term decision not to shave should have contributed to my current, extreme social discomfort. It had been his ridiculous beard, I reflected, which had caused me to so badly misjudge my whole approach to the situation. I sat up and decided to focus on the 'never again' aspect of this encounter.

'Well, you know, *Daniel*, maybe I do keep fixating on your chin,' I said, staring at my now empty glass, whilst pushing back my chair and preparing for an exit, stage left. 'But it's hardly surprising. I mean, it's not a little 'tache or a touch of stubble, is it?' I forced a tense smile. 'To tell the truth, I actually keep expecting you to whip out an accordion and start telling me all about the catch of the day. Anyway,' I continued, determined not to allow him an opportunity to comment on my obvious annoyance, 'thank you for the lemonade but I really should be making a move now.' He made no response and, when I looked up, I was horrified to see him leaning forward, as if in pain. 'Oh my goodness, are you—' I began but was interrupted by his laughter, which suddenly switched from the silent, to the highly audible, variety.

'Catch of the day...' he laughed. He tried several times to say something more but was unable to speak and, in the end, his amusement proved contagious and I unexpectedly found myself laughing along.

We continued to enjoy the joke for several moments before there followed a pause, during which I regretted my uncharitable attitude towards his charitable hair-growth and mused that he looked almost attractive when he smiled.

Eventually, I broke the silence. 'Not that I'm in a posi-tion to mock anyone's appearance, of course.' I swung my feet out from under the table. 'These are rather pitiful, aren't they?' I said, inspecting the huge, sweat-stained Jesus sandals, which I felt sure even Christ himself would have denied.

'Ah, but I have this 24/7,' he said, stroking his beard. 'At least you only wear those for gardening.'

I shook my head. 'Wore them to work today,' I said, surprised at my own candour.

'Oh, I see,' he said, clearly wanting to laugh again but now, apparently, fearful of offending.

'But they are really, *really* comfortable.'

'Oh well then… so long as they're comfortable. And they look like one size fits all, which is handy,' he said.

'Footsy,' I corrected.

'Yes, footsy,' he said, smiling.

I smiled back and there was another pause. 'I should be going,' I said, after a moment.

He politely offered me some more lemonade, which I, politely, declined, despite a certain conviction that I would enjoy the second glass considerably more than the first. As it was, he made no attempt to convince me to change my mind. 'Yes, well, I do have phone calls to make,' he said, sighing and standing up. 'But thanks for coming round Ros, and making me feel better about, you know, the incident.' I stood up and followed him to the front door. 'Really nice to meet you. Again,' he said, holding out a hand.

'Yes.' I shook his hand and, as he opened the door for me, we exchanged a last, brief nod and smile of farewell, before I stepped outside and walked away, hearing the front door click shut behind me.

I turned onto Clarendon Road and headed for home, smiling down at my comfortable footwear and resolving to go shoe-shopping at the earliest opportunity.

Chapter 8

I placed the large, white cardboard box containing the cake onto the passenger seat beside me, prodded it a little, in an attempt to simulate sudden braking, and, once I was satisfied that it had at least a fifty-fifty chance of reaching its destination intact, I started the engine and began the thirty minute drive to my parents' home.

My father was turning seventy and, true to type, he 'didn't want a fuss'. 'He would just love you, Celia, David and the boys to come for the weekend,' my mother had said, 'if you're free. But don't change any plans you may already have made.' I had raised my eyes at this. My father was selfless, almost to the point of irritation – but not quite. Besides, his request for a small, intimate family gathering came as a huge relief to me. I had dreaded the thought of aunts, uncles and cousins, whom I hadn't seen since the abortive wedding, turning up and offering me belated condolences.

I turned into the close at about midday and experienced the usual sense of increased comfort and security I always felt as soon as the house came into view. The exterior had changed little in the thirteen years since I had left to go to university in London; the door had changed colour a couple of times and the ornamental cherry tree at the top of the drive had gained in height but, other than

46

that, it was the same house and garden I had come home to from the age of ten.

By the time I pulled up outside, my parents were standing on the drive to greet me and Celia was waving madly from the living room window. Confronted by such affection, I swallowed hard and clenched my fists, determined not to cry.

'Hello, little one,' said my father, walking over and hugging me. 'It's so lovely to see you and,' he said, holding me at arms' length and looking me up and down, 'don't you look beautiful. You look as if you've started to take a bit of care of yourself again.'

'Oh for goodness sake, Ted,' said Mum, taking me from him as if I were a baton in a relay race and hugging me in turn. 'What a thing to say.' She kissed my cheek. 'Hello darling. Good journey?'

'I'm just saying she looks lovely,' said Dad, in a hurt tone. 'She went through a period of not washing much and not changing her clothes and now she's looking lovely again. That's all I'm saying.'

'It's fine, Dad,' I said. 'I took it as a compliment. Like the new shoes?' I turned my foot to better display the neat, black pumps, purchased a few weeks earlier.

'Lovely. Your mother will kill me later, you know,' he grinned.

'Why wait 'til later?' she said, miming clubbing him.

'Anyway,' I said, aware that the waving at the window was ongoing, 'shall we go in? When did Ce get here?'

'Only about half an hour ago,' said Dad. 'You go in and say hello. Give me your keys and I'll get your bag.'

My sister came to the front door. 'Is anyone coming in? Or shall we just party on the drive?' she smiled. 'Hurry up, Ben and Stephen are dying to see you.'

I didn't quite believe this to be true. At eight and six respectively, Ben's and Stephen's primary, recollectable experience of their aunt had been as the lady who either sat in a corner crying or, on a good day, sat in a corner staring into space – in both circumstances they were usually brought in, made to say a quick hello and then hurriedly escorted from the room. So, for Celia to claim they were desperate to see me was kind but, unless they had been told that I would be handing out Xboxes on arrival, an untruth. My incredulity must have been apparent in my expression. 'They *are!*' insisted Celia, laughing.

'Why? What have you told them?' I asked.

'Goodness, Ros, don't be so cynical. They're just excited to see their aunt.'

In the living room, Dad's elaborate Scalextric track was taking-up most of the floor space, whilst Ben and Stephen sat perched on the window seat in the bay, with the controls in their hands. David was seated on one of the sofas, a copy of *The Times* open on his lap. He smiled as I walked in. 'Hello, Ros! Gosh, you look well.' He edged forward but didn't get up. 'I'm afraid I'm terrified of treading on this fantastic track of Ted's. How's St Albans? How's Andrew? Boys,' he said, turning to his sons, 'it's Aunty Ros.'

'Hello, Aunty Ros,' said Ben, with a smile, 'I am very excited to see you.' I heard a slight groan from Celia behind me.

'Hello, Ben,' I said. 'What a great track.'

There was a clicking sound which, I realised, was Celia prompting Stephen to speak.

'Hello Aunty Ros,' he said, whilst examining the underside of a red Scalextric car. 'My name is Stephen Hawthorn. I live in Barnstaple. I enjoy football and—'

'Stephen…' said David, quietly. Stephen lowered the car and looked up at me.

'Hello Aunty Ros,' he began again. 'I, I… You always cry when you come to our house, don't you?'

'Stephen!' said Celia, laughing nervously. 'Don't be so silly! Aunty Ros does not always—'

'Now, Ce,' I interjected, 'to be fair to Stephen, I do tend to cry when I visit you in Devon. But, you know what, Stephen,' I said, turning to him with a smile, 'I feel much better now and I don't feel like crying half so much as I did.'

'Why not?' asked Stephen.

'Never mind why not, Stephen,' said Celia, sternly. 'Aunty Ros needs a cup of tea.'

'I know why not,' said Ben.

'No you don't, Benedict,' snapped Celia. 'Ros, come and get a cup of tea,' she said, putting an arm around my shoulders.

'I do know, Mum' insisted Ben. 'I heard you and Dad talking. You said that—'

'Come on, Ros,' said Celia, applying gentle pressure to my arm.

'—that Aunty Ros really liked where she lived and where she worked and that, even when the neighbour had killed her guinea pig, she—' Whilst Ben continued with his explanation, and Celia tried frantically to curtail it by means of squinting and not-so-discreet hand gestures,

49

I glanced across at Stephen and was horrified to see his lower lip trembling uncontrollably. I tried to alert Celia to the situation but she was at that point too pre-occupied with attempting to stem the flow of reported speech emanating from her eldest son's mouth to listen. A moment later, little Stephen's face contorted into a gargoyle-like expression of utter horror and distress as he dissolved into very vocal tears.

'Mr Edward!' he wailed. 'Why did they kill Mr Edward?'

'Oh God,' said Celia. 'No one killed Mr Edward, I was only joking with Daddy, wasn't I, Daddy?'

She turned pleadingly to David who, in response, raised his eyes, and then his newspaper and muttered, barely audibly above Stephen's sobs, 'Yes, that's right, Stephen. Not one of your mother's best comedic moments, but there you go.'

'Was it really a joke, Mum?' persisted Ben, raising his voice above the din. 'So that man didn't run over Mr Edward with his lawnmower then? You were just joking?' His expression was one of surprise and anxiety, combined with strained amusement, as if he was seeing his mother in a whole new light and wasn't quite sure whether to rejoice in her quirky sense of humour, or place himself in the care of the local authority.

'A... lawn... mower!' screeched Stephen, in a series of hiccoughs. 'Why... did... he... chop... up... Mr... Edward?'

'Hmm, I wonder what Nanny is up to,' I said quietly, and left the room to the sound of Stephen's continued whimpering.

I followed the sound of clattering crockery and found my mother, making tea and setting out cups and saucers, in the kitchen. 'What on earth is all that noise about?' she asked, as I entered. 'Has Stephen hurt himself on your father's track? I told him that he was squashing too much in with that second figure of eight.'

'Hmm... where *is* Dad?' I looked out of the kitchen window and noticed scaffolding wrapping itself round the back of the house. 'He's not up there, is he?'

'No, he is not,' said Mum in an irritated tone. 'He's been up there every sunny day for the past two weeks, re-pointing, and I've told him he's not to go up on his birthday.'

'Where is he, then?'

'I don't know. Probably on the toilet. So, anyway,' she turned away from the cups and saucers and looked up at me, 'it is so good to see you like this.'

'Like what?'

'Smart shirt, new shoes. My Ros.' She hugged me and it was a moment or two before I realised she was crying.

'Mum!' I said 'Please don't cry. That's my role and it seems everyone's after it today.'

'Oh, I'm sorry, Ros,' she said, letting go of me and dabbing her eyes with her apron. 'It's just that we've all been so worried about you for such a long time and, you know, talking to you on the phone over the past few months and now seeing you looking just so beautiful, well, it's wonderful.'

Celia now came into the kitchen, looking a little red. 'Sorry about that, Ros.'

'What happened?' asked Mum.

'Ben told Stephen about Mr Edward,' sighed Celia.

'What about him?'

'You remember, Mum, the neighbour ran over him in the garden. Remember?' I said.

Mum looked horrified. 'I didn't know that! Oh my goodness, poor Mr Edwards. Is he in hospital? Why did no one tell me?'

Celia and I looked at each other and tutted. 'I'm shocked at you two,' said Mum. 'Poor Mr Edwards. His wife must be wondering why we—'

'Mum,' said Celia, 'not Mr *Edwards*. Mr *Edward*, Ros's guinea pig. Remember?'

My mother looked momentarily confused and then started to laugh. 'Oh yes! Ha, ha, ha! Of course. I had forgotten that that was his name. Oh dear me,' she gasped, 'I was wondering what a car was doing driving through Mr Edwards' garden.'

At this point, David came into the kitchen, accompanied by Stephen who, whilst still blotchy, had calmed down considerably.

'Oh, come on in and see Nanny, darling,' said Celia, bending down and kissing the top of his head.

'Oh yes, my peach,' said Mum, still giggling. 'Come and have one of Nanny's special biscuits.'

'What are you laughing at, Nanny?' asked Stephen, smiling up at her.

'Oh darling,' she said, 'Nanny got a bit muddled and now just can't stop laughing at the thought of poor Mr Edwards being mown down in his own garden. Isn't that silly?'

Stephen turned a trembling, anxious face enquiringly towards his mother. I didn't wait for the tears but instead made a hasty exit in search of my father.

I found him, or rather his legs, protruding from the hatch into the loft. 'What are you up to?' I called.

'I'm coming down now,' he replied. 'I just wanted to get the Lego down for the boys. He emerged carrying a blue crate, full of the small, plastic bricks, which I took from him.

'For the boys or for you?' I asked with a grin.

'Well…' he laughed, descending the last few rungs and pushing the ladder back into the loft.

'Happy Birthday, Dad' I said, kissing his cheek. 'How, are you enjoying the day so far?'

'You've made my day, Ros,' he said, smiling, 'looking so happy and so beautiful.'

I sighed. Between them all, they were determined to make me cry.

'I do feel better,' I said, quietly. 'I just don't know how you've all put up with me.'

My father shook his head. 'We're all very proud of you, Ros. You mustn't be so hard on yourself and you mustn't dwell on what has been and gone.' He took the crate from me, put it down and placed an arm around my shoulders. 'You must treasure the best memories, whilst looking forward.' He gazed down the hallway and wagged a finger towards an unseen horizon, before adding, with a puzzled look, 'There seems to be an awful lot of wailing and gnashing of teeth going on in the kitchen. I wonder if Stephen has had a fall?' He gestured towards the box of bricks. 'What do you say we just pop this lot down to the conservatory and wait for Mum to find us with the tea?

Or,' he said, taking my hand between his own and looking at me with a dangerous gleam in his eye, 'we could go up the scaffolding. The view is marvellous, you know.'

Mum had booked a private dining room in a local hotel for an early dinner, which concluded with the cutting of my football pitch cake and the blowing-out of a modest, but representative, seven candles. By 9.30pm we were back home, the boys were in bed, David was in the study with Dad, helping the latter to solve an IT problem, and Mum, Celia and I were lounging on the living room sofas, quaffing glasses of champagne.

'What a lovely, lovely, day,' sighed Mum. 'Your father said to me that he has never had a better birthday.'

We sat in silence for a moment before I noticed Mum pursing her lips and making small, jerking movements with her head in Celia's direction.

'Is there something wrong?' I asked.

Celia tutted. 'Oh for goodness sake, Mum,' she said. 'Sorry, Ros, Mum wants me to ask—'

'You want to know too, Celia,' interrupted my mother.

'Want to know what?'

'Well,' Celia hesitated, 'we just wondered if there may be… if there might be someone new in your life.' Celia smiled and my mother leaned forward expectantly.

'I'm afraid not,' I said, simply. My mother sat back in her seat but managed to keep her smile in place.

'Oh,' said Celia, 'well, never mind. We just wondered because you seemed—'

'But,' I said, surprising myself, 'I think there could be someone new. I mean, the idea doesn't seem ridiculous. You know, if I met someone.'

Celia looked at Mum and the latter nodded. Celia shook her head.

'Oh for God's sake, what is it?' I asked. 'It's like being at a blooming Marcel Marceux convention.'

'Mother, you have no subtlety or timing' said Celia with a sigh. 'What it is, Ros, is that my friend Katrina's husband has a cousin, Sam, who has just recently moved to Harpenden and Katrina wondered if she could give him your phone number.'

'What? So that I could show him the sights and sounds of Harpenden and St Albans?' I laughed.

'He sounds everso nice, Ros,' said Mum encouragingly.

'Does he? Katrina's the one with the ears, isn't she?' I asked.

'If what you're asking me is whether his ears stick out then the answer is, I don't know. I have never met him,' said Celia, draining her flute and reaching for the bottle on the coffee table. 'However, he has no genetic link to Katrina, so it's unlikely.'

'What do you think, dear?' said Mum.

'Well, I do need someone to take to George's party, so I guess if I could get to know him a little beforehand, and his ears were in proportion to his head, I could drag him along to that...' I paused, feeling a little woozy and trying to focus upon how I would actually feel, should he call me. 'Does he know about... you know... what happened?' I asked.

Celia looked horrified. 'Absolutely not. That's for you to tell, if and when you feel you can – or should.'

'Tell her some more about him, Celia,' said Mum, topping up her glass. 'Tell her about the dog.'

'He has a dog,' said Celia, with a shrug of her shoulders.

My mother beamed, 'There, Ros. A dog.'

'OK, so he has a dog. Why is that a clincher? I don't understand.'

'Well, silly,' my mother continued, now slurring slightly, 'he has a dog, you have – sorry, you *had* a whatsit… a pig… a thing pig. You both like animals. Perfect,' she concluded, raising her glass.

'Perfect,' agreed Celia, winking at me and joining the toast.

'Oh, go on then,' I sighed, clinking my glass against theirs, 'give him my number.'

Chapter 9

'Are you OK, George?' I asked, as she sat hunched over a printout at the small table in the kitchen at the back of the shop.

She looked up and smiled an uncharacteristically tired smile. 'I'm fine,' she said, running her pen down the list of figures. 'Just doing this for Andrew.'

'Split it with me,' I suggested. 'The shop's quiet.'

'Goodness, no. It's fine – he's done most of it.'

'OK,' I said, 'so long as you're sure. You just look a bit pooped today.' I made to leave the kitchen but stopped when she spoke.

'It's a very silly thing, really,' she said with a sigh, leaning back in her chair. 'It's Mike's party. Usually, I love organizing this kind of thing but, this time... I'm just not sure what he wants.'

'But you think maybe he doesn't want a party?' I asked, sitting down next to her.

'He insists he does,' she leaned forward, with her elbows on the table and resting her chin on her hands, 'but he's not interested in any of the preparations, which is fine, but, you know, disinterest can just be a little dispiriting sometimes, can't it?' She hesitated and then shrugged and smiled. 'But, never mind, he doesn't seem unhappy – more pre-occupied, really.'

'Could it be work?'

She looked doubtful. 'Could be, I suppose.' She shrugged again. 'Oh, I don't know what it is. Maybe it's just the whole turning forty thing.' She nudged me and smiled. 'But, hey, your date is tomorrow, isn't it? Have you decided what you're wearing yet?'

'All I know is that I won't be wearing the stockings and suspenders Joan brought in for me yesterday.' I tutted. 'I wouldn't have minded but the stockings are those Scholl support ones.' George laughed. 'She said something about 'hidden treasures' but I wasn't convinced. Anyway, we're just going for a drink at that new wine bar round the corner and then maybe for dinner. It's no big deal, really.'

George smiled mischievously, 'Isn't it?'

'Oh God,' I said despairingly, 'I don't know. I'm trying not to let it be a big deal but, however I sell it to myself, it's a blind date and that terrifies me.'

'He sounds nice,' said George.

'Well, he has a pleasant telephone manner, and no criminal convictions, I suppose.'

'Well, those are both excellent qualities. Now,' she leaned back in her chair and tapped her lower lip with her pen, 'what to wear...'

'This?' I pointed to the fitted white t-shirt, grey skirt and black boots I was wearing.

'Well now, Ros. That's fab for work but you're so gorgeous. You could knock the guy dead.' She punched the air with her fist.

'I guess I could try on a few things this evening.' I said, somewhat unenthusiastically.

'Sorry to interrupt fashion week,' said Andrew, poking his head round the kitchen door, 'but have you finished with those figures yet, George?'

'She hasn't and it's my fault,' I said, getting up. 'I'm distracting her.'

'I like the green blouse you wear with those lovely new jeans of yours,' said George. 'It's a great fit, sets off your eyes, and won't look like you're trying too hard. Just add a chunky necklace or bracelet.'

'Sorry, I could have sworn I had *interrupted* fashion week,' said Andrew.

'Oh Andrew,' said George, pulling a face, 'don't be so miserable. Ros has a date tomorrow and we women need a little support and encouragement before that kind of thing.'

Andrew sighed, 'OK. Well, Ros, good luck. I guess if it goes well then I'm off the hook about finding you someone reassuringly ugly to take to George's party and, if it doesn't go well, never mind, I'll resume the search.'

'Andrew!' exclaimed George. 'How on earth is that supposed to help?'

'No, it's all right George,' I said, holding up a hand and turning to Andrew. 'Thanks for that. You should be a life coach, you know.' I walked past him and into the shop.

I heard George speaking in low tones, before Andrew followed me and said, 'Sorry, Ros. I was just attempting to lighten the mood. I think maybe I should leave this kind of thing to George.'

'No, no, it's fine,' I smiled. 'And you're right. I need a sense of humour over this. It's just a date – not even that really.'

'I think I understand, you know.'

I looked at him in surprise. 'Do you? You've been on blind dates?'

'No,' he shook his head, 'that's not quite what I meant.'

'Oh,' I waited for some further explanation and, when none came, I said, 'Well, would you consider a blind date?'

He looked up briefly from the pile of letters and documents he had begun to sort. 'I don't think a manufactured situation would work for me,' he said, before resuming his task and consigning several sheets of paper to the bin. 'I seem to be the kind of person who's always taken by surprise – and that's not, of course, without its difficulties.'

I was about to enquire as to the nature of those difficulties when the bell above the door jingled and two elderly couples entered the shop.

'Looks like we've got a rush on,' said Andrew, nodding towards the door. 'Oh and George is right by the way,' he straightened the pile of papers and started to walk towards the new arrivals, 'you know – about the green blouse.'

–

That evening, I stood in front of the full-length mirror in my bedroom and took stock. My hair had been cut into a bob just before Dad's party and still looked OK. Body-wise, I decided, things weren't too bad either. I had put back on some, but not all, of the weight I had lost before moving to St Albans and was now a safe size ten. Fine. Clothing: hmm, not so good. I was wearing a very old, beige padded bra, which, judging by its heavily contoured surface, had had a rather traumatic experience in the tumble dryer at some point, and which was pretty representative of every other bra I possessed. A large pair of faded black knickers, more appropriate as

1940s gym-wear than as 21st-century lingerie, completed my current ensemble. On the bed to my left, lay four mountains of clothes, which I had spent the past hour categorizing as: 'Too Big', 'Too Old', 'Too Formal' and 'Too Heavily Associated with The Rat.' A fifth pile, consisting of my most recent purchases of a pair of jeans, a white shirt, black trousers and the green shirt so favoured by George and, apparently, by Andrew too, lay on a chair to my right. I sighed. Not a lot of options then.

I popped on a bathrobe, went downstairs, poured myself a glass of wine and sat down at the kitchen table, wondering briefly whether I should go clothes shopping the next morning, before quickly dismissing the idea as ridiculous and deciding to go back upstairs and try on the various permutations of jeans, black trousers, white shirt, green shirt.

I had reached the bottom of the stairs when the phone rang. I hesitated and then picked it up. 'Hello?'

'Ros?' said a male voice.

'Tom!' I said, breaking into a grin, genuinely pleased to hear from him. 'I was just thinking about you!'

'Were you? I'm flattered. Or were you chopping up sausages?'

I laughed. 'No, actually, you'll never guess. I have a date tomorrow evening and I was wondering whether I should buy a new tea-cosy or just wear my old one.'

'Ooh,' he sounded thoughtful. 'Well, you know what a fan I am of bag lady couture. And it's a look you wear undeniably well. But when I saw you last month, you were hovering on the edge of actually looking rather attractive again, so it might be a mistake to change direction just yet.'

I smiled and felt myself flush a little, pleased with the casual compliment. 'So, anyway,' I said, taking the phone into the living room and flopping down on the sofa, 'what's new with you?'

'Oh,' he said, 'you know. Same old, same old. How's Andrew?'

'Bookish, Irish…'

'No new women on the horizon for him, then?' he asked.

I paused; this wasn't one of Tom's usual topics of conversation. 'I don't think so. Why do you ask?'

'Oh, no reason,' he sounded evasive. 'How did your Dad's party go?'

'Hey, hey, hey,' I said. 'Not so fast. Why the question about Andrew's love life? Am I missing out on some gossip here? You saw him last week, didn't you?'

'Now look, Ros,' he sounded stern, 'let's be clear right now that Andrew has not said one word to me about a new woman. Do you understand? I know what you're like with your extrapolations.'

'Fine, I understand that. Now quit stalling and tell me what you know.'

'OK but you promise me you won't say or hint anything to him. In fact, don't even tell him we spoke.'

'Fine, fine, fine. Now tell me.'

'Well, it was just that he was asking me lots of questions about Amy and whether I thought there was only ever one right person for everyone. You know, soppy stuff like that.' He paused.

'Yes… and…?'

'Well, that's it, really.'

'That's it?'

'It was just odd and out of character. He has never discussed relationships with me before and it was clearly on his mind.'

I had to admit that, limited though the information was, it was interesting. I resolved to run it past George on Monday. 'Hmm…' I said. 'Well, if there is anyone, he hasn't mentioned her to us or brought her to the shop. And I haven't noticed him wringing his hands, spouting poetry or—'

'Spending longer in the lav than usual.' Tom let out a guffaw at his own joke.

'You are *so* crass.'

'But you love me anyway.'

'Yes,' I said truthfully, 'I do.'

'Anyway, look,' he cleared his throat, 'there was actually something else I wanted to tell you.' He sounded anxious.

'Is everything all right?'

'Yeah, yeah,' he gave a nervous laugh. 'Everything is really great. In fact, so great…'

'Yes?' I said. 'Come on, what is it?'

'There's going to be a wedding. I'm getting married.'

I felt as if a cold, lead weight had dropped suddenly from my throat into my stomach.

'Ros?' he said, sounding worried. 'If you're uncomfortable at the thought—'

'God,' I said. 'I really wasn't expecting that.'

'What?'

'You getting married.'

'Not ever?' he asked. 'I'm hurt.'

'Well, not until you were a bit richer. You know, a better catch.' He laughed. 'I'm assuming it *is* Amy,' I said. 'Or did you order one off the internet?'

'Aah, thanks a lot for all those votes of confidence,' he said. 'I was going to ask you to be my best person but now you can just fuck right off.'

'I'm devastated,' I said. 'But seriously, Tom,' I took a gulp of wine, followed by a deep breath, 'I am really, really, happy for you and Amy. I know how much you love her.'

'I do. Thanks, Ros.'

'Hey and even if I'm not now best person, I am looking forward to my invite. I promise not to fall down in the aisle and beat my fists on the floor, screaming, "It should have been me!"'

'Promise?'

'Yeah. I'll do that on the church lawn.'

'Fair enough,' he hesitated. 'And, Ros, you must say if the idea of the wedding… well, you know, after what he did… If you would prefer us not to—'

'Oh shut up, you silly bugger,' I laughed but felt tears springing into my eyes. 'But thanks for being so uncharacteristically sensitive. It's really made my evening.'

Half an hour later, I was back upstairs, with my distressed bra and outsized knickers now hidden beneath my new jeans and the green blouse. This minimalist ensemble was accessorised with one of the many necklaces George had kindly dropped off for me to try. George, I thought, as I fingered the heavy, silver creation, had impeccable taste, a heart of gold and loads of money.

On an impulse, I went into the bathroom and began to apply make-up; concealer, foundation, blusher, eyeliner, mascara, lipstick, lipliner. I stood back to assess the end result. There she was. Other Ros. God, she looked together, and with an air not dissimilar to

Daniel McAdam's Cinders. She was taller, of course, and brunette, but yes, she was similarly, unnervingly *together*.

Before I had time to decide whether to be horrified or impressed by this transformation, I was distracted by the sudden glare of the security light in the garden and, turning off the bathroom light, I peered out in time to see what looked like my fox, dragging something across the lawn and into the undergrowth. My curiosity awakened, my inhibitions dulled, and my confidence heightened, by two large glasses of wine, I hurried into the bedroom and took my camera from the top drawer of my bedside cabinet. Stopping only to check that it was charged, I trotted downstairs into the kitchen, grabbed a torch from under the sink, slipped my feet into the wellies which stood just inside the back door, and went out into the garden to investigate.

The security light which had, by now, gone off, flickered into life again, illuminating the lawn and the trees and bushes which surrounded it on three sides. I stood still for a moment, straining to hear rustling which might give me a clue as to the fox's whereabouts but was frustrated to hear only the sound of conversation and light laughter coming from the far end of the garden. I tutted and walked towards the noise. As I moved further from the house, the security light once again went out and I switched on my torch, strobing it wildly around me in an attempt not to stumble amongst the tangle of branches and brambles I was now entering.

There was by now, of course, absolutely no sign of the fox but my attention was caught by the clearly audible conversation being conducted in the garden backing onto my own. I was vaguely aware of the dividing hedge being considerably lower than I had remembered during my last foray this far into the depths of my garden and, upon reaching it, I had to stoop slightly in order to avoid being seen. Having crouched down, I could, by parting the leaves a little, not only hear but also see two figures, one male, one female, silhouetted against the lights situated in a border behind them.

'God, you're stunning,' he said, slurring slightly.

'And you,' responded the woman, 'are pissed.'

'Maybe,' said the man, 'but I know you're stunning, even when I'm stone... cold... bloody... sober.' An ugly slurping noise formed the punctuation between each word, as he leaned towards her.

'For God's sake, Charlie,' she said, with a laugh, 'get off me and shut up. Someone will hear.'

'Ah, so that's the only reason you want me to get off, is it?' he rasped. 'Because, if it is, let's just find somewhere a little more private next time, shall we?'

She giggled and began to demur but, at this point, I unfeelingly interrupted the tender exchange by screaming loudly and falling painfully forward into the hedge as something, I assumed the fox I had so hoped to encounter, rushed past me.

She screamed, he swore and, as I struggled to disentangle myself from my woody snare, I was aware of a number of other people hurriedly arriving on the scene. When I did, finally, stand up, it was to quite an audience – eight or nine, at least.

'Hello everyone,' I said, sheepishly peering over the hedge and waving my torch in greeting. 'I'm tracking a fox.'

There was a brief silence, during which I swept my torch around the garden and held up my camera in order to lend weight to the 'tracking' claim.

'This is my neighbour, Ros,' I directed my torch towards the voice and illuminated a tall man, with an impressive amount of facial hair. 'Hello, Ros,' said Daniel.

'This is the guinea pig neighbour,' said Charlie's conversational partner, whom I now recognised as Cinderella.

There was a general murmur, indicating comprehension.

'I saw a fox,' I said, weakly, 'and I decided to… track it.'

'He comes into my garden too,' said Daniel.

'Hmm…' I said, as the rest of my audience maintained their silence. 'Well, I think I've lost him now.' I looked to my left and right. Someone sniggered.

An excruciating silence now descended and remained unbroken for what seemed like a day or two at least. In desperation, I opted for small talk.

'It's a lovely evening, isn't it?' Another snigger, this time politely, but poorly, disguised as a choking cough.

'OK, well, it's nice to see you again, Ros, isn't it, Tish?' Daniel directed this question to Cinderella.

'Absolutely,' said Tish. 'It's always an event.'

Charlie laughed explosively.

'Charlie,' she admonished, playfully, 'you're just dreadful. You'll have to excuse Charlie, Ros. He's had rather a lot to drink.'

'Yes, so I witnessed,' I said, determined to score at least half a point.

I couldn't see her expression but she and the small crowd now turned and started to make their way back towards the house, talking in whispers, punctuated by laughter. I bent down to unhook the left leg of my jeans from a particularly vicious bramble and, on straightening up, was surprised to discover Daniel still standing there.

'You've had your hair cut,' he said. 'It looks nice. Even after being dragged through a hedge backwards.'

I sighed. 'Thank you.'

'I'd invite you to join us,' he gestured towards the retiring group, 'but I'm wondering if maybe you've already been to a party this evening.'

'Why do you say that?' I asked.

'Oh, I don't know. Just something about your... manner.' His hand moved to his mouth. 'Oh and your choice of attire, of course – more nightlife than wildlife, I'd say.'

'Well, I'm sorry,' I said, simply. 'Again. Sorry, sorry, sorry. Do apologise to your friends for the disturbance to their evening.'

'No need to apologise, Ros' he said.

'Hmm...' I turned towards the house. 'Bye then.'

'Bye. Oh and Ros,' he added, peering down over the top of the hedge.

'Yes?'

He gestured towards my feet. 'I prefer the sandals.'

I said nothing and headed again towards the light of the kitchen. I would decide when I got there whether to laugh or cry.

Chapter 10

I sat with my glass of white wine on the table in front of me and waited. It was only 8.25pm and we had agreed to meet at 8.30pm but I knew I wouldn't be able to walk elegantly across the wine bar with him watching me, so I had decided, instead, to be unfashionably early.

I was wearing the white shirt and black trousers, having torn the sleeve of the green shirt during my midnight safari the previous evening. However, despite wearing my second-choice outfit, I felt good. George had popped round at six to approve my choice of accessories, and to give me another 'you're gorgeous' pep talk and, whilst I wasn't exactly bursting with confidence, I wasn't a quivering wreck either. I took a sip of wine, placed my mobile on the table in front of me, relaxed back into my chair and considered getting out the book I had brought along, just in case Sam was running late.

My phone vibrated. It was Joan. I hesitated before finally pressing 'Accept'.

'It's Joan, my darling,' she said. 'Is he there yet? Am I interrupting?'

'No, you're fine, Joan,' I replied, raising my eyes slightly.

'Good, now, I just wanted to tell you that I've read your horoscope in three different publications today and all the

69

signs are good.' I heard the rustling of paper at the other end of the line.

'Thanks, Joan. You are thoughtful.' I meant it.

'Nonsense, my darling. It's nothing. Now, Jonathan in *The Mail* says—' Oh my God, she was going to read them all out '—your signs are on a collision course.'

'Is that a good thing, Joan?' I asked, doubtfully.

'Oh yes, dear. That means that both your auras are highly sexually charged. Which reminds me, did you remember the stockings, my darling? I find they give one just that little extra bit of confidence in one's allure.'

'Um, yes, stockings and suspenders all in place,' I said, absently, reaching under the table and searching for the book in my handbag, 'and that's really good news about the whole, er, astrological sex thing.'

'We must stop meeting like this,' said a smooth, male voice, which I recognised instantly. I looked up to see Daniel McAdam standing next to the table. He was looking amused and was dressed casually, but impeccably, in a purple and black striped shirt and dark jeans; the beard was as incongruous as ever.

'Er, sorry Joan, but I'll have to go,' I said into the phone.

'Ooh, is that him?' she squealed. 'Have fun, my darling.' She signed-off with kissing noises down the phone. I quickly hung up and slung the phone into my bag.

'Oh hello, Daniel,' I said, as calmly as I could, praying that he had heard neither end of the conversation.

'I always thought suspenders were traditionally worn with a skirt.' He glanced at my trousers.

Bugger.

'Actually, I'm not wearing suspenders,' I said. 'A well-meaning, slightly eccentric, friend gave me a pair and I didn't want to hurt her feelings by telling her that I wasn't wearing them. Also, despite what you might have overheard, I will not be having sex with anyone this evening.'

He hesitated. 'Now, as I'm not quite sure whether to congratulate or commiserate, I think I'm just going to accept that statement and move on.' He drank from the large glass of red wine he was holding and put his other hand in his pocket.

'I'm here with my big brother, Miles – he's down from Edinburgh for the weekend.' He nodded his head towards a tall, fair-haired, extremely attractive man leaning against the bar. The latter raised a hand in greeting and smiled. I was suddenly very pleased that I had made an effort. I waved and returned the smile. 'Yes,' continued Daniel, 'Miles was amongst my guests last night. So you've already met really.'

My smile froze. 'Fabulous,' I said, lowering my hand and taking a large gulp of wine. 'Well, it's great to see you again, Daniel, but I'll let you get back to Miles. I'm sure you want to make the most of your time together.'

He didn't move. 'Oh we know each other inside out. He won't mind me chatting to you for a moment.'

I groaned inwardly. 'Lovely,' I said.

'So,' he smiled, 'what are you up to this evening?'

'I'm meeting a friend for drinks and then we are off out for dinner.'

'Anywhere nice?'

'Yes.'

He continued to smile and sipped his wine. I looked at my watch. 8.40pm. 'An old friend?' he asked.

'Sorry?'

'This friend you are meeting. Is she, or he, an old friend?'

'Oh... no. It's a new friend.' I took another gulp.

'Miles and I aren't running to a timetable,' he said. 'Would it be all right for us to join you, while you wait? Only, there don't seem to be any other free tables.' He gestured at the increasingly crowded room.

I considered telling him the truth. I considered telling him about The Rat, about James T. Gaville, about the effort I had gone to tonight, for the first time since my wedding day, to appear attractive to a member of the opposite sex. I considered begging him to please just go away.

'Of course, that would be fine,' I said.

'Great!' He beckoned Miles, who grinned, presumably at the prospect of some light entertainment courtesy of the mad woman let loose from her attic, and came over to join us.

'Hi again, Ros,' he said, in a voice identical to his brother's.

'Hello,' I said.

'Ros is meeting a friend and kindly said we could share her table,' said Daniel.

'Great,' said Miles, sitting down. 'So, Ros, what do you think of this?' He tugged at Daniel's beard. 'Personally, I can't cope with it. It's as if my brother has been partially swallowed by a Brillo pad.'

I continued my assault on the contents of my wine glass. 'When I first met him, I assumed he was a recovering alcoholic,' I said.

Miles laughed. I remained stony faced. 'I don't think she's joking, Dan,' he said.

'I didn't think for one minute she was, Miles,' his brother replied.

I looked at my watch. 8.43pm.

'What time are you expecting your friend?' asked Daniel. I thought I detected a look of pitying concern behind the facial hair.

'Eight thirty,' I said, draining my glass.

'Check your phone,' suggested Miles, 'maybe they're stuck somewhere.'

My phone! It was on vibrate. I reached down into my bag and took it out. Two missed calls from Sam.

'Damn,' I said. I put the phone to my ear. No message the first time. I played the second message. '*Hi Ros.*' He sounded hesitant. '*Look, I hoped to catch you before you set off. I have left a message on your landline. I'm afraid I won't be able to make it tonight. I'm not very well. I was fine up until about half an hour ago and then I suddenly felt rather unwell and threw—*' I pressed delete and placed the phone back in my bag.

No one spoke for a moment and then Daniel said, 'How about another drink, Miles? Can I get you one, Ros?'

I took a deep breath and swallowed hard. 'No thanks. My friend is ill. I think I'm just going to go.'

'That's a pity about your friend,' he said, 'but why not stay and have another quick drink with us. We have no fixed plans.'

Miles smiled and nodded his agreement with the proposal but I shook my head. 'No thanks,' I mumbled, getting to my feet. 'I'm tired anyway.'

Daniel stood up too. 'I'll walk you to the door.'

I wanted to protest against this faintly ridiculous suggestion but decided not to risk a lengthy sentence, opting for 'OK' instead. I retrieved my bag from under the table, managed to say goodbye to Miles and then walked, with Daniel, to the door, which opened out onto the pavement.

'Can I get you a taxi?' he asked.

'No thanks, I'm going to walk.'

'Sorry your evening didn't quite pan out,' he said. 'Are you absolutely sure—'

I experienced a sudden rush of irritation and hurt pride. 'Look,' I said, turning to him, 'I know you think of me as quite a comical and—' I held up a hand as he tried to interject. 'Just let me finish. I know you think of me as quite a comical, and somewhat pitiable, figure and that's fine. That's not an unreasonable conclusion for you to have reached based on our very unfortunate interaction to date. However, for whatever reason, I would like you to know that, actually, beneath all the guinea pigs and the ugly footwear and the foxes and the blokes who stand me up… beneath all that, I am bright and intelligent and I was, to boot, once, extremely successful, both profession-ally and personally. I made money and I had sex.'

'Er, Ros, I think that maybe you don't—'

'You are a very successful person, Daniel. You have a lovely home, a sexy brother and a girlfriend with a remarkable bottom and I don't think for one moment you mean to hurt my feelings but I find pity very hard to take, especially from someone like you, so I'd really like you not to feel sorry for me. I don't need you, or anyone else, to feel sorry for me.'

I turned away and started to walk, at speed, in the direction of home. I was relieved that he didn't attempt to follow me and, as I turned the first corner, I began to cry. Not wanting to get into a taxi, or to continue the walk home, in such a conspicuous state of distress, I decided to head for the shop. I had the keys. I would pop in, make myself a cup of tea and then call a cab, or walk home, once I was feeling better.

–

I arrived at *Chapters* less than five minutes later. A further two minutes of fumbling for the keys in my handbag and I was inside and wondering why the alarm hadn't been set. It was only after I had re-locked the door and put the keys back in my bag that I realised I wasn't alone.

'Ros?' Andrew was standing in the doorway of the illuminated kitchen, a can in one hand and a mobile phone in the other. I remained motionless and silent in the darkened shop. He spoke into the phone. 'Er, Donal, would it be OK if I called you back? My business partner has just turned up at the shop and I think we may have some issues to run through. Yeah... yeah... we'll speak then. All the best.' He hung up. 'Aren't you supposed to be mid-date, right about now?' he asked, quietly.

I said nothing. I had stopped crying and was in no hurry to start again. 'Ros?' he tried again. 'Ros, do you fancy a drink? There's some wine in the fridge and you'd be keeping me company with my Guinness.' He held up the can.

I walked towards him and, as I reached the entrance to the kitchen, he opened his arms. I dropped my bag and leaned into his chest. He closed his arms around me and we stood there for a moment or two. 'Someone told him,' I said into his blue and white checked shirt.

'Someone told who what?' he asked.

'Someone told Sam about me and so he stood me up.' I took a deep breath in an attempt to prevent the return of tears.

'Did he say that?' he asked, softly.

'He didn't have to. This afternoon on the phone, he was flirtatious, happy and healthy. Six hours later and he's suddenly got dysentery.'

'Well, maybe he has got dysentery.'

I pulled away from him, picked up my bag and fumbled for a handkerchief, into which I blew my nose very noisily. 'I'd put money on the fact that he hasn't.'

'Come and have a drink,' he said. 'We don't have to sit in the kitchen. We can sit in the shop, where your red eyes and runny nose won't be so well-lit.' He smiled down at me.

'OK. Thanks,' I said, managing a wobbly smile in return.

'Right. You go and sit on the stairs and I'll bring you a glass. Grab Joan's cushion from behind the till.'

I did as he said and waited for him to re-emerge from the kitchen. After a moment, he returned with my wine and sat quietly next to me whilst I drank it and filled him in on the evening's events. When I had finished my account, he leaned back, opened a fresh can of Guinness and said, 'Yes, not the best of nights, Ros. But, you know, when you look at the situation objectively, maybe Sam was sick, and,' he said, ignoring my attempt to lodge a protest, 'even if he wasn't, even if, as you say, he'd heard what had happened to you in the past and was anxious about that, even then, that doesn't mean that he is representative of the majority of the male population.' He paused to drink his Guinness. 'It just means he's a bit of a sad, narrow-minded guy, who probably has multiple issues of his own and without whom you are much better off.'

'I just,' I downed the remainder of my glass in two gulps, 'I just feel a bit like I'm being seen as damaged goods, just when I'm starting to feel whole again.' He nodded sympathetically and refilled my glass. 'God and then there's my bloody neighbour who keeps popping up like a hirsute jack-in-a-box and treating me like I'm a candidate for care in the community.'

'My God,' said Andrew, with a despairing shake of his head. 'I just don't know who the hell that guy thinks he is with his kind concern for your welfare and offering to keep you company and buy you drinks. He sounds like a right arse and no mistake.'

I laughed. I didn't know whether it was the wine or Andrew's analysis of the situation, but I was beginning to feel a little better. 'Oh no,' I giggled.

'What?'

'I told him that his girlfriend had a nice bottom.' I blinked, as the room rippled slightly.

'Jesus, Ros, how did you manage to crowbar that one into the conversation?'

'Dunno…' I sighed, 'but I did.'

Andrew smiled. 'Quite an achievement.'

'Hmm… Hey,' I said, turning towards him and prodding him with a finger, 'you haven't told me what you're doing here yet.'

'Oh, you know, I had a few things to go over – a few phone calls to make. That kind of thing. And sometimes,' he stared into his Guinness, 'I just don't fancy going home.'

'Do you mean you don't fancy going home alone?' I asked.

'Maybe,' he said.

'I think I understand,' I said, holding out my glass for a further refill.

'I think you probably do.' He smiled and poured me another half glass. 'Slow down a bit, Ros.'

'Oh but God, you know what this means!' I cried.

'What?'

'It means you're going to have to fix me up with a rugged gay friend!'

'Oh dear,' he said, 'that is bad news.'

'And why?'

'Because,' he said, gravely, 'I've thought about it and none of them are quite as rugged as you.'

I felt deeply wounded for a moment, before grinning and wagging a finger at him. 'Aah, you're just pulling my legs, aren't you, you legs puller, you,' I said, with some difficulty, noticing that my tongue suddenly seemed to be suffering some sort of partial paralysis.

'I can't fool you, can I, Ros? Yes, I am pulling your legs.'

'So you've found me a date?'

'The truth is, Ros, I didn't even bother asking round because I knew that, once you put your mind to it and gave up dressing like Anne Widdecombe, and giving off those all-men-are-the-devil vibes, you wouldn't have any trouble finding someone.'

'Anne Widdecombe?' I said, frowning. 'Really? Gosh. But, anyway,' I shook my head and tried to focus, 'more important than that, Andrew, is the fact that I now have no one to take to George's party.'

'There are over two months to go yet. You'll have a date by then,' he said, smiling in what I guessed was supposed to be a reassuring fashion.

'Oh God but I haven't got the energy for all this dressing up and fussing all over again. I don't want another blind date for at least *three* months.' I held up four fingers to emphasise the point.

'OK,' he said, 'just come with me then.'

I missed my mouth with my wine. 'Why? Where are you going?'

'It's running down your chin, you muppet,' he said, taking my handkerchief from me and dabbing my face. 'I mean, come with me to George's party.'

'You mean… go together? With each other?'

He stopped dabbing and looked at me. 'Why not? I haven't got anyone to go with either.'

'Isn't there someone else you'd really like to go with?' He didn't reply. 'What about Sandra?' I pressed.

'Funny thing is,' he said, handing me the handkerchief and returning his attention to his drink, 'it turns out she doesn't enjoy parties.'

I was silent for a moment before the joke hit home. 'Oh yeah,' I laughed, 'because she's gay. You are so funny, Andrew. Why have I never noticed all the funniness before?' I lay back on the stairs, holding my glass high above my head. 'I'm tipsy, you know.'

79

'You don't say,' he said, taking his mobile out of his back pocket. 'Come on. I'm calling us a cab. I'll drop you off on the way.'

Chapter 11

I hadn't seen Alan Bullen for about six months, when he phoned to suggest a drink. I was quite curious as to how old colleagues were faring, especially as I had heard rumours of imminent cutbacks, and I knew that Alan could be gloriously indiscreet. We agreed to meet at six-thirty, the next evening, at *The Poet*, just around the corner from his office. I was no more than about ten minutes late but, when I arrived, he was sitting in a corner booth, already over half-way down his pint of beer. Even from a distance of twenty feet, I could tell something was wrong. The possibility of redundancy sprang immediately to mind. I took a deep breath and walked to join him.

'Hi, Alan,' I said, touching his shoulder as I reached him.

'Ros!' he said, getting to his feet and giving me a kiss on the cheek. 'It's been way too long. But look at you! You look fabulous! Love the shoes.'

'Thanks,' I said. 'Can I get you a drink while I'm at the bar?'

'I'll get you one.'

'Nonsense. A beer?'

'That'd be great. Thanks.' He sat back down and I went to fetch our drinks. I stood at the bar and sneaked another look at him while I waited. He was staring straight ahead and seemed to be miles away. I decided that, on this occasion, it was to be my turn to lend the listening ear and if necessary, I thought, as I watched his torso rise and fall with the effort of an enormous sigh, offer a shoulder to cry on.

I paid for the drinks and returned to the table. 'There you go, Alan.' I handed him his beer and sat down opposite him. 'So, how are you?'

Up close, he looked even worse. Dark circles hung under his eyes and a light stubble covered his chin. He offered me a weak smile. 'Actually, Ros,' he said, 'things aren't too great.'

'Is it work?' I asked. 'I heard the new chairman was making a few changes.'

'Work?' He looked genuinely bemused for a moment. 'Oh, no, work is fine. I mean, Newman, Youngman and Marshall have gone from our division. And Wendy Haynes and Kate Woodruff got the boot too. But I'm fine.'

My jaw dropped slightly. 'My God. But that's awful. It must have been so hard for you to see them go – and it means a lot of extra pressure on you.'

'Not really,' he finished his first pint.

'Alan,' I leaned over and put my hand on his, 'whatever's wrong?'

He looked up with tears in his bloodshot eyes. 'Oh, Ros. You are absolutely the last person I should be burdening with this.'

'Nonsense,' I said. 'You were so supportive of me during my darkest days. Of course I want to try and help – if I can.'

'It's all just such a dreadful mess,' he said, a tear finally escaping and trickling down his cheek. 'It's not something I ever wanted, you know. Hurting people left right and centre.'

'Good God, Alan. What on earth has happened?'

'Anne and I are… are getting divorced.'

'Oh, I'm so sorry. That is such sad news.' I recollected Anne as a short, solid woman in her late thirties. I hadn't really met her often enough to form much of an opinion of her personality, or of her relationship with Alan, other than that they seemed perfectly happy in each other's company.

'I shouldn't be bothering you with it all. I just thought that… God, well I don't know what I thought.' His hand trembled as he started his second pint. 'I feel I need forgiveness. That is what's torturing me. I can't sleep, thinking about everything. I just need absolution, Ros.'

'From Anne?'

'From Anne, from – well, from everybody. I just feel I have let everyone down, Ros. I let you down, so very badly, didn't I?'

'Not at all, not at all. You did everything you could for me, Alan. I only ever let myself down and, you know what, leaving was the best thing that could have happened to me. A friend told me at the time that it was a new beginning, a new opportunity, and he was right.' I smiled encouragingly.

'Really?' He looked a little less despairing.

'Absolutely,' I said. 'And your divorce, horrific as it may seem at this moment, could be a new beginning for you, and for Anne too. I mean, I don't know the circumstances…' I paused to allow him to elucidate if he

83

wished. When he didn't, I pressed on with my pep talk, '…but I do know that good can come from the most awful of situations.'

'And what about forgiveness, Ros?'

'Forgiveness?'

He hung his head and then raised his blood-shot eyes and looked at me. 'Have you forgiven him?'

I sat back. I simply could not tell this man on the edge, desperate for his wife's forgiveness, that no, I hadn't forgiven The Rat and that I never would. That, actually, I would like to take his testicles, put them through a mincer, add a little basil, fashion them into a couple of ball burgers and then serve them up, with a green salad, to… hmm, I'd have to think about who I'd most like to serve them up to.

'Of course I have forgiven him, Alan,' I said, brightly. 'He had his reasons for what he did and I forgave him long ago. Tina, my therapist, made it clear to me very early on that harbouring feelings of hatred and resentment merely serves to obstruct the process of personal healing.' That's it, I thought, I would serve the bollock burgers up to Tina.

Alan looked massively relieved and even managed something approaching a smile. 'Ros, you can't begin to imagine how much that helps me. It really gives me hope for the future.'

I took my first sip of wine and congratulated myself. If a little white lie kept Alan from jumping into the Thames then so be it. I was glad to help.

—

The rest of the evening went relatively well, considering Alan's less than buoyant mood. He didn't provide any further details regarding the divorce but instead insisted upon hearing about my improving circumstances. As the latter seemed genuinely to make him feel better, I was happy to oblige and, after an evening of relentless positivity on my part, I headed for Blackfriars, still concerned about Alan but rather appreciative of my current blessings, having spent most of the evening counting them for him.

I arrived on the crowded platform, with five minutes to spare before the next train to St Albans. I spied an empty seat to my right, on the end of a row of three, and sat down next to a dark-haired, besuited young woman who was busy texting at impressive speed. When the train pulled in a few minutes later, I stood up and followed her towards the nearest set of double doors. As the doors opened, and the waiting commuters began to embark, she stumbled slightly in her heels and her male companion reacted quickly, catching her by the elbow to prevent her falling. They exchanged an 'oops', and a light laugh, and found a pair of seats near the exit.

It was only when I sat down opposite them, that I realised I knew the man she was with. 'Mike!' I said, with a smile. A momentary flicker of shocked surprise crossed his faced before he broke into a grin.

'Hello, Ros! What have you been up to this evening?'

'I've just been for a drink with an old work colleague. How about you?' I smiled at the woman next to him. She returned the smile, revealing a set of perfectly aligned, whitened teeth, and leaned forward slightly, in anticipation of an introduction.

'We had a late meeting. This is India Morne, one of our in-house solicitors at Marsh,' he said, turning towards her. 'India, this is Ros Shaw. She co-owns the bookshop where George works.'

'Lovely to meet you, Ros,' she said, maintaining her smile and holding out a manicured hand for me to shake. 'So, you work with Mike's wife?'

'Yes, we feel very lucky to have her,' I said.

'Well, I've only met Georgina a couple of times but I have no doubt she would be an enormous asset to any organisation – big or small.'

Mike nodded at her and smiled proudly.

'You're so right,' I said, 'and she's a lovely mother to boot. She's got it all, really.' I sighed. 'I should loathe her by rights.'

Mike laughed and India continued to smile.

'So, you work with Mike then?' I asked.

'Not on a daily basis but our paths do cross,' she said, turning to look at him.

'So Ros, how is business?' Mike loosened his tie and undid the top button of his shirt.

We talked bookshops and mergers and time passed quickly, with Mike in good spirits, simultaneously relaxed and buoyant. Consequently, our arrival at West Hampstead took me somewhat by surprise.

'This is my stop,' said India, suddenly. 'It was really nice to meet you, Ros. I'm going to make a point of popping into *Chapters* next time I'm in St Albans.'

'Please do,' I said. 'I'm sure George would like that too.'

She bade us goodbye, reminding Mike to email her a document for a meeting the following morning, and was gone.

'So, Mike,' I said, once we were alone, 'are you looking forward to your party? I didn't know whether to mention it in front of India – I wasn't sure whether she'd be there.'

'I don't think so,' he said, looking out onto the platform as the train pulled away, 'she's more of a colleague than a friend really.'

'Well, she seemed very nice,' I said casually.

'Really?' he asked, raising his eyebrows.

'Yes,' I said, 'You look surprised. You're now going to tell me that she's a total bitch, aren't you?'

'Not at all,' he laughed. 'It was just a kind thing for you to say.' I smiled and shrugged, amused at his reaction to the throw-away compliment.

For the remainder of our journey, we chatted about his forthcoming birthday and I entertained him with tales of my father's recent party. Arriving at St Albans, we shared a cab from the station, and, not more than ten minutes after waving him off, I was make-up free, in my pyjamas and brushing my teeth.

It had been an interesting evening and, despite Alan's sad news, not an unenjoyable one. And yet, as I scrubbed my teeth, and unconsciously assessed myself in the bathroom mirror, I found myself overwhelmed by a sudden sense of unease. What was it? Was it Alan? Well, I had left him in a much better state than I had found him. And I felt no real concern for his immediate welfare; he had already texted me to thank me for coming out, and to say that he had arrived safe and sound at his sister's home in Dulwich. So no, it wasn't Alan. Unable to come up with an explanation for my sense of foreboding, I decided, instead, to focus upon reaching that tricky, lower left molar with my brush.

A moment later, I had satisfactorily dealt with the molar, and was mid-floss, when my hands froze and I stared in horror at my wide-eyed, open-mouthed, newly-enlightened reflection.

It had come to me. During the minutes I had been sitting next to India Morne on the platform at Blackfriars, she had been holding hands with the man next to her. With Mike.

Chapter 12

I went into work the next day, relieved that it was George's day off. Both Joan and Andrew asked me within the first half-hour whether something was wrong. Andrew immediately accepted a 'No, everything's fine' and didn't enquire again; Joan, however, persisted and I was eventually forced to tell her that I felt a little under the weather.

'Is it cystitis again, my darling?' she asked, as she handed an elderly gentleman his change, 'because, if it is, I can get you a carton of cranberry juice when I pop out for my break.' I was aware that the customer was lingering, interested as to the cause of my symptoms.

'No, it is not cystitis,' I said, addressing him directly. He smiled in relief, raised his hand in silent salutation and left.

'Ooh, well, perhaps something you've eaten then,' she said, slipping on her coat. 'Or perhaps,' she added with a wink, 'it's something entirely different, which you'll tell me all about another time.'

I smiled. 'Perhaps.'

'Well, that's absolutely fine, my darling.' She rubbed my arm. 'Now, when I get back, remind me to tell you some more about our forthcoming production of *Oklahoma!*. I know you'll be wanting tickets.' I smiled and nodded as she bustled from the shop.

'Yes, and let's hope Joan doesn't wave to us from the stage this year,' said Andrew, coming downstairs. 'It was like being at an infant school nativity last year.'

'I expect you're right...' I said absently.

He came over to the till. 'So, are you going to tell me what the matter is, or just continue to give the appearance of being on Mogadon all day?'

'What? Oh...' I glanced down and, seeking an uncontroversial excuse for my continued distraction, tapped a magazine which Andrew had left lying open on the counter. 'Sorry, Andrew, I was concentrating on this article in your mag.' I stared at the page. 'Quite absorbing. Yes... very interesting.'

'OK,' he reached over and gently rotated the magazine through one hundred and eighty degrees, 'but you're reading upside down, Ros. And, whilst I admire the additional challenge you're setting yourself there, it does make understanding the corollary effect of high investment levels in China that much harder to understand.' I looked up. He smiled and raised his eyebrows questioningly.

I closed the magazine. 'I'm not sure I understand anything these days.' I sighed, before adding, on an impulse, 'Andrew, you're not free for a drink after work, are you?'

'Er... I think so.' He sounded hesitant; apparently slightly disconcerted by the suddenness of the proposal.

'Don't worry if you're not. It's nothing major,' I said, feeling suddenly awkward.

'No, no, that'd be fine. Yes, let's do that. Where do you fancy?'

'How about The Six Bells?' I suggested, before real-ising that there remained a delicate logistical issue to be overcome. 'Can we meet there half an hour or so after closing? I don't want Joan to feel left out but there's something I need to talk over with you alone.' I knew how awful that sounded but Andrew seemed to have recovered from his initial discomfort and now just shrugged and nodded.

'That's fine with me,' he said, picking up a pile of books and heading back towards the stairs. 'I'll see you there at six-thirty.'

I arrived at the pub first and ordered a large white wine for myself and a Guinness for Andrew. He turned up about five minutes later and I waved to him from my corner seat.

'Hi,' he said, coming over and placing his jacket on the back of the chair opposite me before sitting down. 'Thanks for this,' he raised his glass and took an appre-ciative sip. 'So, Ros,' he said, getting immediately to the point, in what was, I reflected, typically male fashion, 'what's wrong? Hope it's not the job because you've just got the hang of it.'

'No, it's not the job,' I smiled. 'I like the job.'

'Good,' he said. 'Although,' he added, with feigned solemnity, 'if it's not the job, then you may be talking to the wrong person. I mean, before you kick off, are you sure you wouldn't rather be talking to George about whatever the problem is.' He saw my expression change. 'George isn't the problem, is she?' he asked, now looking genuinely concerned. I nodded and he put down his

Guinness and pushed it away from him. 'Off you go, then,' he said.

I told him about my journey home the previous evening. He listened impassively, staring fixedly at his hands, which were folded on the table in front of him. When I had finished, he maintained his silence and gave no immediate clue as to his thoughts. I began to wonder if he perceived my account as gossip.

'I'm sorry,' I said. 'Perhaps I shouldn't have told you but it's been on my mind ever since it happened and I just wanted to discuss it with someone who knew everyone involved and—'

'Are you sure?' he asked abruptly.

I looked at him, surprised by the sudden interruption. 'Sure about what I saw? About whether she was holding his hand?'

'Yes.'

'Absolutely. I remember thinking she must be left-handed because she was texting very quickly, whilst holding the hand of the person to her right. I spent a long time last night thinking about scenarios in which you might innocently hold the hand of a member of the opposite sex – when you're distressed or when they're a good friend.' I began again the process of trying to find a comforting explanation for what I had seen. 'I mean, I link Tom's arm whenever we go out but Mike was very clear that they were primarily colleagues, not really friends – certainly not close enough to invite her to his birthday party. God and now I have this horrible thing in my head which I want to explain away but can't. And I think maybe it's something I should talk to George about as soon as possible, because if—'

'My advice would be not to,' said Andrew quietly, still staring at the table.

I hesitated; disconcerted by both the manner and nature of his response. 'But it's—'

'What do you want to do?' He raised his eyes to look at me and I struggled to read his expression. 'Instinctively, I mean? You don't want to have that conversation with her, do you?'

'No, of course not.'

'Then follow that instinct.'

'That's so male,' I said, bristling slightly at his unexpectedly simplistic analysis and matter-of-fact tone. 'You know, it might actually be helpful if you explained your thought processes to me a little. George is one of my best friends. Wouldn't you expect a best friend to tell you if they saw your partner snuggling up to someone else on the daily commute?'

'But *is* that what you saw?' He looked at me questioningly. 'Are you absolutely certain?'

'I told you what I saw. I've tried to think of another explanation but I can't.'

'You said yourself, when people are distressed, they seek comfort.'

'She didn't look remotely distressed.'

He shook his head. 'Not everyone carries a sign declaring their feelings, Ros. Some people are exceptionally good at keeping their feelings hidden. And just because you can't come up with a satisfactory alternative explanation for what you saw within twenty-four hours, doesn't mean there isn't one.'

He reached for his drink and, for one ridiculous moment, a flicker in his expression made me think that he might actually throw the glass. But instead, of course, he simply took a sip of the Guinness, before replacing it carefully on the table in front of him. 'Just take a step back and give yourself a chance to reflect. Don't do anything without serious, careful thought.' He paused, before adding, in a gentler tone, 'And I'm sorry.'

I looked at him and was surprised to see something resembling vulnerability. 'Sorry? What on earth for?' I asked.

'For not making it any easier for you to see George on Monday morning.'

'It's OK,' I said. 'It's not your dilemma. It's just hard to know the… the least wrong thing to do.'

He sighed. 'I can only speak from my heart,' he said, unconsciously using that turn of phrase and tone of voice that endeared him to so many of our female customers. 'And I'm afraid that, whatever the facts, there'd be no point in anyone telling me that the person I loved had feelings for someone else. I wouldn't believe it until the moment I discovered it for myself. And,' he continued, with a sad smile, 'I have no doubt that I would shoot the messenger. Twice.'

'OK,' I said.

By unspoken, mutual consent, we changed the topic of conversation, the mood gradually lightened and we avoided any further mention of George until we had finished our drinks and decided to head home, neither of us feeling like a second.

'I just hate the possibility of what's to come for her,' I said, as we stepped out onto the pavement.

'She deserves much better, that's for sure,' he replied. 'Mind you,' he added, 'I really can't believe there's any man who could fail to appreciate what he's got there.'

I smiled and nodded in an optimistic manner but, as I made my way home, I was feeling anything but optimistic for George.

Chapter 13

'Girls' weekend away!' said Celia, as I opened the front door.

'Well, actually, if we're going to be strictly factual about this,' I said, giving her a kiss, '*you* are a girl away. *I* am a girl at home. But I know what you mean. Come on in.'

We walked through to the kitchen. 'Oh Ros, this all looks lovely,' she said, stroking the cloth on the kitchen table and admiring some sketches I'd bought at an affordable art fair.

I smiled. 'I think you mean, this all looks clean, Celia.'

'No,' she insisted, 'I mean this all looks lovely. And you've put up new curtains,' she said, going back out into the hallway and peering into the living and dining rooms. 'It all just makes such a difference.'

'Actually,' I said, 'I'd love to be able to buy a place.'

'Have you been looking?' asked Celia.

I shook my head. 'No… I think I'll need another year or two of the shop doing well before thinking seriously about buying and then it will be somewhere smaller than this. It's just that I love the garden so much,' I said, looking out of the kitchen window.

'Ah, if only you loved gardening too,' said Celia, joining me by the sink and looking out at the shrubs running riot.

I laughed. 'Cheeky! Rome wasn't built in a day, you know.'

'I know,' she smiled, 'I'm only teasing. Now, tell me about the shop. Is business good?'

'It is actually,' I said, taking a bottle of rosé from the fridge and waving it at her, enquiringly. She nodded. 'Andrew works very hard and I feel I'm starting to be more of a help than a hindrance now. We sat down with the bank last week and everyone seemed very pleased with the way it's all going.'

'Wonderful,' she said, as I poured her a glass of wine. 'And, dare I ask, have you recovered from the Sam debacle?'

'Oh yes,' I said, sitting down and waving a hand dismissively. 'I'm glad he didn't turn up really. If he was that uncomfortable with the situation, the whole thing would have been a disaster.'

'Hmm,' she frowned. 'I was a bit cross with Kat over all that, you know.'

'I understand that she felt she needed to tell him,' I said. 'I think I would have done the same in her position.'

'Yes, but tell him the week before – or two days after,' she said. 'Don't blooming tell him as he's putting on his shoes to go out the front door.'

'He called a couple of days ago, actually, I meant to tell you.' I said.

'Gosh, did he? What did he say?'

'He suggested meeting up but I said I thought we should just leave it for a while. Besides,' I said, taking my first sip of wine, 'I'm going with Andrew to George's party, so the pressure's off re finding a date.'

'Andrew?' She eyed me suspiciously.

'Celia, I can assure you that there is nothing between Andrew and myself. But we are much more relaxed with each other these days.'

She gave me a sly grin. 'Really? More *relaxed*, are you?'

'You're awful, Muriel.'

'Again, only teasing. But you know that I've always thought that he's rather lovely.'

'Yes, you've told me many times and you're not alone in that. And he is. But he doesn't do it for me.'

'Who does?'

I hesitated, surprised to find myself giving the question serious consideration. 'Actually, the guy who killed Mr Edward has a rather gorgeous brother.'

'Ooh, does he?' said Celia, with interest.

'Yes, but,' I said, holding up a finger in an attempt to quell any premature celebration, 'he lives in Edinburgh.'

'Oh.'

'*And* he witnessed me fall into a hedge and run off crying after being stood-up.'

'So not overly auspicious then.'

'No.'

'Shame.'

'Yes, it is,' I sighed.

We were momentarily subdued before Celia rallied. 'So...' she said, 'take-away, plonk and,' she rummaged in her bag and took out a DVD, 'movie tonight. And then clothes shopping tomorrow, for your party and my Christening – followed by cocktails and dinner out. Yes?'

'Sounds like a plan!' I was pleased that this was, at last, a genuinely enjoyable weekend getaway for her, rather than just a mercy dash to check up on her needy sister.

'Fab,' she beamed. 'Chinese or Indian? You choose.'

Celia and I didn't surface until about ten the next morning, having stayed up talking until two the night before. We spent until lunchtime lounging around in our dressing gowns, drinking tea and talking some more.

She was assured enough of my ongoing recovery to tell me some of her own troubles, something she hadn't done for almost two years. Most of her worries were for her children: were they making and retaining friends at school; did she push Ben too hard academically; would they get into the local state secondary school when the time came? She had, seemingly, no concerns for herself and the incidental references to David and their relationship, were reassuringly benign. She was, I decided, on the whole, exceedingly happy with her lot. I didn't resent her that, being, as she was, the author of her own contentment.

After a light lunch, we walked into the centre of St Albans, at which point Celia insisted that the first order of business simply *had* to be finding me a party dress. I didn't argue as I knew the idea of dressing me up like a cut-out paper doll was something she would genuinely enjoy. We spent the next hour and a half browsing the High Street names and the small boutiques. After rejecting at least a dozen dresses as either too bright, too tight, too short or too *Strictly Come Dancing*, I eventually found an on-the-knee, fitted, purple silk cocktail dress, with which even I could not find fault.

Celia declared that it must be worn with heels, or not at all, and thus a pair of filigree silver, ridiculously high, spike-heeled shoes were added to my haul, despite the fact that, with them on, I was approximately 6' tall and could barely walk a step. 'Just practise walking up and down the hallway when you get home,' said Celia, when I attempted a weak refusal. 'You'll be fine – and they make your legs look like spaghetti.'

'And that's a good thing?' I said, looking down. 'Where are my ankles in that simile?'

'Oh you know what I mean,' she said. 'Just buy them, Ros.'

Celia, as I knew she would, managed to kit herself out perfectly from head to toe in under half an hour but then spent over twice as long choosing gifts for the boys. It was five o'clock before we agreed a time-out for a cup of tea and a slice of cake.

We adjourned to the small café, down a quiet side-street, in which I sometimes took refuge, following a busy morning in the shop, and flopped down on a sofa by a low table, placing a mountain of bags on the floor at our feet, and ordered our refreshments.

'Thanks so much, Celia,' I said.

She brushed a stray curl from her forehead and waved away my gratitude. 'No, thank *you*,' she said. 'This is so much more fun than spending a Saturday wandering around Exeter shops on my own.' She picked up the pot of tea, which our waitress had just placed in front of us, and began to pour.

'I don't just mean for coming shopping with me,' I said, quietly. 'I mean for it all. For everything. I only wish that, for your sake, and everyone else's, I could have pulled myself together a little sooner.'

She put down the teapot and put a finger to her lips. 'Shhh…' she said and leaned over to embrace me. 'I'm so very proud of you, Ros. I'm not sure I would have survived it.'

I smiled. She just couldn't help herself. 'Shut up,' I said.

'OK, I will. I'll finish pouring the tea instead. And hey,' she said, looking over her shoulder, 'where are our cakes?'

—

We had our first champagne cocktail at 8pm and were mixing ourselves Cosmopolitans at home around midnight. The food in between had been palatable but incidental to the conversation and the alcohol. We had talked about Mum's diet, Dad's scaffolding, David's job and Celia's lack of confidence in her abilities as a mother, with each topic being satisfactorily, and optimistically, concluded, with the exception of the diet – we both agreed that that was doomed to failure.

We then moved onto gossip and Celia told me about an old school friend, and mother-of-three, who had recently moved out of the marital home in Blackheath to live with someone called Regina, who had multiple piercings and a market stall in Brixton. I managed to greet this news with the appropriate level of shock, gravitas and devastation for approximately forty-five seconds, before dissolving into fits of laughter.

Suddenly, I remembered about Tom. 'God, Ce, I completely forgot to tell you that Tom's getting married. I hadn't told you that had I?'

'No,' she hiccoughed, looking surprised, 'you hadn't. When's that then?'

'January.'

'Brrrr…'

'I know! Hey,' I laughed, 'we'll have to go shopping again.'

'Hurrah!' She grinned and toasted me with the remains of her cocktail. 'Is he marrying Anna?' she asked.

'Amy.' I sipped my drink.

'Amy. Of course. And are you OK with it all?' I had been inspecting a cocktail spillage on the sofa and now looked up to see that Celia's smile had dropped.

'What, with him getting married?' I laughed incredulously. 'I never fancied him, Celia.'

'No, no, I meant with going to the wedding.'

'Oh yes,' I said, 'just because mine didn't happen doesn't mean I can't be happy for someone else. I went to Florence's, didn't I? And that was fine.'

'That's not what I meant, Ros,' she said, unsteadily placing her empty glass on the coffee table. 'I meant because, well, I presume Tom will invite...' her voice trailed away and she looked at me with concern in her eyes; her first anxious moment of the weekend.

Suddenly, I understood what she meant and she was right. That was why Tom had been so worried about telling me he was getting married. Not because he thought I had a problem with weddings, or may be harbouring unexpressed feelings for him. He was worried because The Rat would be there.

Chapter 14

I waved Celia off after brunch the next morning, having reassured her, I hoped to her complete satisfaction, that I was not at all concerned about the prospect of seeing The Rat after all this time. In fact, the truth of the situation was much more confused. Whilst the thought of seeing him didn't terrify me, I couldn't claim to be totally at peace about it. I felt as I had when sitting an exam for which I had prepared moderately well; an equal measure of eagerness and reluctance for the moment to come when I would discover whether success or failure was on the cards.

What I *was* sure about was that I had to know, one way or the other, whether he would be there. I simply could not spend the next six months in a state of anxious uncertainty. Consequently, about half an hour after Celia left, I picked up the phone and called Tom. I was in the middle of leaving a message, asking him to call, when Amy picked up the phone.

'Hi, Ros.' Her tone was clipped. 'How are you? We haven't spoken in months, although Tom keeps me up to date, of course. It sounds like the bookshop is surviving and that you are coping a little better.'

I decided to ignore the inferred slights. 'Yes, business is booming,' I replied, whilst frantically searching for a reason for phoning and at the same time cursing myself for not calling Tom on his mobile, 'but I must just congratulate you on your forthcoming nuptials.'

'Thank you, we're very excited.'

There was a slightly uncomfortable pause.

'How are the preparations going?' I ventured.

'Great.' she said. 'Venue, catering and entertainment are all in place.'

'That's wonderful… well,' inspiration came, 'I phoned because I wanted to pick Tom's brain actually. He has a financial adviser he's always banging on about – Laurence someone…'

'Laurence Feehily.'

'Yes, that's him. I just wanted to get his number if I could. It's for my dad…'

'Sure. I'll get Tom for you. I think he's in the study – actually he's just walked in.' There was a slight distortion in sound as she put her hand over the receiver, although not enough to prevent me from hearing her end of the conversation. 'It's Ros,' she said, tonelessly. Tom said something indistinct to which she replied, 'God, I don't know. She gave me some balls about wanting Laurie's telephone number.' I cringed and waited for Tom to come on the line.

'Sorry about that,' I said, when he took the phone.

'No, no, that's fine, I'll look up the number for you,' he said, jovially.

'I don't want the number.'

'I know that,' he said. 'Here it is. Have you got a pen?'

'No.'

'Great. It's 077— hang on a minute, Ros. I just have to say goodbye to Amy.' I heard rustlings, indicating a hand over the receiver again.

'I don't know why you pretend,' she said.

'Pretend what?' he asked.

'Never mind. See you later.' I heard a door close.

'Sorry, Ros. I'm back now. What's up?' he asked.

'You know that thing you two do with putting a hand over the receiver,' I said.

'Yes.'

'It doesn't bloody work. There's a mute button for that kind of thing, you know.'

'I'll bear that in mind. Now, what do you really want?'

'Well, I'd quite like not to be terrified of your fiancée for starters.'

'Wouldn't we all but there it is,' he sighed. 'Now, really, get to the point. I need a wee.'

'OK.' I took a deep breath. 'I'm going to ask you a question but I want you to know that you needn't worry about the answer you give me.'

'I'm worried already.'

'Don't be. It's fine. I just need to know.'

'OK.'

'Is he coming to your wedding?'

'What?'

'Is he coming to your wedding in January?' There was silence the other end of the line. 'Tom?'

'I thought you realised that.' He sounded appalled.

'Oh yeah, yeah,' I tried to sound casual. 'Of course I knew he'd been *invited*, I just wondered whether he'd accepted, that's all. I just wanted to know. You know, so I could be prepared.'

'Prepared in what way?' he asked. 'Prepared as in: ready emotionally? Or prepared as in: arrive armed with a handgun?'

'Oh Tom,' I laughed.

'I'm serious, Ros' he said. 'I'm not laughing. Do you hear me laughing? Listen to this.' There was a pause.

'I don't hear anything.'

'That's the sound of me not laughing.'

'Oh go and have a wee, for God's sake, and stop worrying,' I said. 'I just needed to know, that's all. I'm cool about it.'

'Great and keep it that way,' he said. 'He's cool about it too. So it's all good.'

'Is he? Good. Good.' I was desperate to know more. Had they had a conversation about me? Had he been worried? Was he bringing a "plus one"?

'Ros?'

'Yes?'

'You are certain you're OK with this?' His tone was gentler now. 'Because, if you're not, we will fix it. God knows how but we will fix it. I don't want you upset and, above all, I don't want Amy's day spoiled.'

'Of course I wouldn't spoil her day! It's some time since I was the sniveling sofa wreck, you know,' I said, a little offended. 'I am very aware of other people's feelings these days.'

'I know, I know. I'm sorry,' he said. 'It's just that Amy is quite, well, uptight about the whole thing anyway. She couldn't cope with a chipped nail, let alone fisticuffs at the reception.'

'I appreciate that,' I said. 'And I assure you, there will be no fisticuffs.'

'OK. Well, I'd better go but do you fancy a drink in the next week or two? Your neck of the woods?'

'Sounds good.' I said. 'Text me a couple of dates.'

'Great. Will do,' he said. 'Hey, and when I see you, you can look me in the eye and tell me that you don't have murder on your mind.'

'Go and pee, for God's sake.'

'Too late – a little bit has already leaked out. You know, with the stress of this conversation.'

'Just go.'

'OK. Bye.'

I hung up and immediately decided to call my mother. I was in need of some inane conversation regarding the trials and tribulations of living with my father, in order to distract me from the weighty issues of betrayal and an inability to forgive and forget.

'Hello?' My mother's tone was the usual mixture of expectation and mild excitement.

'Hi, Mum. It's me.'

'Ros! How lovely. And how are you my darling?'

'I'm fine. How are things there? How is dad?'

She sighed. 'Well, you know the old greenhouse? Your father has taken it to pieces and is currently in the back garden trying to construct his own solar heating system. I said to him, "*Ted, if you want to knock something down, knock down that monstrosity of a shed you built last summer*". Honestly Ros, how many people do you know who have a shed with windows from a Ford transit?'

I sat down on the sofa and relaxed. This was exactly what I needed.

Chapter 15

I watched George carefully over the next few weeks, in particular looking for signs of anxiety or distress when Mike's name was mentioned. But she seemed her usual self, and appeared, if anything, a little brighter as Mike had suddenly developed an interest in, and a new enthusiasm for, celebrating his birthday. I began to feel that there simply must have been an innocent explanation for the hand-holding after all and was grateful that Andrew had cautioned me against acting on impulse and telling George what I had seen.

If Andrew had been female, I would have been able to share my ongoing observations, musings and conclusions with him. As it was, he proved to be disappointingly male about the whole thing; steadfastly behaving as if we had never discussed the matter. His attitude, and demeanour, in George's presence, were unchanged and he never once raised the subject of Mike, even when we were alone.

My concern regarding the hand-holding incident ebbed until it was no more than an occasional nagging doubt, and female conversation and attention in the book-shop began to centre increasingly, and uncontroversially, on Mike's party and on Joan's imminent appearance in *Oklahoma!*. Indeed, the two topics were now conveniently segued by the fact that Joan planned to bring Ali Hakim, aka, her co-star, Robert Lochran, as her date to George's bash.

None of us mentioned the fact that, at the ages of 62 and 67 respectively, Joan and Bobby, as she called him, were a little older than one might have expected Ado Annie and Ali to be. However, as Andrew pointed out, Joan had, time and time again, recounted anecdotes which confirmed her to be a woman with a complete inability to say 'no', and this, together with an impressive vocal volume, if not range, had no doubt influenced casting.

'Oh Bobby is so naughty!' Joan gushed one afternoon, as she updated us, at length, regarding the production, whilst Andrew feigned deafness less than ten feet away. 'He takes any and every opportunity to slip an arm round my waist or to pat my behind. Arthur even had to insist on a slightly less tactile performance at the final dress rehearsal.' Joan giggled like a schoolgirl.

'Arthur?' asked George.

'The director, dear,' beamed Joan. 'Actually,' she chuckled, 'between you and me, I think there may be a little bit of jealousy there.' She nudged George and winked at me.

'Really?' said Andrew, deciding to join the conversation. 'So Arthur is gay?'

'I'm afraid not, my darling,' replied Joan. 'But Binky Breslow, in the chorus, hopes to have the op one day, although he just tucks it all in for the moment. I can introduce you to him after the show this evening if you like.'

Andrew smiled, in what seemed to be genuine amusement. 'Oh yes, I'd almost forgotten that tonight was the night.' He turned to George and me. 'Shall we meet for pre-show drinks?'

'What a lovely idea, Andrew!' exclaimed George. 'I shall ask the sitter to come early. You know, Joany, I'm really looking forward to this evening. Last year was such fun.'

'I'm sorry but am I the only one who wants to know more about Binky Breslow?' I asked, incredulously.

'We've met him before, Ros,' said George, absently, whilst applying some lipstick in preparation for the school run. 'He was Sister Berthe in that production of *The Sound of Music* Joan took us to in Hatfield last February. Remember?'

'Was he the tall nun in the horn-rimmed specs?'

'No, dear,' said Joan. 'You're thinking of Pauline Fisher. She has polycystic ovaries.'

'So who… You know what, never mind,' I said. 'Anyway, I'm really looking forward to it too, Joan. Hey and sneak us a wave, if you can. It makes me feel all backstage pass-ish.'

Joan smiled and her eyes flickered briefly towards Andrew. 'Of course I will, my darling. Of course I will.'

Chapter 16

We sat with our drinks, near the unlit fire, in the relatively quiet mid-week bar of The Six Bells, with forty-five minutes still to spare before we had to take our seats for Joan's opening night performance. It was a warm, still evening and I felt an unexpected rush of something like contentment, as I sipped at what had been, half an hour ago, a large glass of white wine, and listened to George's tragic tale of Lottie's recent poor showing in the school talent contest.

'Yes,' continued George, 'she was a little disappointed, as we had practised the poem endlessly and I mean,' she finished her gin and tonic, '*endlessly*. But, I said, "*Lotts, it was a first attempt and, next year, we'll try something a little more stand-out*".'

Andrew smiled. 'What do you have in mind?'

'Oh, I don't know. One sweet little boy performed a magic trick and another child did paper-folding. She was very good actually. She made a little bird and launched it into the audience.' George hesitated. 'Well, I think it was a bird. It was either a bird or a crucifix'

'Did it glide?' I asked.

'No. That's why I'm wondering if it was a crucifix.'

I was puzzled. 'Why would she throw a crucifix into the audience?'

'Isn't that a scene from '*The Exorcist*'?' asked Andrew. George laughed.

'So, who won?' I tried not to be concerned that I was genuinely interested.

'Oh, a very bendy child called Alicia. She taped a hairbrush to her foot and gave herself a centre parting. But, as I said to Mike on the phone, that's not actually a talent, is it? It's just a physiological fact.' George elbowed Andrew. 'It's not talent, is it, Andrew?'

'I'm not sure, George, but I would certainly rate an interest in poetry above an ability to bite your own toenails. Now,' he said, standing up, 'who would like another drink?'

George and I both accepted the offer and he headed for the bar. George watched him go.

'He's so very lovely, Ros' she said, smiling. 'I just wish he'd find someone, you know.'

I looked over at Andrew, leaning across the bar to give his order and noticed the barmaid flick him a second, surreptitious, look, as he glanced down to take cash from his wallet. There was no doubt that he was a good-looking guy. 'And it's not only that he's good-looking,' continued George, 'he's intelligent and caring to boot. A real catch. I tell you Ros, if I wasn't happily married... Not that he'd be interested in someone of *my* age, of course. He'd want someone much younger – about your age.'

I smiled inwardly. It wasn't the first time that George had extolled Andrew's virtues in an attempt to play cupid. I shook my head. 'George, we both know that he has had many, many opportunities. Half of our business is from thirty-something females looking for love with Andrew, but he's simply not interested. His heart is broken, or lost, or something. Oh and,' I added, finishing my wine and prodding her upper arm with the index finger of my free hand, 'the fact that you're six, or, is it, a whole *seven* months older than Andrew, doesn't exactly make you a geriatric.'

'Here you go,' Andrew placed our drinks in front of us. 'So, what have I missed? Have you moved on from flying crucifixes and freakishly supple limbs?'

'Yes, actually,' I said, wickedly. 'George raised the subject of relationships, didn't you, George?' Andrew looked unconcerned. 'And she was just wondering,' I paused, prolonging George's agony, 'whether Joan and Bobby are serious, or whether it's just a fling.'

George narrowed her eyes at me in admonition before turning to Andrew. 'Yes, Andrew,' she said, sipping her second G&T appreciatively. 'Lust or love?' He glanced first at George and then at me and flushed slightly for a reason I couldn't fathom. I looked at George to see if she had noticed his discomfort but her head was lowered, her attention now focused on the contents of her bag as she searched for her mobile phone whilst muttering something about the babysitter. When I looked back at Andrew, he appeared as impassive as usual.

'Well, you know,' he said, as George, herself now looking a little flustered, finally found the phone and placed it on the table in front of her. 'I tend to think a mix of the two is rather nice.'

She picked up her drink again. 'Sorry, Andrew, that was so rude of me.' She paused. 'You know, I've completely lost track of what we were talking about.'

'Acquired talent versus being a freak of nature,' I said, quickly, not quite certain what had just occurred, but instinctively feeling that a change of subject was required.

'Oh yes,' said George, with a smile. 'Now… let me tell you about Lottie's friend, Monty, who played the recorder with his nose. *And* he had a streaming cold, poor little love. Now, I'm not sure that's talent exactly but it certainly shows a dedication to one's art.'

–

Joan managed to wave to us no fewer than three times during the performance, which delighted George and me and, in the end, as Joan would have wished, elicited a loud 'Jesus Christ' from Andrew. As she had requested, we went backstage after the show to congratulate her on a dramatic triumph and to be introduced to Bobby and the rest of the cast. She was waiting for us outside the women's dressing room door and waved all three of us in, with a wide sweep of her arm. 'Come in, come in, my darlings!' she cried.

'I think I'll just wait out here, Joan, until you're ready,' said Andrew, unable to avoid the sight of several bulging bodices through the half-open door.

'Oh you can come along in, Andrew. Nobody minds,' said Joan, touching him lightly on the arm. 'Nobody minds, do we dears?' she added, addressing the other occupants of the room. A dozen or so pairs of female eyes turned on Andrew and he was greeted with a cacophony of encouragement and shrieking laughter.

'Ooh, no, I don't mind *at all*. Not for a lovely young man like that, Joany.'

'I'm sure this isn't the first set of stockings that he's seen. Is it, dear?'

'Do you think he'll help me with my zip, Joany?'

Poor Andrew. A room full of Joans and no obvious, polite means of escape. He stood, as if made of marble.

Joan threaded her arm through his and pulled him across the threshold, addressing the room as she did so. 'Now, leave him alone, ladies. This young man is spoken for. Come on in, Andrew.' She then leaned towards him, turning her back slightly on her fellow cast members. In a barely audible whisper, she said, 'They're all quite covered up, Andrew, and I'm not trying to embarrass you, my darling, but I would like you to meet my friends. I talk about you and your lovely shop all the time.'

Over a period of no more than a second, Andrew's expression flickered from astonishment, through bewilderment and pleasure, before finally settling into affected resignation. He raised his eyes heavenward. 'Oh, go on then,' he sighed, loudly. 'But do be gentle with me, won't you, ladies?' The shrieking began again, along with the introductions.

We finally left the theatre just over an hour later, at the weary behest of the caretaker. Following Andrew's trial by ordeal in the ladies' dressing room, Joan had taken us along the corridor into some sort of office, where Bobby was waiting with a bottle of Prosecco and five plastic cups. We toasted their first-night success, whilst Joan told Bobby all about us and then told us all about Bobby, at one point placing a hand on his chest and rejoicing in his 'heady masculinity' which, bearing in mind his largely bald head and 5'6" frame, smacked slightly of exaggeration. But no one seemed to mind the rose-tinted nature of her spectacles and we all, even Andrew, laughed along and made no attempt to correct her highly-complimentary deviations from the truth in respect of us all.

At around eleven thirty, Andrew and I waved Joan, Bobby and George off in a cab, before walking back to *Chapters* to collect our bicycles. En route, we discussed the show, the possible outcomes of a forthcoming rent review and whether Binky Breslow would ever make a convincing woman, before Andrew raised the subject of Tom's wedding. It hadn't occurred to me that he would be going but, of course, as one of Tom's closest friends, it was unthinkable that he wouldn't have been invited.

'I'm quite looking forward to it,' he said. 'Knowing Tom, it'll be no expense spared.'

'Hmm…' I said, noncommittally.

We stood at a pedestrian crossing, waiting for the lights to change. I pressed the button repeatedly.

'You not so sure about it?' he asked.

'Oh, I know I'll enjoy it when I get there. But I'll have the usual plus one problem.' I held up a hand to stymie the offer which I knew was imminent. 'No. Not necessary. But, thank you anyway. I'll sort myself out this time and you can take a proper date. But I do hope they put us on the same table.'

'Maybe I'll ask Mary,' he said, as the lights finally changed and we started to cross.

'Mary who?'

'Mary whose boots I untied and removed this evening. Mary who can't bend down because of her arthritic hip.'

I smiled. 'Of course. Well, she was very taken with you.' I hesitated and then decided to risk making the conversation a little more personal. 'But, lovely as Mary was, we all know that you can aim a little higher than that, Andrew. George was singing your praises again this evening. She'd have you married a hundred times over, you know.'

He said nothing, but a quick glance didn't reveal any signs of irritation regarding the subject, so I pressed on. 'And she's right, you know. You must notice the women batting their lashes at you daily across the counter. No one take your fancy?'

'I could ask you a similar question, you know,' he said.

'And I'm happy enough to answer it, if you want to know. The truth is, I'm no longer averse to the idea of a relationship. I just haven't been tempted yet.' I looked at him and saw that he was smiling. 'Is that how you feel?' I asked.

'No. My situation is quite the reverse.' We had arrived at the shop. 'Have you got your keys to hand?' I retrieved my keys and handed them to him.

'Is that all you're going to say?'

'Sorry?'

'That your situation is quite the reverse to mine?'

He shrugged. 'Well, that's the truth. There you go.' He held the door open for me but I didn't move.

'Sorry, Andrew. It's just that I'm female. So, I need more detail.'

'Jesus, Ros,' he sighed. 'Look,' he pushed me gently through the door and deactivated the alarm, 'you say you're not averse to a relationship. Well, I am averse.' We headed towards the back of the shop to collect our bikes. 'And I know that's not likely to change anytime soon.'

'Am I allowed to ask why you're averse?'

'Of course you can ask.' We lifted our bikes back through the shop and out onto the pavement outside.

'But you're not going to tell me, are you?'

He locked up and handed me the keys. 'You know me so well, Ros,' he said, mounting his bike and raising a hand in farewell.

'Far from it,' I sighed, completing the conversation alone as he headed off down the hill. 'Far, far, from it.'

Chapter 17

The week before Mike's party, George had planned to spend a few days at her parents' holiday cottage in Wales with Mike and Lottie. Unfortunately, the dates coincided with the completion of a merger involving a Marsh subsidiary, and Mike was reluctant to delegate responsibility for the final stages of the deal to anyone else. It was therefore agreed that George and Lottie would go to Wales, and share the cottage with friends, whilst Mike remained at home to oversee completion and then relax into a weekend of general celebration. George seemed philosophical about the change of plan when she told me about it on her last working day before heading off.

'It's a shame because I wanted Mike and Lottie to spend some time together before his birthday,' she said as she slipped on her jacket and prepared to make a note of our mid-morning coffee and cake orders. 'Especially as Lottie won't be with us on the day.' She paused and addressed the ceiling. 'What will you have today, Andrew?' she called. On receiving no reply from the first floor, she wrote *Americano* on her slip of paper. 'I'm sure that's what he'll want.' She smiled and continued to scribble. 'I'm going to get him a muffin too, to cheer him up. He's a bit snuffly this morning, isn't he?'

'Is he? I hadn't noticed,' I said. 'So you're OK about Wales, then? I'm sure you'll have a great time.'

'Yes, Lottie and I will head off tomorrow morning and then I will drop Lottie with Mum and Dad on Wednesday evening. It will be fine.' She sighed. 'And I know Mike well enough to realise that he'd be totally pre-occupied with the deal, even if he did come with us. So he might as well stay at home and then be able to enjoy the party, knowing that everything has gone through without a hitch.'

On those rare occasions when I found myself wondering whether I missed the pace and challenges of the City, conversations such as this with George served to remind me of the benefits of my new, low-key occupation.

'I'm assuming you're a cappuccino, Ros?' she said, stepping out onto the pavement.

'Lovely, thanks.'

She waved and smiled at me as she walked past the window and then turned to cross the road, looking as beautiful and well-groomed as ever but, I thought, a little more tired than usual. I put this down to increased hours as a single mother, as Mike was forced to spend more and more time in the office, in an effort to push the deal through on time.

'Did someone call me?' I started and turned to see Andrew standing a few feet away.

'Good God, Andrew,' I said, placing a hand on my chest. 'You gave me such a fright. You're like those twins in 'The Shining'.'

'I've never read it or seen the movie.'

'You don't say,' I muttered, before adding a more loudly, 'Anyway, yes, George was asking if you wanted a coffee.'

'Damn. I wanted an Americano'

'Well, you're in luck then,' I said, flicking through his copy of the *LRB*, 'because that's what she said you'd want, so that's exactly what you're getting.'

I looked up. He stood motionless, staring at me with an unreadable expression on his face: a mixture of discomfort and something else.

'What's the matter? Are you OK?' I asked.

'What? Sorry, I was miles away, Ros. What did you say?'

'I told you that George is getting you an Americano and then I asked if you were OK,' I said. 'You looked worried.'

He shook his head. 'No, I was just thinking about the rent review.'

'Well, there's nothing to be concerned about there,' I said, returning my attention to the magazine. 'It's looking favourable for us and, business-wise, we're still bucking the trend – the collectables side of things is doing really well and footfall is up... apparently,' I added, scanning the deserted shop.

'Hmm...' I thought he sounded unconvinced.

I closed the magazine. 'Look, Andrew. If you have a problem with the way things are going, it would be as well for you to tell me about it now. I know that from a commercial point of view we are doing quite nicely, but if you have another kind of concern then let's sit down and talk about it. Maybe you'd like me to work some more hours and take some of that pressure from you. I had been thinking about that myself and it's something I would be more than happy to do. And the business can afford for you to take a break if that's what you want to do. You certainly deserve one.'

'I love coming to work,' he said.

'OK,' I said. 'Well, that's good to hear but, regrettably, I am of a somewhat paranoid disposition and I can tell there's something wrong and, if you don't tell me what it is, I will assume it's something to do with me and that's not going to be good for anyone.'

'You're not making me miserable, Ros,' he said, looking out the window.

I followed his gaze and saw George waiting to cross the road with her tray of coffees and a small, paper carrier bag. 'OK, Andrew, that'll do me for now. But if whatever is wrong has anything to do with business then you owe it to me to sit down and discuss it with me.'

He turned to me and smiled. 'Christ, when did you get so corporate?'

'It's been coming on gradually.'

'One could almost say imperceptibly.'

I wagged a finger at him. 'Thin ice, Andrew O'Farrell.'

George set the shop bell ringing as she entered. 'Ta-da!' she beamed, proffering the tray and waving the bag. 'Andrew, I have a special treat for you to take away the Thursday blues.'

I watched as he took the bag from her and peered inside at its contents. 'Banana wholemeal,' he said, looking at George. 'My favourite. How did you know?' She huffed on her fingernails and polished them on her lapel, enjoying her success and, in return, he flashed her the easy smile which kept so many of our female customers coming back for more. The smile remained in place, as he made his way into the kitchen with his gift but, as he turned to close the door behind him and momentarily glanced back into the shop, I saw unmistakable anxiety in his eyes.

I began to worry about what it might be that Andrew knew and I didn't.

Chapter 18

'Bugger.' I blinked, sending a brushful of waterproof mascara arcing up towards my eyebrow. 'Bugger, bugger, bugger.'

I looked at my phone on the bathroom windowsill. Andrew would be here for pre-party drinks in less than ten minutes and I was still in my bathrobe. I removed the black streak from my eyelid with a cosmetic wipe and decided to wait until my fingernails were properly dry before attempting a second assault on my lashes.

I went into the bedroom, where my dress and tights were lying on the bed. No, I would leave those too, until the fingernails were absolutely bone dry. I looked in the mirror. Well, with the exception of the eyelashes, the dress, the tights and the shoes, I was ready in every other respect – as ready as I would ever be. I had, that morning, had my hair cut and, for the first time in a long time, highlighted too and I was rather pleased with the result. I sat down on the bed, with my hands splayed on my lap and began to count to sixty – another minute should do it.

The doorbell rang. Trust Andrew to be early. I hurried downstairs and, on reaching the front door, tentatively tested the nail on the index finger of my right hand, before deciding it was safe to attempt to turn the lock. I opened the door.

'Interesting choice of attire,' said Andrew, looking me up and down. 'I'm relieved I didn't attempt to complement that look with a corsage. However, I did bring this instead.' He produced a bottle of champagne from behind his back.

'Neither of us get out enough, do we?' I said, taking the bottle from him with a smile and kissing him lightly on the cheek.

'Nowhere near,' he said.

'Anyway, come on in. You go and pour us out a couple of glasses and I'll go and finish getting ready. I've only got my lashes to do and then I'm good to go.'

'And perhaps you could put on a clean dressing-gown while you're at it,' he called after me as I ran up the stairs. 'That one seems to have something on the hem. I'm praying its Marmite!'

'Glasses are in the top cupboard to the left of the fridge!' I called, unscrewing the lid of my mascara.

I heard the clinking of glasses downstairs and the pop of a cork as I pulled up my tights and stepped into my dress. I picked up the clutch purse, kindly loaned for the occasion by Celia, and the ridiculously high silver shoes and went downstairs into the kitchen, where Andrew was mopping up a minor spillage with some kitchen roll.

'I just pray to God I don't break my neck in these things,' I said, placing the shoes down on the kitchen table. 'I've been practising in them for weeks but one dodgy knot in George's oak floor and I'm bound to come a-cropper.' I laughed and looked up to see Andrew standing with a flute of champagne in each hand and a look of apparent horror on his face.

'God, what's the matter?' He was staring at my dress. 'Andrew, what's wrong?' I demanded, experiencing a rising panic. 'What is it? Is it too short? WHAT?'

'Ros,' he said, suddenly grinning, 'you look amazing.'

An unanticipated tear escaped and I disguised its removal by scratching my cheek. 'Really?' I said, quietly.

He walked over and handed me my glass. 'You are going to be fighting them off with a big stick tonight.'

I put my glass down on the table and hugged him. 'You,' I said, 'remarkably infrequently, say just the right thing. Thank you.'

'You're welcome,' he said, as I released him. 'Now, drink this,' he returned my glass to me. 'We have a party to attend.'

–

We arrived at the party about an hour after the official start time, to find things well underway, with a surprising number of early dancers already enjoying the disco in the largest of the downstairs rooms.

Our coats were taken, and drinks placed in our hands, by uniformed staff. We wound our way towards the back of the house past groups of loudly chatting guests and a rather impressive buffet, laid out in what was usually the dining room. In my heels, I was almost eye-level with Andrew and, as such, was one of the tallest guests, men included. Without the pre-party champagne, I would have teetered self-consciously through the throng. As it was, I simply enjoyed the view. Andrew and I recognised a couple of faces from one of George's dinner parties but no one else.

'I think we should let George know we're here,' I said, peering over the crowd in an attempt to spot her. 'And I'd like to ditch this as soon as possible, too.' I waved the blue, red and yellow striped bag which contained cufflinks, my gift to Mike.

'OK,' said Andrew, 'but we've done a complete circuit of the ground floor already and I can't see either of them. Are you hungry? We could head back to the buffet and see if we bump into one of them on the way.' A passing waiter relieved us of our empty glasses and replaced them with fresh ones, brimming with champagne, advising us, as he did so, that there was a bar in the basement offering a variety of alternative refreshments.

I raised my eyebrows at Andrew. 'Well, that's where your Guinness will be, and maybe George and Mike too, but,' I held up my glass, 'I think you're right about food. I really need something to eat soon, otherwise you'll be carting me home in a wheelbarrow.'

'You're preaching to the converted,' he said. 'Let's go and eat.'

We returned to the dining room and joined a small queue at the buffet. I scanned the table, deciding that George really knew how to throw a party and, as my plate was artistically piled with food by yet another member of hired staff, it occurred to me that no expense had been spared by George in her attempt to give Mike a party to remember.

Our quest for food achieved, Andrew and I took our plates and joined the crowd in the large, square entrance hall, which was this evening draped in silver fabric and fairy lights. The noise of the disco escaped through a door to our left but didn't preclude conversation. We had just been greeted by two of the few guests we knew, when I finally spotted George, standing near the entrance to the dining room, talking to an older, grey-haired couple.

The man had clearly just finished telling an amusing anecdote and George was laughing appreciatively. She was beautiful, in a pale blue, beaded chiffon shift dress. Her hair was up, magically held in place, it seemed, by a single, sparkling silver clip, shaped like a butterfly. A moment later she turned and, seeing Andrew and myself, looked gratifyingly delighted, made her excuses to her friends, and fluttered over to greet us.

'Ros!' she said, embracing me. 'Oh my goodness have I got a surprise for you. And Andrew!' She placed her hands on his shoulders and stood on tip-toe to kiss him. 'I've been looking everywhere for you.'

She was so good at making people feel important. I looked at Andrew and could tell that he was as touched by the welcome as I was.

'How are you getting on?' she continued. 'Are you being looked after? And I see you've bumped into Fi and Jeremy,' she turned to the other half of our foursome.

'We're just taking the opportunity to catch-up, George,' said Jeremy. 'You sound like you're still a happy band of pilgrims at that little bookshop of yours.'

'Oh we are, aren't we?' said George with a smile. 'I simply love going to work.'

'God, I wish I did,' said Fi. 'You haven't got room for me, have you, Andrew?' I blinked, uncertain as to whether she had actually licked her lips as she said this or whether I had just imagined it.

'Well, I'm not sure. I'd have to confer with Ros, of course.'

I smiled, grateful for his nod towards our partnership.

'Our other colleague, Joan, is here too... some-where...' said George, looking round. 'You must meet her, Fi, she's a gem.'

'Is Bobby with her?' I asked.

'Yes,' said George, 'and they both look absolutely marvellous.'

'Oh dear,' said Andrew, under his breath, and I knew he shared my concern as to what 'marvellous' might actually constitute.

'So, Ros,' said Jeremy, nudging me, 'I'm loving the dress. You look fabulous. When did that happen?'

'You mean, when did I transform from the troll I was the last time we met?' I laughed.

'Far from it,' he said quietly, as Fi continued her attempted seduction of Andrew. 'You were sexy then but you're sexy as hell, now.'

And you, I thought, are a sweaty drunk. I smiled politely and asked after his children, which seemed to have the desired effect of re-directing at least a degree of blood-flow to his brain. He was beginning to tell me about his eldest son's recent selection for some 'A' team or other, when we were distracted by a shriek from George.

'Oh my goodness, here they are now! Joan! Bobby! Over here, over here!'

Ado Annie and Ali Hakim emerged from the disco. It was a testament to the breeding, or perhaps the early inebriation, of George's guests, that Joan and Bobby's full theatrical attire provoked no more than the odd smile. As far as I could tell, the only widened eyes and open mouths belonged to Andrew and myself.

'Hello, my darlings!' I was embraced first by Ado and then by Ali, before the pair moved onto Andrew. 'We thought you two would never get here. Bobby has twirled me round that dance floor a dozen times already. I trust,' she said, tugging at Andrew's chinos, 'that these are your dancing pants.'

'Regrettably these are my Guinness pants, Joan,' said Andrew dryly.

'Oh, don't be such a stick-in-the-mud, Andrew,' chimed George. 'I demand a bop.' She took his plate and glass from him, placed them on a nearby table, and then took his hand. 'Now,' she laughed.

He looked momentarily appalled and then, to my utter astonishment, and Fi's apparent chagrin, he retrieved his glass, downed its contents in a single gulp and said, 'OK. Let's go.'

'Fabulous!' said Joan, clapping her hands. 'Come along, Bobby.' She grabbed his hand and he dutifully prepared to follow. 'Come on, Ros, darling. We can be a threesome!'

I weighed up my options, which seemed to be limited to dancing a reel, in impossible heels, with a cow-girl and a geriatric tinker, or chatting to a couple of would-be swingers. I looked at my shoes. Swingers it was. 'I'll be there in a moment, Joan,' I said, 'I'll just finish my plate. I'm starving.'

'That's fine, my darling,' said Joan, squeezing my arm and beckoning me down to her level so that she could whisper in my ear. 'Only do let me know if you meet a nice young gentleman, won't you? I don't want to miss anything exciting.'

I straightened up and nodded. 'I'll be sure to let you know immediately,' I said, solemnly.

'Super! Bobby! Let's dance!'

They scuttled off to the disco and I turned to resume my conversation with Jeremy and Fi, only to find that they had, in the meantime, turned to join an alternative group. I briefly considered following Joan, before remembering that I had yet to deliver my gift to Mike. I retrieved the striped bag from a nearby chair and headed towards the basement and the bar.

—

The basement, which George usually referred to as 'the den', was similarly festooned to the hall. A bar, strewn with lights, had been set up in one corner and the room was about half-full of couples standing in small clusters, or taking the opportunity to lounge on one of the long sofas or beanbags. I scanned the room. There was no sign of Mike. I ordered a glass of white wine, took a sip and was just beginning to feel conspicuously tall and alone, when I was tapped lightly on the shoulder.

'My, how you've grown.' I turned and was pleasantly disconcerted to find myself being addressed by a tall, highly attractive man, whom I recognised but couldn't immediately place. I felt momentarily at a loss before it dawned on me.

'Miles?'

He laughed. 'I'm afraid that Miles is in Edinburgh, Ros.'

I looked up into the amused, blue eyes. 'Daniel?' I said in astonishment.

'I knew you'd get there in the end,' he said. 'Shaved it off last week.' He rubbed his chin. 'I miss it, actually.'

'You… you just look so different.'

He took a step back and looked me up and down. 'You look pretty different yourself,' he said. 'I mean, you always look great, of course…' He hesitated. 'It's just that, you know, I haven't really seen you when…' He concluded the sentence with a shrug and, having recovered from the shock of his shave, I now recalled our last encounter, including the bitter monologue which I had delivered to him, on the pavement outside the wine bar, several weeks earlier.

Oh God. Suddenly, the prospect of a conversation with the swingers upstairs seemed rather attractive – as did the idea of being twirled around the dance floor by an Ali Hakim, twice my age and half my height. Anything, in fact, would be preferable to being forced to embark upon yet another humiliating round of apologies and explanations to Daniel McAdam.

He was smiling – rather smugly, I now thought – down at me, his newly-revealed, handsome face making the situation even more unbearable. However, it was clear that, short of feigning a seizure, there was no alternative but to attempt conversation. I arranged my features into a polite smile. 'So, how have things been since… since I last saw you?' I heard my voice trail off into a near whisper. I cleared my throat. 'Are you here alone? No Tish?'

'You mean Tish with the perfect bottom?'

I groaned inwardly. He wasn't going to let me off the hook and he clearly remembered every syllable of my rant. Had he been taking notes? Or perhaps there had been a small recording device concealed in his beard. Whatever his preferred method of recall, this was going to be even worse than I had thought.

'Actually,' he lowered his voice conspiratorially, 'Tish has moved on to pastures new.'

A miracle. The news enveloped me like a fluffy blanket on a winter's eve. I was no longer bottom of this two-person heap. I resisted the urge to jump and clap my hands.

'She dumped you for someone else?'

He appeared both surprised and amused. 'What a refreshingly unminced series of words. Oh and thank you for looking so astonished at the possibility. I'll take that as a compliment.'

'I just mean… why now?' I felt my confidence returning. 'With the beard, maybe, but not…'

He raised an eyebrow. 'But not without the beard?'

'Oh, you've found each other. How wonderful.' A glowing George glided down the stairs, closely followed by Andrew. 'I've brought Andrew to the Guinness. He deserves it after what I've put him through.'

I glanced at Andrew. He didn't look like he'd been put through anything particularly unpleasant. George moved to the bar, whilst he remained beside me and held out his hand to Daniel.

'Hello, I'm Andrew O'Farrell. Ros and I are colleagues.'

They shook hands. 'Daniel McAdam. Ros and I are neighbours.'

'Really?' said Andrew. 'Close neighbours?' I studied his face but detected nothing but polite interest.

'Not next-door neighbours,' explained Daniel. 'Our gardens back onto one another.'

'So, how did you meet?'

Daniel looked at me. 'I'll leave that one to you, Ros.'

I mumbled an explanation into my glass.

'Sorry?' said Andrew, cupping his hand to his ear and leaning towards me. 'He did what?'

'Oh, Andrew,' said George, rejoining us and handing him a Guinness. 'You remember. Daniel ran over Ros's guinea pig with his lawnmower.'

Andrew, just about to take his first sip, lowered his glass and looked at me in bewilderment. 'Him?' He stared incredulously at Daniel.

'I know!' exclaimed George. 'I didn't put Daniel together with Ros's description of a smelly simpleton either.' I cringed. She was clearly drunk.

I smiled at Daniel apologetically. 'The beard... the sweater...' I said weakly.

'I was being sponsored not to shave, Andrew,' explained Daniel, smoothly. He seemed thoroughly unconcerned by George's description. 'And I had just killed her pet. Mind you, she did manage to get her own back,' he continued. 'She disrupted a very civilized dinner party of mine by falling into my hedge,' he drank his beer and shot me a side-long glance, 'whilst fox-hunting at midnight.'

I sighed and felt my earlier sense of *schadenfreude* begin to evaporate. He had been dumped by his girlfriend, publicly described as a simpleton and outed as a guinea pig murderer and yet, somehow, inexplicably, he had the audience onside and I was suddenly feeling like a child at the grown-ups' table.

Andrew frowned. 'You forgot to tell us about falling into your neighbour's hedge, Ros.'

'Maybe it's *my* hedge,' I said, truculently, 'and I just let him trim and maintain it.'

Daniel nodded. 'Ros is quite right. I should really check the boundaries before declaring ownership of the hedge into which she fell… head-first… in front of almost a dozen people.' He smiled broadly at me and, for a moment, I found myself too fascinated by the sight of features previously obscured by facial hair, to focus on forming a decent riposte. He was certainly as attractive as his brother but there were several quite definite differences. The mouth was fuller and the jaw more square and his eyes, which I had never properly noticed before, were actually, if anything, more – 'Ros?' Andrew was waving a hand in front of my face. 'Ros, are you still with us?'

'Sorry… I was just…' I turned to George. 'I was just wondering where on earth Mike is. I'll be taking this home with me at this rate.' I held up the bag.

'Yes, where is the birthday boy, George?' asked Daniel. He was talking to George but looking at me, his smile gone. I decided not to attempt to read his expression. Instead, I looked at George.

She was turning around, wobbling slightly as she did so. 'I wonder where he is,' she said. 'I saw him about half an hour ago, chin-wagging in the kitchen. I would have expected him to have found his way down here by now but I think he's having too good a time mingling upstairs.' She smiled, as if pleased at the thought. 'Talking of mingling,' she said, 'I'd better do some myself, although,' she nudged me, 'truth to tell, I should actually rather like to just flop down on one of those beanbags and talk shop. Literally.' She laughed and headed back upstairs.

And then there were three.

I made a few light comments about the food and the decorations and the music, all of which were met with heightened eyebrow movement and nods from Daniel, and no reaction at all from Andrew. A mildly awkward silence followed, during which I grinned inanely and shot several, meaningful say-something-for-God's-sake looks at Andrew. However, as it turned out, it was Daniel who finally filled the conversational breach.

'Do you wear contacts, Ros?'

'No,' I smiled, happy to talk about anything, even impaired vision. 'Why?'

'It was just that the way you were looking at Andrew, I thought maybe one had rolled under your eyelid.' He was smiling benignly at me. 'I've heard that that can happen.'

'Ros,' said Andrew suddenly, seemingly oblivious to this exchange, 'I spotted Richard Webster earlier and I thought I might just—'

'Oh God, Andrew, it's a party,' I said, panicked at the thought of him deserting me. 'Forget about business until next week. Richard Webster will still be on the end of a phone on Monday.'

He smiled and put a hand on my arm. 'Two minutes, Ros. It's really important.' I recognised in his eyes the same sudden, inexplicable anxiety he had recently shown over the rent review.

I forced a smile. 'OK but you'd better tell me all about it later. And I mean *all* about it. Off you go.'

He winked at me, kissed me on the cheek, and turned to Daniel. 'Good to meet you, Daniel,' he said, holding out a hand. 'And all the best with that boundary dispute.' They shook hands and Andrew headed for the stairs. I watched him go before turning to Daniel.

'It's OK,' I said. 'You're allowed to go and mingle too. I do know a few other people here.'

He smiled and shook his head. I looked at his chin – he had had a remarkably close shave. 'Yes, I spotted you with Jeremy earlier. But I'm quite happy talking to you, Ros. Although, you've got to stop staring at my chin. It's making me nervous – makes me think I must be drooling or something.' He pointed at my empty glass. 'Refill?'

I hesitated, spotted a free sofa and realised that my feet were killing me. 'Yes, please.' I gestured towards the sofa. 'I'm just going to slip my shoes off for a moment.'

'OK. And they are great shoes, by the way,' he said. 'Do they cross over into gardening?'

'Yes. The heels are excellent for aerating the soil.'

He laughed and went to get the drinks.

I flopped down, removed my shoes, folded my legs up onto the sofa, leaned back and waited for my drink. I hoped Andrew was OK. I decided that I would sit him down on Monday and demand to know what the problem was. I couldn't think of anything: unless he had run up massive debts and managed to hide them from both myself and our accountant. I mentally dismissed the idea. That wasn't Andrew.

I sat up, rubbed my forehead and looked across to where Daniel was waiting for our drinks at the bar. He had fallen into conversation with a sophisticated-looking blonde. She was repeatedly placing her hand on his arm, in a calculatedly casual fashion, as she laughed, confident, I thought, that he was hers for the rest of the evening. I sighed. No one would dare dump her at the altar. And, as for him, well, he wouldn't be single – or at least celibate – for long. I wondered if he'd even last the night. He handed her the drink he must have ordered on her behalf and she thanked him with a smile and a look so intense that I wondered if she was attempting to convey the satnav co-ordinates of her bedroom telepathically. I bent down to refasten my shoes and decided to go in search of Andrew and Joan upstairs.

'I thought you wanted to give your feet a break.' Daniel was standing in front of me, proffering a large glass of white wine.

'Er...' I leaned to the left, in order to see past him to his friend at the bar. She was laughing with the barman, whilst casting an occasional glance towards Daniel. 'Yes, they're fine now.' I took the drink and, along with the blonde, waited for him to make his excuses and return to her.

He sat down beside me. I looked at him.

'What?' he asked.

'What?'

'Well, you're looking at me like I've got two heads. Honestly, Ros, it was just a beard. If I'd known that shaving it off was going to have such a traumatic effect on you, I would have posted a few pre-beard photos through your letterbox before you saw me again. You know, broken you in gently.'

I looked across to the bar. Her astonished expression mirrored my own.

'Thanks for bringing me a drink,' I said, tearing myself away from her.

'You're welcome,' he said. 'Now, I know how you know George. Don't you want to know how I know George?'

I realised that I did want to know exactly that and was surprised that it hadn't yet occurred to me to ask.

'Go on then,' I said.

'Through Mike.'

'OK.'

'He was my first boss.' I looked back to the bar. She threw him one last, incredulous look and then stalked off up the stairs.

I slipped my feet out of my shoes once more and tucked my legs back under me. 'That's interesting. What was he like to work for?'

'About as ruthless as you'd expect.'

'I wouldn't expect anyone George loved to be ruthless at all.'

'You're right,' he said. 'Ruthless was the wrong word. He was fair but he didn't let friendships get in the way of the job.' He paused. 'He doesn't tend to make friends with colleagues.'

'Except you?'

'I moved on from Marsh within eighteen months. We kept in touch.'

'And now you're friends?'

'I would say we're firm acquaintances. We enjoy each other's company over a drink.'

'And George?'

His face softened. 'George is great. You should have seen her reaction when she realised that I was the neighbour who ran over your guinea pig.'

'When exactly did she discover that, incidentally?'

'About ten minutes before I came down to look for you in the bar.'

'Did she laugh?'

'Well, more than I bloody did. How the hell did you describe me? The way George tells it, you made me sound like a cross between Brian Blessed and the poor guy in *My Left Foot*.'

I laughed. 'Sorry.'

'Forgiven.' He clinked his glass against mine.

'Daniel, my boy, where on earth have you been hiding all evening?' I looked up and recognised one-half of the older couple with whom George had been talking upstairs. He smiled, genially, down at us. 'And you must introduce me to your beautiful friend here.'

'Hello, Phil,' said Daniel, standing up. 'Come and join us. This is my neighbour, Rosalind Shaw. Ros, this is Philip Wainwright, a colleague of Mike's at Marsh.'

'Hello, Rosalind,' he said, shaking my hand vigorously, as he and Daniel sat down. 'Are you here with Daniel?'

'No, no,' I said, surprised to find myself blushing at the suggestion. 'I'm here with my friend, Andrew. We both work with George.'

'Ah, the lovely George,' he laughed. 'She invites all the best people, eh Daniel?' Daniel smiled. 'Unfortunately, Daniel and I are on the other guest list.' He lowered his voice to a whisper. 'The dull one.'

'I'm sure that's not true,' I laughed.

'I assure you it is, my dear.' He turned to Daniel. 'So how are things, with you, Daniel? Molly was so very sorry to hear about you and Letitia, my boy.' He winked and I thought I noticed Daniel stiffen slightly. 'Actually,' Philip nudged me and grinned, 'Molly wasn't sorry at all, Rosalind. Said it was the most sensible thing Daniel had done all year. Eh, Daniel?'

'Now, Phil, I—'

'Oh, now, don't be coy about it, Daniel.' Philip held up a hand. 'I know you are a gentleman but there's no shame in ending a relationship when things aren't working out. Cutting and running is much better than stringing a young lady along for years, eh?' He turned to me. 'Don't you agree, Rosalind?'

I looked at Daniel. He was studying his glass.

I turned to Philip and forced a smile. 'Sorry, Philip. I'm afraid I'm not up to date with all the details. I had thought that it was Letitia who had cut and run.'

'Oh no. Far from it. Isn't that right, Da—' He paused, mid-sentence, looking uncertainly first at Daniel and then at myself. 'Oh dear. Are you a friend of Letitia's, Rosalind? Have I perhaps spoken out of turn?' He put an anxious hand to his mouth. 'Molly will have my guts. "*Do not attempt to chat, Philip. Stick to business.*" That's what she says to me, you know.' He looked at his glass, still three-quarters full of beer. 'Time for a top-up, I think,' he said, standing up. 'Lovely to have met you, Rosalind. Daniel.'

'Great to see you, Phil,' smiled Daniel. 'And no harm done, so don't worry.'

Philip managed a worried smile, sighed and headed off in the direction of the stairs.

When he was out of earshot, Daniel spoke first.

'Poor Phil,' he began, with a smile, 'he's a great guy but not the most tact—'

'You know,' I interrupted, 'it really doesn't matter to me how your relationship ended.'

He appeared momentarily taken aback and then looked serious. 'I'd be surprised if it did. And yet your tone would indicate that you're actually rather irritated by it, for some reason.'

'Perhaps that's because *you* felt a need to lie to me about it, *for some reason*.' I glared at him and took a large, fortifying gulp of wine, my grip on the glass tightening to a strangle hold.

He looked at me blankly. 'I think, perhaps, I need you to explain your issue,' he said calmly.

He was, I was certain, being deliberately obtuse. 'It's really very simple,' I said, slightly more breathlessly than I would have liked. 'You see me as a sad, lonely neighbour, who spies on your dinner parties and gets stood up in wine bars and my *issue*, as you put it,' I took a second, large draught of wine, 'is that you invented a tale of personal rejection in a patronising attempt to make me feel better about my state.'

'An intriguingly complex, theory,' he said, his face impassive. 'It's just a shame that I haven't got the faintest idea what you're talking about.'

'I've told you before,' I hissed, feeling increasingly indignant that he should remain so apparently unmoved, 'I don't need pity. It is as unnecessary as it is offensive.' I drained my glass and awaited the enlightened, apologetic denial of any intent to offend, which I felt certain must now follow. However, after several seconds of excruciating silence between us, during which he drank his beer and studied first the room and then, rather disconcertingly, my shoes, my confidence regarding the validity of my complaint began to waver and it dawned on me that it was just possible that his response might not be quite as apologetic as I had hoped.

'You're quite right,' he said at last, shifting his attention from my shoes to my face. 'You have mentioned the pity issue before. In fact, that whole 'don't pity me' thing is pretty much your tagline, isn't it?' He frowned. 'Why do you assume that every element of my behaviour towards you stems from pity?'

I opened my mouth to respond but he continued without a pause.

'That was a rhetorical question and now I have a theory of my own to impart.' He didn't raise his voice but the tone hardened. 'You see, I think that you feel so sorry for yourself all the time, that you assume everyone else does too. And your rather impressive levels of self-absorption prevent you from recognising that that is simply not the case.' I swallowed hard, shocked by the quiet force of his now obvious annoyance.

'Well, I hope it will be of some comfort to you, Ros,' he continued, 'when I tell you that I don't feel sorry for you at all.' He finished his drink. 'Other than, of course, with regard to your guinea pig. But, that aside, I have felt not one ounce of pity – not over your imaginary relatives, or your failed attempts to track wildlife and not even over your no-show friend in the wine bar. Life's full of disappointments but you had options; you could have chosen to have a drink with myself and Miles, or – how about this for an idea – dialled a number or two and found yourself another friend, instead of choosing to deliver a melodramatic rant about foxes, footwear and, oh yes, your sexual history and previous earning capacity.'

He leaned towards me, his blue eyes now devoid of any warmth. 'And, lest you should go away suffering under the weight of any further misapprehension,' he continued quietly, his voice barely above a whisper, 'I should make it clear that I certainly do not pity you tonight.' His expression flickered and he seemed about to say more but, instead, stood up and offered me a cold smile, which perfectly complemented his eyes. 'Well, I have no doubt that you're enjoying this encounter even less than I am, so I trust you won't mind if I go and find someone slightly less hostile to talk to.' I tensed, as the final verbal blow hit home. 'Enjoy the rest of your evening.'

He walked away up the stairs, whilst I looked around me to see if anyone had overheard the lecture. Apparently not. That was something at least. I leaned back, and put a hand to my forehead, immediately feeling the truth of what he had said. My mind filled with alternative explanations for a white lie regarding Tish: the most obvious one, of course, being a chivalrous desire to preserve the dignity of an ex-girlfriend. Added to that, when I tried to recall the details of our original conversation, I was now not sure whether he had ever claimed she had ended the relationship, or whether that had simply been my assumption. I hesitated for just a moment, slipped my feet back into my shoes, picked up the gift bag, and hurried up the stairs.

–

The entrance hall was heaving and, even with my extra height, I couldn't see him. I looked into the disco, but a smoke machine was now in action, obscuring the dancers. In any case, I couldn't imagine him delivering that damning assessment of my personality and then immediately trotting off to strut his stuff to *The B-52s*. I continued through into the kitchen, where a waiter offered me a pinkish cocktail from a tray. I downed one, coughed a little, and then took another.

The kitchen and day room were as crowded as anywhere else. How many people had George invited?

I had just decided that the search was hopeless, and was about to give up, when I saw him. He was standing by a fireplace, talking to the blonde from the bar. She was clearly delighted to have regained his attention and was laughing in a come-to-bed kind of way, although she was probably, I mused, the kind of woman who did absolutely everything in a come-to-bed kind of way. She probably pouted and fluttered her eyelashes at the carrots and cucumbers in the veg section of Waitrose.

I finished the second cocktail and looked at Daniel. He appeared relaxed. There was no hint of the anger or irritation he had displayed just ten minutes earlier. He was clearly mid-anecdote – probably involving a hedge and a fox. There! I was doing it again – assuming it was all about me. He was right. I was self-obsessed. I looked back to her. Still laughing. And why not? That was what normal people did at a party; relaxed, flirted and had fun. Why couldn't I have managed that?

I turned away and immediately spotted Mike. He was standing just a few feet from me, a Scotch in one hand and an unlit cigarette in the other, talking with two men, neither of whom I recognised. I sashayed over. 'Mike.'

He turned, smiled and took my hand.

I froze as the image of a besuited young woman, sitting texting on a train platform, suddenly, and very unexpectedly, entered my increasingly fuzzy consciousness. I fought hard to dismiss it, and the accompanying sense of unease, resolving as I did so to adopt a positive, determinedly *non*-hostile, approach to the remainder of the evening. I was not here to argue with Mike. My fears regarding his behaviour had come to nought. I looked at him smiling benignly down at me. He was happy. George was happy. And now I was going to shrug of all neuroses, paranoia and self-pity and be happy too. I was going to relax, flirt and have fun if it was the last thing I did.

'Ros.' Mike opened his arms for a hug and I kissed him lightly on the cheek.

'Happy Birthday to you!' I said, holding out the gift bag. 'Don't worry about opening that now, just pop it with the others – or tell me where to put it.'

'I'll look after it,' he said. 'Thanks so much.' He turned to his companions. 'Ros, this is Keith Hayward and William Jessen, both old school friends of mine. Gentlemen, this is Ros, one of George's very best friends.'

I was touched and moved by the introduction coming, as it did, hot on the heels of two cocktails and the dressing-down from Daniel. I smiled at Mike and it struck me that he looked a little emotional too.

'It's not at all difficult being a friend to George,' I said to my new acquaintances, as I shook their hands.

'She's a wonder,' said the taller of the two, 'and call me Will, Ros.' He held onto my hand a second longer than was strictly necessary and matched the grip with extended eye contact.

Relax, flirt, have fun. I smiled at him and fought an instinct to pull my hand away.

'So, Mike,' I said, turning from Will. 'How are you enjoying your party?' I raised my voice slightly, so as to be heard above the laughter and conversation around me, and also the music from the disco, which had gone up considerably in volume. 'It doesn't look like you've had many refusals, Mr Popular.'

'I think they come for George,' he laughed and drained his glass. 'She's got loads of friends, hasn't she, Ros?'

'She certainly has,' I smiled, looking round the room, wondering where Andrew was.

Mike touched my arm. 'No, but, Ros, she really does have loads and loads of friends, doesn't she?'

I looked at him. He seemed anxious, even anguished, suddenly. Clearly as tipsy as me. But I realised that I found his obvious love and concern for George welcomingly reassuring. 'Yes, of course,' I said brightly. 'She is much loved.'

He looked relieved. 'Yes,' he said. 'She's fine.' He turned to Keith and Will. 'Now, anyone for a top up?' Keith nodded but Will shook his head and addressed me.

'Actually, I rather fancy the look of that disco. How about you, Ros?' He grinned and my thoughts turned to the proposed re-introduction of the wolf to the British Isles.

'Er...'

'Oh come on,' he said. 'Here,' he grabbed a glass of champagne from a passing tray, 'you can refresh yourself with this on the way.'

Relax, flirt, have fun.

'Why not,' I said, laughing, and we threaded our way through the throng.

I wasn't sure how long we danced but the physical activity was punctuated with periods of relaxation and flirtation, aided by alcohol, on the various chairs and sofas scattered around the ground floor. Yes, I thought happily, after one particularly long conversation about fishing, regarding which I knew absolutely nothing but seemed suddenly very well informed, I was certainly ticking all the relaxation, flirtation and fun boxes now.

We had just finished dancing, very energetically, to *The Fratellis*, when Will suggested we go into the garden to cool off.

'But I'm not that hot and I haven't got a wrap,' I objected. He removed his jacket and placed it round my shoulders. I thanked him and decided that I really liked Will. He was actually very gentlemanly.

He led me out onto the patio and down the steps to the lawn, before suggesting a detour. 'Hey,' he laughed, 'Ros, come round here. I've got something to show you.'

'I bet you have, you naughty boy,' I said, sniggering.

He took my hand and led me round to a darkened passage way at the side of the house. Once there, he pressed me against the wall and pushed his tongue into my mouth. After experiencing momentary shock, I kissed him back, letting my tongue do battle with his and wondering if Daniel had got this lucky with his relaxed, flirty, come-to-bed blonde. Will's mouth moved down onto my neck, whilst a hand moved up my thigh. I couldn't picture Daniel McAdam snogging in a dark alley, though. No. He'd be more of a white sheets and champagne on ice type. And Daniel didn't drool or reek of Benson and Hedges. He smelled of – I was lucid for a moment. Will's head was now level with my waist. I put my hands either side of his face. 'Hey, you, get back up here,' I laughed.

'No way,' he groaned, both hands pushing up under my dress, 'it's so much nicer down here.'

'Now, now,' I said, trying to pull him up.

'Just relax, Ros.' He stood up, leaving his hands where they were. 'Relax.' He slobbered the word against my neck. 'Relax.'

I stopped laughing and shook my head, as it continued to swim. 'Stop now.' I began to push him away but he leaned heavily against me, trapping my arms by my sides and forcing the breath from my lungs.

'Just relax. I'll help you relax,' he rasped, his breath uncomfortably hot against my ear.

I fought to focus. He was right; relaxation was key. I had to stay calm, try to breathe and relax. Stiletto into toe, knee to the groin. Stiletto – toe. Knee – groin. I shifted, positioning my spike heel above the toe of his shoe. I might not be able to quite knee his groin but I was pretty sure I could move my arm enough to execute a grab and twist.

Suddenly, he cried out and stumbled backwards, landing heavily, flat on his back. I felt confused. I hadn't touched him. In spite of the circumstances, I instinctively bent down to help him up, extending an arm, which was grabbed gently but firmly, not by Will, but by Andrew, who was standing at my side, looking down impassively at the moaning heap at our feet.

'Leave him, Ros.' He turned. 'I'll be a moment. Can you take her inside?' I was blearily aware of two figures standing in the shadows behind him. The shorter of the two stepped forward.

'Of course I can. Come on, my darling,' said Joan, taking my hand. 'Ooh, but let's just get you looking beautiful again.' She smoothed my dress and dabbed my eyes and mouth with a handkerchief from her gingham clutch purse.

'I don't feel very well, Joan.' I said, leaning heavily on her as she led me inside.

'Don't you, dear? Well, never mind, because Bobby is just over there with a nice glass of iced water for you and, once you've drunk that, Andrew is going to take you home.'

'Thank you,' I said. 'God, I'm such a bother to everyone. I love you, Joan, you know. And Andrew.'

'And we love you too, my darling,' she said, giving me a squeeze as I sat down unsteadily on a stool near the breakfast bar. Bobby prudently took up position behind me, to prevent me from crashing to the floor, and then placed the glass of water on the counter in front of me.

'Thank you, Bobby,' I croaked. I picked up the water and took a gulp. 'Joan?'

'Yes, dear?'

'I feel a bit silly, you know. I think I have made the most terrible mistake.' I replaced the glass on the counter, lowered my head into my hands and began to sob quietly.

'No, no, dear,' she said, bending down and stroking the top of my head. 'You *almost* made the most terrible mistake. And that's not the same thing at all.'

Chapter 19

When I awoke for the second time it was midday. The first time, it had still been dark outside and I had remained conscious long enough only to run to the bathroom, vomit, brush my teeth and retreat back under the duvet. The second time, I felt a little better physically but much worse psychologically, as it took less than a minute for me to recall that I had attended George's party the night before and had been escorted home in disgrace. The specifics regarding the exact nature of the disgrace, took a little longer to fall into place but, once they did, I decided that the only course of action was to pack my bags, quit St Albans and join a convent in the Outer Hebrides. I was sure there had to be one.

A cup of tea, two paracetamol and a piece of lightly-buttered toast later, I decided that an alternative to the convent option might be to write lengthy letters of apology to everyone whose evening I had spoiled. I sat in my bathrobe at the kitchen table and listed them in my head: Andrew, Joan, Bobby, Daniel, George… George. Had she witnessed my disgrace? I struggled to reconstruct the sequence of events, whilst trying hard not to think about the details of my encounter with Will.

Joan had taken me inside. Who was in the kitchen? It had still been quite busy and I remembered seeing at least a couple of people sitting, or slumped, on the floor. Sitting or slumped? It made a difference. If they were slumped then I may not have been the only sad drunk and therefore less conspicuous. And, thank God, most of the 'action' had taken place outside. Had I seen George before I left? Or Mike? Well, if I had, I couldn't remember.

Hopefully, they'd been in another room but I found it hard to believe that Andrew and Joan would have left without saying goodbye, so, even if George hadn't seen me, she would probably know what had happened. Still, focusing on the positive, at least I hadn't actually been sick in George's home. I had saved that for the taxi. Poor Andrew. I would have to insist he let me pay for all that dry cleaning. And I was pretty sure that he had carried me upstairs – I had a vague recollection of trying, and failing, to walk up – and then put me into bed, still wearing my dress. He was such a good friend. My letter to him was going to be pretty long; I wondered how much it would cost to have it bound.

And then there was Joan. How embarrassing for her in front of Bobby. And after she had told him so many lovely things about me. Perhaps I would send them a joint apology. And flowers for Joan. Yes, flowers. It was the least she deserved.

As for Daniel McAdam, well, my altercation with him now paled into insignificance in the light of my later misdemeanors. But I would still write. I might as well get all the self-abasement over with in one go. Or had I already apologised? Why would I think that? I tried to remember whether I had spoken to him after our argument in the basement. I had seen him laughing with The

Blonde by the fireplace but no, I hadn't spoken to him again.

I got up, switched on the kettle and rubbed my forehead. God, this really was the mother of all hangovers; my head was pounding and there was even a ringing in my ears. I held my nose and blew down it for several seconds in an attempt to stop the ringing before I realised that it was actually the doorbell. Marvellous. I looked down at my robe to see if I looked decent enough to answer the door. Well, it had Marmite along the bottom of it but, other than that, it was fine. I went to the front door and opened it just wide enough to see who it was. I experienced a fresh wave of nausea, sighed, and opened it fully.

'Hello, Daniel,' I said.

He was unshaven and clearly exhausted. My thoughts returned to The Blonde. He offered me an empty smile, which I found unexpectedly painful. 'Hi, Ros. I'm sorry to bother you. I know you can't be feeling great today but I really need to talk to you. I would have called Andrew, or Joan, but I'm afraid I don't have any contact details for them.'

I looked at him and experienced a sudden, horrifying recollection. I opened my mouth to speak but no sound came out.

He looked concerned. 'I'm sorry. Are you OK? If I could just get Andrew's number from you then I needn't bother you any longer.'

'You were there,' I said.

'Where?' he asked, looking confused.

'You were in the garden. With Andrew and Joan.'

'Oh,' he looked down. 'Yes. Yes, I was. Had you forgotten that?'

I nodded.

'Well, yes. I was talking with Andrew and Joan, when I noticed you go outside.' He hesitated. 'We talked about it briefly afterwards.' He looked at me. 'Do you remember that conversation?'

I shook my head.

'OK.' He cleared his throat. 'Well, it doesn't matter.'

'You met Joan?' I said.

He nodded.

'She's such a lovely person.' I said.

'Yes, she is, Ros. But I have something quite important to sort out.' He looked past me into the hallway. 'Perhaps I could come in?'

'Oh God, yes,' I said. 'I'm so rude. Come in, come in. This is Marmite on my robe.' I pointed to the dark brown streak on the hem.

'OK,' he said and we headed towards the kitchen.

'Have a seat,' I said. 'Would you like a cup of tea or coffee? I'm just having one. Another. I think I might need another couple of paracetamol or ibuprofen, or something, too.' I opened a cupboard and took out several boxes of pills. 'I feel so awful.'

'I'll have a cup of tea, please,' he said.

I made the tea in silence, too hung-over, confused and ashamed to bother with small-talk. He didn't seem to have the heart for it either and it wasn't until I handed him a mug and sat down that he spoke again.

'I'm here about George,' he said.

I swallowed. Had he come to tell me that she never wanted to see me again because I had ruined her party?

Had I been sick on a rug after all? Had Will been injured in the fall and decided to sue them for negligence over an uneven pathway? I decided not to attempt a guess but, instead, to let him finish. A few moments later, I was enormously grateful for this uncharacteristic display of prudence.

'Mike has left George.'

I stared at him uncomprehendingly. 'Where has he left her?'

He sighed. 'He has left her at home, Ros, and he has gone to live with someone else.'

I felt like a cartoon character who has just been hit in the face with a frying pan. I was again unable to speak.

'Ros, I want to make sure she is OK but I don't think I'm the person to do that. I don't have phone numbers for her family or her friends and I think that's what she needs right now.' I sat, staring unblinkingly at the table. 'Ros… Ros!' He spoke sharply and I jumped, knocking my tea and causing a minor spill. I looked at him.

'I'm sorry,' his voice was smooth again, 'but someone has to check on George and if you're not up to it I would like to call Andrew. I think we should call him anyway, actually. I assume he may have contact details for her family on file.'

'Yes, yes, I'm sorry. You're right, I think we should call Andrew but I don't think he's the best person to see George today.'

'No?'

'I don't think it should be a man.'

He nodded. 'Of course, you're right.'

'I'll call her and then I'll go round. But actually,' I paused, 'I think her parents are bringing Lottie back today.

In fact,' I glanced at the kitchen clock, 'they may be here already.'

He looked relieved. 'But you will check?'

'Yes, of course.' I stood up. 'Right. I'm going to go and shower and throw on some clothes. Are you able to stay for a few minutes and tell me what happened? I think the more I know before I try to speak with her the better, really.'

'Of course. You go and sort yourself out and I'll drink my tea. Oh and Ros,' he looked up at me as I stood up to leave, 'I'm sorry about what happened last night.'

'Oh, I'm fine,' I said, waving away his concern. 'I've met far worse than that toad.'

'Right,' he said and I went to get dressed.

—

Even before Daniel told me, I could have hazarded a pretty good guess as to whom Mike was with: India Morne. Inevitably, I wondered if there was anything I could have done to have prevented the situation, but I quickly decided that such hypothesizing was not a sensible use of time or energy, so, instead, I tried to put the 'what ifs' and 'if onlys' from my mind and concentrate upon what I could do to help George. The first thing of course, was to talk to her. Not surprisingly, there was no answer when I rang, so there was nothing for it but to try to see her in person.

We went together in my car to George's house, with Daniel planning to walk home whilst I saw George. On the way, he added some detail to the brief account he had already given me of the events of the previous evening. Apparently, it had been about 1.00am when Andrew and

I left the party. Things were beginning to peter out around then and, after a brief chat with Joan and Bobby – I guessed about the drunk who had just been carried out with her underwear, if not her dignity, thankfully intact – Daniel had decided to head off too. Before he left, he went in search of George and Mike but, finding neither of them, assumed that they had gone to bed, leaving the stragglers to sort themselves out.

Daniel had elected to walk home 'to clear his head' and, a short distance from the house, on the opposite side of the road, he had noticed a woman, leaning heavily against a lamppost, apparently in tears. This, of course, turned out to be George, rather the worse for wear but coherent enough to explain that Mike had left her for India Morne and was never coming back. Uncertain what to do, Daniel had returned to the house with George and put her into bed where, presumably due to a high alcoholic intake, she quickly fell asleep. He then cleared the house of the last remaining party goers, trying, as he did so, to find a personal friend of George who would perhaps be of some use. Failing in his quest, he had repeatedly called Mike's mobile but to no avail. He then called Phil and Molly Wainwright, and one or two other former colleagues whose wives he thought may be able to help but, again, got no reply. Not wanting to leave George alone, he spent the night on the sofa in her room. However, when she woke she, quite under-standably, hadn't wanted to discuss her feelings with him and was keen for him to go, so he had merely stayed long enough to be reassured that she didn't intend to do anything stupid and had then taken a taxi home, showered and come to see me.

Daniel concluded this depressing account just as we pulled up outside George's house. I gave him Andrew's number, so that he could bring him up to date regarding George, and watched him as he entered the new contact details into his phone. To say he'd had a rough night was an understatement and I had certainly played a part in that. I stared out of the front windscreen of the car and decided that, for better or for worse, I had to try and put at least one part of it right. I took a deep breath.

'Daniel…' My mouth was dry. Just one word in and my courage was already deserting me. I gripped the steering wheel for support and began again. 'Daniel, I just need to say something before you head home. I just need to tell you that I'm sorry about getting so cross over nothing last night and… well, you should know that I did try to find you to make amends but, by the time I found you, you were busy talking and I didn't want to interrupt. And also,' my voice caught, forcing me to clear my throat 'and also, just to add, about Will, well, I have never, just never, put myself in such a stupid position with a man before and…' I despaired at my inability to articulate. 'Well, it was all just a dreadful mess and I'm sorry.'

He said nothing in response and, unable to bring myself to look at him, and feeling exhausted, I closed my eyes and leaned my head forward to join my hands on the steering wheel. 'I'm going to go and try and see George now,' I said quietly. 'But if, at some point, you would like to come round for a cup of tea and a normal, neighbourly conversation about anything and everything other than my insecurities, I would really like that. If, on the other hand, I have exhausted your patience and interest then, well, frankly, who could blame you?' Without looking at him, I sat upright, got out of the car and started to walk up George's drive. A few seconds later, I heard the passenger-side door open and close and I experienced a momentary, indefinable optimism. However, not for the first time, he chose not to follow the babbling woman and, by the time I had reached George's front door and looked back, he was gone.

Well, that was that. I focused on the matter in hand, rang the door bell and waited for a reply, noticing, as I did so, a silver BMW estate which, as far as I knew, belonged to neither George nor Mike, parked in front of the garage. I waited for a minute or so and was just beginning to consider going round the side of the house, or peering through the letter box, when the door was opened by an attractive woman in, I guessed, her mid-sixties. I had no doubt she was George's mother. She looked strained.

'Can I help?' she asked, attempting a smile.

'Oh hello,' I said. 'My name is Ros Shaw. I'm a friend of George. I just popped round to see if she was all right this morning but, as you're here, I won't disturb you. If you could just tell George that I called and give her my love and if she needs anything to just let me know.'

'Thank you, I will, and, sorry, your name is?'

'Ros Shaw. We work together at *Chapters*.' I saw sudden comprehension in her eyes.

'Ah, yes. George speaks of you often. Thank you, Ros.'

'OK, well, goodbye.'

'Goodbye.'

I walked back down the drive and wondered about what to do next. I doubted if Daniel would have spoken to Andrew yet, unless he had decided to call him on the way home. Maybe I should go round and see Andrew in person, both to apologise and to talk about George. Or perhaps I should take those flowers to Joan. I opened the car door.

'Ros! Oh Ros!'

I turned to see George's mother beckoning to me from the doorway. I closed the door, locked the car and walked back up to the house.

'George would very much like to see you,' she said, smiling and ushering me into an entrance hall which was clearly suffering from the morning after the night before. Streamers from party poppers littered the floor, along with balloons, glasses, a pink pashmina and the odd item of buffet fare. 'I'm sorry about the mess,' said George's mother. 'The contract cleaners turned up an hour or so ago but George apparently sent them away. We'll get them back tomorrow, when the house is empty.'

'Are you taking George with you?' I asked.

'Yes, we are. Just for a little while. I'm going to do a little tidying up and Alistair has taken Lottie to the park but as soon as he gets back and George is ready, we'll be on our way.'

I thought about my own mother and her similarly practical approach to a crisis and nodded. 'Of course.'

She smiled. 'George is upstairs in her room. It's a little less chaotic up there. Can I get you a cup of tea or coffee or a soft drink, perhaps?'

'No, no, I'm fine. Thank you.'

'Well, if you know the way, I'll leave you to it.' She turned towards the kitchen.

'Mrs...' It suddenly struck me that I didn't know George's maiden name.

'Do call me Ruth.'

'Ruth, is there anything I should know before I go upstairs?'

'You do know that he's gone?' She looked concerned.

'Yes.'

'Well,' she sighed, 'I'll leave George to explain the rest. I don't want to put words into her mouth.'

I nodded and began to climb the stairs.

Chapter 20

I arrived home at 5pm, walked into the living room and, without stopping to take off my shoes, flopped down onto the sofa. I felt physically and emotionally exhausted. My concerns which, I now realised, had until this weekend been exceedingly few and far between, were now jostling for attention in my brain and I felt at a loss as to where to begin. I wanted to apologise sooner, rather than later, to both Andrew and Joan for my bad behaviour but any conversation with them would have to involve George and I just didn't know how I would summon up the energy for that today. Nevertheless, it would have to be today. I knew that. It certainly couldn't be at work tomorrow.

I felt my phone vibrate in the back pocket of my jeans. I retrieved it and sighed. There was a text from Andrew to call him as soon as possible and two missed calls, also from Andrew. It was no use. I couldn't put this off. I dialled his number and he answered immediately.

'Hello, Ros.'

'Hi Andrew. I'm sorry I missed your calls. I've only just got home.'

'I've spoken to Daniel,' he said.

'Oh.'

'Yes. So, how was she? I'm assuming you did get to see her?'

'Yes, I did. She's not great, Andrew.'

'Right. Look, I'm actually in the car at the moment. Would it be OK if I called round to see you later?'

Exhausted as I was, I thought that sounded like a good idea. I didn't want to have this conversation over the phone.

'Of course. When were you thinking?'

'In a couple of hours or so? Have you eaten? I could pick us up a pizza.'

He was lovely. 'That sounds great.'

'OK. Well I'll see you sometime around seven then. Bye.'

'Bye.' I hung up and lay back on the sofa. I wasn't looking forward to this.

—

He arrived at 6.45pm, carrying several Pizza Express boxes and a couple of beers.

I raised my eyebrows at the beers. 'You recover fast,' I said, letting him in and directing him towards the kitchen, where the table was already laid.

'Some of us stopped drinking quite early on, actually, Ros,' he explained, with a smile. 'I moved onto mineral water at about eleven.' He sat down at the kitchen table.

'I wish I had,' I said, taking a glass from a cupboard and pouring his beer. 'I must just say sorry, about that incident in the garden, Andrew. I really am.'

'Look, Ros,' he took the beer from me with a nod of thanks, 'you had too much to drink, you met an idiot who didn't understand the meaning of the word 'no'. That's all. I know it was embarrassing for you. God knows you told me that enough on the way home. But, at the end of the day, no real harm was done.'

I wasn't quite sure that I concurred absolutely with that last statement but I was happy that he seemed to have drawn a line under the matter. 'Thanks,' I said, fetching myself a glass of tap water, in preparation for topping up the analgesics in my system, 'and I will pay your dry-cleaning costs.'

'That's generous of you, but I don't actually have any.'

'But—'

'You were sick on the cab driver when he came round to help me get you into the house.'

'Was he cross?' I asked.

'Was he *cross*? Let me think. Yes. "Cross" or "fecking furious" probably covers it but he didn't suggest compensation and I didn't bother putting the idea into his head.'

I groaned and rested my forehead on the table.

'But I'm not here to talk about you, Ros,' he said, quietly.

There it was again. Another man appalled at my apparently unswerving focus on self.

I didn't lift my head. 'I know that. But what you want to talk about is so dreadful, I can hardly bear it.'

I heard him sigh gently. 'I'm sorry,' he said. 'But I need you to tell me because I need to know if she's OK and, if she's not OK, what we need to do.'

I looked up at him. Absolutely everyone looked exhausted today. I had never seen Andrew look so tired. The anxiety in his eyes brought to mind his insistence upon talking with Richard Webster the night before. I really had to make him tell me what was going on. But, for now, I had no choice but to let that concern bump around up there with all the others. George had to come first.

'OK, Andrew,' I began, 'well, George is not OK. I spent an hour or two with her this afternoon and she is crushed by the loss of her husband to India Morne, the woman I saw him with on the train that night.' I paused, waiting for a reaction – perhaps some echoing of my increasing conviction that I should have informed George of my fears at the time – but he said nothing and his face conveyed no hint as to his thoughts. 'George's parents arrived just after midday today and have now taken George and Lottie to be with them in Oxford.'

'Is George hopeful that she and Mike can sort this out?' He placed a slice of pizza on my plate and reached for a piece himself.

'No, she isn't...' I hesitated.

'But that may be simply the early reaction of someone who—'

I interrupted him with a shake of my head. 'I know what you're going to say, Andrew, and it's what I said to George but...'

'Yes?'

'India is three months' pregnant and Mike is, apparently, happy with that situation. And that's not just the beer talking last night. He's repeated that assertion, very soberly, to George on the phone this afternoon, in addition to requesting a divorce.'

Andrew still showed no reaction but simply sat, staring into his beer. When he did speak, it wasn't what I expected. 'I should have known he was lying,' he said quietly.

'What?' He looked at me steadily. I wondered if I had misheard. 'Sorry, Andrew… Who was lying? Are you saying that you had discussed this with Mike?'

'I went to see him,' he said. 'After you told me what you had seen on the train.'

I sat back, astonished. 'But you said—'

'I said you shouldn't tell George. But I went to see him.'

'What on earth did you say?'

'I told him that I had heard through a friend at Marsh that he was seeing a female work colleague. I didn't mention you.'

'I don't care about that but when did all this happen?'

'It was over a pint, the week after you spoke to me about it. He didn't deny it and behaved as if he realised he had made a mistake. He said it had never been anything serious and that he had come to his senses – said it was over and asked me not to tell George. He thanked me for giving him an opportunity to explain things, rather than going to George.'

'Good God, Andrew, why on earth didn't you tell me what you had done?'

'What good would have come of that? I watched George at work and she seemed fine – better than she had in a while, in fact.' He shook his head, as if in disbelief. 'What a complete bastard.'

We sat in silence, leaving the pizza untouched. It seemed neither of us wanted to talk any more about George and yet to talk about anything else was unthinkable. Eventually, he said, 'Do you think I could have done more, Ros?' It struck me that he sounded like Alan Bullen: carrying that same inexplicable burden of responsibility for the happiness of others.

Or perhaps it was something else. Perhaps his concern for George related to his recent apparent business worries. Was he wondering whether we could afford her absence? I looked at him. He was sitting with his arms on the table and his head bowed, the appearance of all other emotions now supplanted by that increasingly familiar anxiety. Whatever the cause of his concern, I suddenly feared for him almost as much as I did for George. I decided to tread carefully.

'Look, I think you did as much as you possibly could,' I said, reaching out my hand and placing it on his. 'There were only two people capable of putting a stop to all this and you weren't one of them.'

He looked up and nodded. 'I know,' he said. 'It's just that, sometimes, things are complicated.'

'Andrew, why don't you tell me what's complicated?'

'Because I don't want to complicate things for you.'

'Is that statement supposed to make me feel better? To set my mind at rest? Because it bloody doesn't, you know.'

He laughed. 'I'm sorry.'

'OK, so tell me.'

'I will.' He threw me a tired smile. 'I promise. But not tonight, eh? It's been quite a weekend. Let's just eat our pizza.'

I sighed. 'OK. But I am going to hold you to that promise, you know.' I looked at him sternly. 'Now, pass the dough balls. You're hogging them.'

Chapter 21

The atmosphere in the shop over the next few weeks was subdued to say the least. Joan and I between us worked the extra hours needed to cover George's absence and whilst, under normal circumstances, I would have rather enjoyed this, every additional hour worked was simply a reminder that George wasn't there.

Joan and I, individually, spoke with George at least once a week, and then updated each other, and Andrew, as to how she and Lottie were getting on. When she spoke to me, she sounded her usual bright self, always pressing to know how I was and what I was up to and, although she was happy to talk about the practicalities of shared custody and the divorce process, she never discussed her feelings. If she felt bitter, betrayed and let down, she never said so – at least not to me.

Emotionally, she was centred upon Lottie and no one else. Every decision she took was made with her daughter in mind and it was clear that she was doing all she could to convince Lottie that, just because her father had left the family home, it didn't mean that he had stopped loving her. None of us wanted to press her on when she might be returning to St Albans, and as the weeks went on, we avoided the topic but took some comfort in her occasional references to missing the shop and to Lottie's school friends, whom, she said, Lottie was looking forward to seeing 'sometime soon'.

I had no doubt that Andrew was saddened by what had happened to George, however, despite the fact that Joan and I passed mutual best wishes back and forth, he didn't, as far as we knew, ever call her. I was disappointed by this, as I knew George was very fond of him, and I attempted, more than once, to encourage him to call, or to email, if he felt uncertain as to what to say over the phone. However, every time I raised the topic, or any topic in fact, he seemed at best unable to focus and at worst disinterested, as if distracted by, or pre-occupied with, a weightier matter which he refused to share. The rent review, which had appeared to trouble him earlier in the year, had come and favourably gone, and yet his anxiety had not.

It was far from constant, and most of the time he simply appeared to be a slightly more distant version of himself, but I was worried about him – not least because I could tell that Joan was too. Rather than trying to make Andrew run away, by talking about her hand-knitted sock fetish or her friend Maureen's hormone replacement therapy, she went out of her way to look after him with cups of tea and kind enquiries. All of Joan's more lurid topics of conversation were now reserved for when Andrew popped out for a breath of air, or to get his lunch, and such uncharacteristic discretion on her part made me more concerned than ever.

–

One Monday, in early November, Andrew called me at home to tell me that he wouldn't be coming into the shop that day because he was feeling unwell. This was the first day's sick leave he had taken since I had known him. However, other than experiencing a little mild surprise, which had resulted in some affectionate teasing, I wasn't overly worried. Joan and I had a busy morning in the shop and it wasn't until I sat down in the small kitchen with a cup of coffee mid-afternoon, that it suddenly occurred to me that Andrew might be ill. Really ill.

Dread flowed through me as I realised that serious illness could account for his odd moods and behaviour over recent months. It would also explain his reluctance to discuss what was wrong and his determination not to enter into any serious relationships. I cursed myself for not considering the possibility before. Why hadn't I just accepted that there was nothing wrong with the business and looked for an alternative explanation, instead of wondering whether he had gone mad and lost his shirt, and our shop, on the three o'clock at Haydock?

I decided to talk it through with Joan. I went back out into the shop, only to find her dealing with a customer and another three waiting. I put down my coffee and went to help. It was a busy afternoon, hot on the heels of a busy morning and I didn't find another opportunity to talk to her until later that evening, when we had closed up and she had offered to stay behind and help me to decorate the shop, with bundles of holly and ivy culled from my garden.

'Are you sure you don't mind, Joan?' I asked.

'Oh no, dear, I love this kind of thing. Besides,' she looked across at me from the step ladder she was climbing in order to weave ivy along the banisters, 'we haven't had a moment to chat today, have we. I wonder if Andrew will be back with us tomorrow. What do you think?'

I took my chance. 'I don't know, Joan.' I hesitated. 'Actually, Joan, I've been a bit worried about Andrew, lately.'

She now seemed fully absorbed in her task. 'Have you, my darling?' she said vaguely, as she continued to wind the ivy around a spindle, with the assistance of garden wire.

'Yes. I think you have too, haven't you?'

She didn't turn around but she stopped what she was doing and sighed. 'Yes, I have, Rosalind. I just hope it can all be sorted out. He's such a good boy.'

I lowered the sprigs of holly I had been attempting to balance on top of one of the numerous pictures around the shop.

'You mean you *know* what the matter is?'

She now turned and looked at me in puzzlement. 'Oh yes, don't you?'

I was in a state of total astonishment. 'He won't discuss it with me at all.'

'Oh my darling,' she smiled sadly, 'that's hardly surprising, is it? He doesn't want to worry you, does he?'

'But he's discussed it with you?'

'Oh no, of course not.' She began to climb the ladder again. 'He wouldn't do that.'

I resisted the urge to scream and opted for counting to three instead.

'So,' I said, as calmly as I could, 'he hasn't actually told you what the problem is.'

'Well…' she picked up the trailing end of the ivy and began to wind again, 'technically, no.' She shook her head.

'But I just wonder how long he'll be able carry on. Don't you? And that has implications for us all.'

I swallowed hard. 'Do you think it's very serious, Joan? He won't tell me anything.'

'Oh, I think it's as serious as it can be, my darling.' She finished winding and climbed down. 'Andrew is not the kind of person to make a fuss over nothing, is he? I think he's hidden it from us as long as he can.'

'Well, why won't he talk about it?' I asked, feeling my frustration rising. 'Then perhaps we could help him.'

Joan looked at me and smiled sadly. 'I'm not sure we're qualified.'

'I realise that but I think talking may help. Do you think I should push him to talk about it, Joan? Do you think that would be the right thing to do?'

'I'm not sure that there's ever any right or wrong in this kind of situation,' she said, bending down to pick up a few stray ivy leaves from the floor. 'It's even perfectly possibly to do something which, initially, seems to be absolutely the wrong thing but, in the long-term, turns out for the best. I remember when we were all waiting for Arthur Tucker to come out of the closet…'

I had a sudden sinking feeling. 'Sorry to interrupt, Joan, but you don't think that Andrew's gay, do you?'

She stood up and looked confused. 'Bi-sexual, you mean? Well, I don't think so. There's nothing… You know, I think we may be talking at cross-purposes, my darling. Do you mean to tell me that you believe Andrew's problem is that he's gay?'

'No, but when you said about Andrew Tucker—'

'Arthur Tucker.'

'That's right, sorry, Arthur Tucker. I thought you were saying that *you* thought Andrew was gay.'

'Oh, I see, no,' she said, laughing, 'I was just using Arthur as an illustration of it being difficult to know what to do for the best when someone is in crisis. You see, it was apparent to us all that Arthur was a Bertie ice-cake but would he admit it? No, he wouldn't. In fact, he spent all his time bowling and drinking double strength Bovril, in an attempt to prove his heterosexuality.' I decided not to request an explanation of the Bovril reference and, instead, let Joan continue. 'So, in the end, Margie Williams said to me, "Joan, go and talk to Arthur. He's tying himself in knots and he's started wearing dungarees and a leather jacket to try and look macho." My attention began to wander slightly as I marvelled again at Joan's alternate universe, in which real men wore dungarees and drank beef-based beverages and I wondered how, if at all, this homily would ever relate to Andrew.

Meanwhile, Joan was still talking. '…and I said to him that if he loved Graham he should just tell him. It might be that Graham was also living a lie.' She was smiling at me in a "do you see?" kind of way. I realised that it was my turn to speak.

'Oh, I see,' I said. 'And did it all turn out well for Arthur and Graham?'

Joan picked up the last of the leaves and began to walk towards the kitchen. 'Oh, dear me, no. Graham knocked two of Arthur's teeth out with a rather valuable toby jug, but at least Arthur was out of the closet. Moved to Rhyl with a boy called Simon Beal who played the clarinet.'

I was just about to ask the crucial question as to whether Joan and Arthur remained on speaking terms, when I was startled by a loud knocking on the window behind me and turned to see Bobby, grinning at me and pointing to the locked door. Joan bustled out of the kitchen.

'Oh, I had completely forgotten about Bobby picking me up. It's a good job I lingered or I would have missed him!' She unlocked the door and let him in. 'Rosalind and I are decorating, Bobby.' She gestured at the staircase and he smiled and nodded appreciatively. 'Why don't you stay and help us?'

'Oh no, no,' I smiled. 'You two go. I'm just going to put up these few bits of holly and then head off myself. We can do some more tomorrow before opening, if Andrew's back.'

'Are you sure, my darling, because Bobby has a wonderful way with décor.' She linked his arm and looked up at him proudly.

'I'm sure. You know, I think I may give Andrew a ring and see if he needs anything.'

Joan slipped on her coat and scarf. 'I think that's a wonderful idea,' she said. 'And tell him my Arthur Tucker tale. How he got it all out in the open. Lost some teeth but found a soul-mate. You tell him that, my darling.'

I hugged Joan and then saw them out of the shop, deciding that I would spend another half-hour getting creative with the greenery before going to visit Andrew. I might not be certain as to what his problem was but I had come to the conclusion that I was with Joan and Arthur Tucker over one thing. Better out than in.

Chapter 22

I waited what I thought was a reasonable time before trying the buzzer again but, after a further minute or two, there was still no answer. I took a step back and looked up at Andrew's lounge window on the second floor. There was a lamp on, so presumably he wasn't in bed. Determined to speak with him, I quickly dismissed the idea that he might have fallen asleep, or gone to bed early and have forgotten to switch off the lamp, and called him on his landline. Just when I thought it was going to switch to answerphone, he picked up.

'Hello?' He sounded croaky and my belief in the wisdom of this visit immediately wavered.

'Er... hello, Andrew. It's Ros. Sorry to bother you. Hope I haven't woken you. I was just wondering how you are and whether you needed anything?'

'Thanks, Ros. Excuse me one moment.' He coughed, putting me in mind of a sea lion show I'd seen with Ben and Stephen at Whipsnade several years earlier. 'Sorry about that. How are you?'

'Oh I'm fine.' I stamped my feet in an attempt to keep warm. 'We were just worried about you, that's all. It's not like you to be off sick.'

'No, that's true. Just hang on.' He blew his nose loudly. 'I just have a very heavy cold. But I'm well stocked up with Lemsip and soup so I'm fine.'

'So, it's just a cold then?'

'Yes, nothing life-threatening. I had wondered if it was going to turn out to be 'flu but I actually feel a little better this evening. I may make it in tomorrow. Is everything OK at work?'

'Yes, all's well. We had a very busy day. The first editions are proving popular for Christmas.'

'Great.'

'Yes.' There now followed a pause in the conversation, during which my confidence wavered further. Coming round unannounced had been a bad idea. I had decided he was terminally ill and had run with the idea like a toddler with a brick truck. It would be much more sensible to talk to him about whatever his problems were when he was over his cold. I cleared my throat and decided to cut and run. 'In fact,' I continued, 'I'm at the shop now. I just thought I'd give you a call to see if you needed anything from Sainsbury's before I went home.'

'Oh,' he said, 'so that's not you standing on my doorstep, then?' I experienced only momentary confusion, before looking up to see him smiling down at me from his lounge window. I waved meekly. 'You're a strange woman, Ros. You know that, don't you?'

'Yes.'

'You coming up?'

'Go on then.'

He buzzed me in.

–

He looked as dreadful as anyone with a streaming cold usually looks. He was in his bathrobe, hadn't shaved, his lips were cracked and the area between his nose and mouth were red raw. But I was reassured to see that he seemed to be looking after himself. The flat was as immaculate as ever, there was an array of medication on the kitchen work-surface and I deduced from the pans and dinner plate draining next to the sink, that he had made the effort to cook something for his tea.

I made a cup of tea for myself and a Lemsip for Andrew and took the drinks into the lounge, where he was lying on the sofa, under a blue and green tartan blanket.

'Did I wake you up?' I asked guiltily.

'No, it's fine.'

'Really?'

'OK, well, I may have been *slightly* asleep but, you know…'

'Sorry.'

'Not at all. It's really kind of you to come round.' He sneezed at impressive volume and then blew his nose. 'Just hope you don't get this. God, I haven't had a comedy cold like this since I was at school. Still, it's only a cold. There are people dying out there, right?' I scrutinised his face and then mentally crossed 'terminal illness' off my list of possibilities.

'Hmm… listen are you sure it's OK for me to be here, or are you desperate for your bed? I don't want you to sit up just to be polite.'

'Don't worry, Ros, I think we're past the stage of being polite with each other, aren't we? Besides, I'd have just let you think I believed your crappy "I'm in the shop" lie if I hadn't wanted to see you.' He said, "*I'm in the shop*", with a fair impression of my English accent, making us both laugh – his amusement terminating abruptly in a further coughing fit.

'God, you poor thing. I think you should probably have another day or two at home.'

'Maybe...'

'Joan and I are fine. We started to decorate the ground floor this evening.' He smiled. 'Well, Christmas is coming, you know. Although...' I paused before deciding to seize the moment, 'you wouldn't think it, looking at your face sometimes.'

He reached for the box of tissues and hid his face in a Kleenex.

'You promised you'd tell me what the matter was, Andrew.'

'Did I?'

'Yes, you did.'

He added the tissue to the mound already in the waste paper basket next to the sofa and took a sip from his mug. 'Is that why you came round?'

'Yes.'

'Not because you thought I might be dying?'

'Actually, as it happens, that was one of my theories but I'm pretty sure now that that's not it.' I hesitated. 'It's not. Is it?'

'No. I'm not dying.'

'OK and it's not the rent review because that was fine and, unless you're cooking the books, it's not George's absence because we can afford that – even if we have to take on...' I stopped, noticing a change of expression. He looked at me and then back down at his Lemsip.

I felt sick. 'Andrew...' He looked up at me again. There was guilt and sadness in his eyes. 'Andrew...'

'Yes?'

'Have you been cooking the books?'

He burst out laughing. I thought, at first, that it might be the reaction of a desperate man; however, after a moment, I realised that he was genuinely amused. He tried to speak but his words were lost in a renewed fit of coughing.

'Ros...' he gasped eventually. 'Ros, you know, you are so lovely. But no, no, I haven't been cooking the books, as you put it. The figures you see are the real figures and we are, as you know, doing well. Very well, in fact.'

'So why, then,' I cried, my patience at an end, 'are you moping round like someone's shot your favourite puppy and put it in a lasagne?'

'That's an interesting image. Personally, I think "puppy in a pie" is more alliteratively—'

'Shut up,' I said, standing up and pointing at him. 'I'm sorry but I've had enough of this. I don't care what the problem is. I want to know what's bothering you and I want to know now. I don't care if you think it's none of my business because I can tell you it absolutely is. You are my business. Literally, in fact. As your friend and your business partner, your welfare is very important to me and your current behaviour is impacting upon Joan and me, and even upon poor George, whom I know must be wondering why you haven't managed to pick up the phone and call her, and that's all going to have a commercial impact somewhere down the line. Enough is enough, Andrew. Tell me what it is and we'll try and sort it out and, if we can't sort it out, we'll work around it.'

He was clearly taken aback by my outburst and looked at me for a moment with widened eyes. There then followed a silence, during which I sat back down and he took to studying the pen and ink sketch of *Chapters* which hung on the wall above the sofa. His tone, when he finally spoke, was matter-of-fact. 'I have feelings for George...' he began, without looking at me.

It took several, long moments, for me to grasp the situation. Of course, I knew immediately that his statement was significant, momentous even; however, my brain, perhaps fearing implosion, seemed determined to resist recognising its full import, forcing me instead to opt for a simple consolidation of the facts. 'You have feelings...' I said weakly, whilst suddenly experiencing a need to blink a lot more than usual.

'...which have become increasingly difficult for me to manage,' he continued.

'Difficult to manage...' I mouthed, before deciding to avoid any further attempts at pointless reiteration and to, instead, let Andrew finish, whilst I focused upon trying to reduce my blinking to something approaching normal levels.

'It is a problem which is rather difficult, if not impossible, to resolve. Consequently, I saw no point in troubling you, or anyone else, with it.' He stopped speaking abruptly and lay, unmoving, on the sofa, continuing to stare upwards at the sketch.

I sipped my tea and, at last, succeeded in organising, and audibly articulating, my thoughts.

'Bloody hell, Andrew.'

'I know,' he said.

'Really, though.'

'I know.'

'I wasn't expecting you to say that.'

'I can tell.'

'How long?'

'A year. Maybe longer.'

'Bloody hell.'

'I know.'

'And that's why you went to see Mike?'

'Yes.'

'And why you didn't want me to tell her.'

'Yes.' He at last turned his head to look at me. 'It was OK for a long while,' he said, wearily. 'You know, I knew I had feelings for her and that was fine. I mean, recognising and appreciating someone's worth doesn't have to be problematic. But, you know, my feelings strengthened and now...' He resumed his scrutiny of the picture. 'Well, now, it's even more difficult and complex.'

I nodded. 'You mean because you can't bear to see her devastated by the break-up of her marriage but, on the other hand, the break-up of her marriage offers you the possibility, no matter how remote, of a relationship with her at some point? All of which results in an impossible and highly distressing emotional dilemma for you.'

'Ros,' he sighed, 'how is it that you can be *that* astute and yet so obtuse as to think I might be dying or cooking the books?'

'It's all part of my charm,' I sighed. 'I'm sorry, Andrew.'

'So, you haven't got a solution for me then?'

'Time.'

'You're right. I've reached that conclusion myself. In a way, the longer she stays away the better. If she were to come back any time soon, that could be difficult. I think if I were to see her unhappy then I might not be able to pretend that that didn't matter to me – a lot. Jesus, I can't even manage to speak to her on the phone. I really need to pull myself together.'

I looked at him. Even with those lips, and that blanket, I had no doubt that women would queue up to take his temperature and mop his fevered brow. What a mess. He could have had almost anyone at all between the ages of twenty-five and one hundred and five. But no. He had to fall for the beautiful, kind, selfless, intelligent, married-with-child, George.

'OK, well, Andrew,' I said, leaning back in my chair, 'we're just going to have to manage this like any other staffing problem and, I'm afraid, the first thing you have to do is re-establish a "normal",' I drew the inverted commas in the air, 'relationship with George. If you can't do that on the phone, you will have to do it by email. You can exaggerate your illness and use that as a part-excuse for your silence. And then, you're going to have to get your head into a place where you can handle seeing and spending time with George, because I know for a fact that however else she feels about you, the idea of not having you as a friend anymore would be devastating to her. And I know you wouldn't be so selfish as to do anything to hurt her more than she has been already.'

'Ros,' he said, raising a hand, 'can I just interject at this point to comment that you are at your most appealing when you are being overbearing and authoritative and that you should use that to your advantage next time you bump into someone you fancy.'

'I'll bear that in mind.'

'OK, now carry on. You're sending me to sleep and I could do with a nap.'

'Actually, I'm going to go now.' I stood up.

'Really?'

'Yes, but can I get you anything before I go?'

'No, I'm fine.'

I stooped down and kissed his warm forehead. 'You're a plum, you know.'

He laughed. 'Thanks for coming.'

'Best time I've had in ages.'

'See you tomorrow.'

'No. The day after tomorrow, at the earliest, but write to George tomorrow. Just a "hello". It's the selfless thing to do, you know.'

'Yes, I do know. I think I've just been too introspective of late. Thanks for helping me with that.'

'Well, I am, after all, an expert on introspection – or self-absorption, as someone put it rather recently.'

He smiled. 'People say lots of things they don't mean. Besides, anyone who thinks that just doesn't know the real you, do they?

'I'd like to think they don't.'

'So, why not just re-introduce yourself?'

'I think they've seen enough. Anyway,' I called, walking into the hallway and opening the front door, 'you're the most pressing case here. We can work on me after Christmas.'

I let myself out and fetched my bike from the bottom of the stairs. I wondered if he would send that email and crossed my fingers.

Chapter 23

Andrew was back at work two days later. It was clear that he wasn't entirely recovered but he was much improved, both in body and, apparently, in mood. One of the first things he told us was that he had been in touch with George and that she would be at work the following Tuesday. A lesser man may have delivered this news with a flicker of self-consciousness, a significant look or a knowing smile, but, in true Andrew fashion, he advised us of her return with precisely the same expression on his face as when he told us that Eric the electrician would be fitting the new ceiling lights on Friday after hours.

All significant looks and knowing smiles were therefore left to Joan. The day after my evening visit to Andrew, she had made no comment, other than to enquire as to whether I had actually managed to see him. When I confirmed that I had, she had simply mouthed the word 'George' at me, accompanied by one of the aforementioned significant looks. I had merely nodded in return, not knowing whether to be astonished at her insight or depressed at my own total lack of it. Other than that, she and I hadn't discussed the matter at all, each feeling, I hoped, that the less said the better. However, this didn't prevent Joan nudging me, tapping the side of her nose, winking and pushing her tongue into her cheek, whenever George's name passed Andrew's lips. I prayed that he didn't notice and wanted to assure him that it wasn't me who had spilled the beans but he appeared oblivious to her twitching and consequently I decided that, if he hadn't noticed, then the last thing he needed was me drawing attention to it.

–

I arrived at *Chapters* at 8am on the day of George's antic-ipated return to find Andrew sitting at the kitchen table with a large mug of coffee and, apparently, absorbed in his copy of *The Guardian*.

'Anything interesting?' I asked, placing my coat on the back of a chair and switching the kettle on.

He looked up. 'There's an interesting editorial on the Copenhagen summit, if you'd like to read that?'

'Gosh, you're dull.'

He nodded. 'Yup.'

'And, so, George is back today, isn't she?' I kept my back to him and started to make myself a cup of tea.

'She is indeed,' he said, absently. I heard him turn a page.

'So... I wonder what time she'll get here.'

'Quarter to eight,' he said.

'What?'

'Quarter to eight, Ros,' said George. I turned to see her standing behind me in the doorway of the kitchen, smiling with her arms outstretched. We hugged each other tightly and I didn't let her go until I was sure I had blinked back any potential tears.

'George!' I said, standing back to look at her. 'You look great.' I gave her another hug. 'We have missed you so, so much, haven't we Andrew?' The minute I had let the casual question slip, I kicked myself for asking it. I cast an anxious glance towards him but he seemed unperturbed.

'Actually, Ros, I have already told George, at length, how miserable we were without her, haven't I George?' His tone was relaxed and he didn't look up from the paper.

'Yes, he has.' George smiled at him. 'And about how sales are well up on last year. It all sounds marvellous. It is just so lovely to be back.'

I looked at her properly. She looked beautiful, if slightly less accessorised than usual, in a sleek, black polo-neck, an olive green pencil skirt and black, suede boots. But I estimated weight loss in the region of about half a stone and noted the suggestion of dark circles under her eyes, which concealer couldn't entirely disguise.

She reached out and squeezed my hand. 'I'm fine, Ros,' she said, quietly. 'I now believe it's all for the best.'

I nodded. 'Anyway,' I said, 'How on earth did you manage to beat me into work? What have you done with Lottie?'

'Mum is with me,' she replied. 'Just for a day or two, so I thought I may as well make the most of it. I have so been looking forward to coming back to work and, you know, if things are busy over the next few weeks, I would be more than happy to work some extra hours.' There was a slight catch in her voice and, I thought, just a hint of desperation, although her smile didn't falter. Andrew started speaking almost before she had pronounced the final syllable.

'That would be an enormous help, if you can manage it, George. Ros and I actually discussed the possibility yesterday but thought you might have trouble fitting in extra days.' He closed and then folded the paper, before pushing back his chair and standing up. 'But if you could work a few extra hours, that would be great.'

'My goodness, yes,' said George, clearly delighted. 'As many as you like, really.'

'Good,' smiled Andrew. 'Well, we'll look at it, and, you know, if you could, perhaps, come in each day, even if just for a morning or an afternoon or, say, from twelve until two, that would work, I think. What do you think, Ros? Perhaps you and George could sit down for ten minutes now and sort it out?'

I had been listening to the exchange, nodding along to Andrew's kind fabrications as necessary, and now reached for my laptop and prepared to put George down for as many hours' company and occupation as she needed over the run-up to Christmas.

'And,' I added, feeling a sudden, early surge of festive cheer, 'while we're at it, I can tell you all about my plans for the staff pre-Christmas dinner and drinks at my house. There will be mince pies and frenzied dancing to Frank Sinatra's Christmas classics. I thought I might ask Joan if she would like to bring Bobby, too, what do you think?'

'Well, that sounds just wonderful, doesn't it, Andrew?' said George, excitedly. 'Just think you, me, Joany and Bobby, quaffing fizz, munching mince pies and rocking around the Christmas tree at Ros's place.'

Andrew threw her a look of resignation and sighed. 'Yes, and with a bit of luck Joan and Bobby will come dressed as elves. I just can't wait, George. I really can't.'

George laughed and I felt more festive than ever, confident that Andrew meant what he said.

Chapter 24

'So you're sure you don't mind, Ros?' said Celia.

I considered it a measure of how far I had come in the past year that this question was a rhetorical one. I knew that Celia had already formed the plan; advised absolutely everybody else of the plan; made all the necessary logistical arrangements required to put the plan into effect; before, finally, 'consulting' me.

'No, it's fine. It'll be fun.'

'Yes, so, what have we got? That's Mum and Dad in your room, the boys in the guest room, you in the study on the futon and David and I on the sofa bed downstairs. That's not too much of a squash, is it?'

Not if you're Toulouse Lautrec, I thought. But it would be fine. My feet would overhang slightly but I could wear bed socks.

'And,' she continued, 'the boys are so excited to see you.'

'What,' I laughed, 'even more excited than they were at Dad's party?'

She was laughing too. 'Oh that was funny, wasn't it? I'll have to warn everyone that we must have no mention of Mr Edward this time.'

'So, when were you thinking of arriving?'

'Well, I've said to Mum that we'd aim to get to you by lunchtime on Christmas Eve and leave after dinner on Boxing Day; David is in work the next day. Mum and Dad would leave the morning after. How does that sound?'

Another rhetorical question. I graced it with a response nevertheless. 'Yes, that's fine. We're being very decadent and not opening on Christmas Eve. Andrew is off to Ireland the night before, George isn't around and Joan is flying to The Maldives with Bobby.'

'The Maldives? Gosh. How much does that cost?'

'God knows. Apparently she has "savings". Personally, I suspect her of running drugs in her spare time.'

'Could be...' I could tell Celia's mind was now on other things. 'Right... well, anyway... are you all sorted for Tom's wedding?' So that was it.

'I think I'm just going to get an old frock altered a bit. There's a lovely lady nearby who takes things in and up, so I'm managing to recycle.'

'Great... great...' I waited for her to get to the point. 'And, so, you're looking forward to it?'

I was deliberately obtuse. 'Yes, it sounds like it's going to be quite a lavish affair. Amy's stepfather imports wine, so everyone is expecting great things.'

'Lovely... lovely...'

'Yes.'

'OK... great...'

'Celia?'

'Yes?'

'Do you want to know who I'm going with and whether I'm at all anxious about seeing The Rat?'

'Er... well, yes, actually.'

I laughed. 'Thought so. Well, I'm definitely travelling down with Andrew but I've told him to invite someone else, so he's not going to be my plus one.'

'Are you going to take a plus one?'

'I doubt it.'

'I could be your plus one.'

'No you could not.'

'OK.' There was a brief silence, then she said, quietly, 'You're not cross with me, are you Ros? You know, for being concerned? I can see that that could be quite frustrating for you, now that you're back to your old self. I shouldn't really be raising concerns that you don't have. Sorry.'

I sighed. 'Ce, I love you for being concerned. And I understand why you think Tom's wedding is a big deal. You're quite right, actually, it *is* a big deal. But I'm not worried about it. There's been a lot of water under the bridge and it's all in the past for me,' I lied. 'I just hope he's found happiness with someone else.' I wondered if she had heard any gossip. I wasn't disappointed.

'Not from what I hear, Ros,' she said. 'I mean, I only get things second and third hand but Megan said Oliver had seen him and there definitely wasn't a new woman on the scene.'

'Oh right. Oh well. Anyway, I'd better go, Ce, I'm meeting Ant. We're off to hear *The Messiah* tonight.'

'Mum would be impressed.' I thought I heard her sigh, and wondered if she hadn't totally accepted the water-under-the-bridge line.

'Yes. It's the choir Alan Bullen used to sing with. Remember we heard them at St Martin's?'

'Alan, your old boss? Ah and how is he?' She sounded suddenly eager. 'He's divorcing, isn't he?'

'Yes, that's right.' I replied. 'He's divorcing.' I waited for the inevitable.

'Well, now, there's someone whom I'm sure would love to go to Tom's—'

'Celia Hawthorn-Shaw, you are absolutely incorrigible.'

There was a pause before she spoke. 'I'm turning into Mum, aren't I?' She sounded appalled.

'Dear God, no,' I laughed. 'You've got a long, *long* way to go before you can hope to match her levels of, well, I'll avoid the words "emotional", "social" and "suffocation", and just call it concern.'

'Well, that's very generous of you,' she sighed, 'but I'm not so sure.'

'Oh, don't be silly. Besides, Alan wasn't a totally dreadful suggestion. He's not exactly a barrel of laughs but he means well. Unfortunately, however, he seems to be quite the social butterfly these days. He hasn't been free to hook-up since he told me about the divorce. We've just exchanged the odd text.'

'So things are on the up for him then?'

'They seem to be, yes. He's certainly not moping at home, that's for sure.'

'Oh, well… that's nice.' She sounded subdued.

'Yes, it is.' I looked at my watch. 'But I'm afraid I'm going to have to run, Ce.'

'Of course, you go. Bye then. And have a lovely time with Ant.'

'I will.' I tried to sound reassuring. 'And all is well. I promise you.'

'I know, I know. And Christmas is going to be so much fun.' She sounded brighter again at the thought. 'Bye, Ros.'

'Bye.' I hung up and reached for my coat and scarf, whilst mentally reviewing the conversation with Celia, and immediately alighting upon the most intriguing piece of intelligence gleaned. *So, The Rat was still single.* I looked forward to indulging myself by dissecting that fact on the train.

Chapter 25

It was four weeks before Christmas, and I was upstairs at *Chapters*, rearranging the books back into alphabetical order by author after another busy day whilst Andrew sorted out the ground floor. He had suggested, earlier in the day, that we go for a drink after work and I was looking forward to mulled wine and the possibility, no matter how remote, that he may raise the subject of George. He had displayed no hint of his feelings for her since she had returned to work and this, coupled with the fact that Joan, on her very best behaviour, had ceased all nudging and winking from the moment George arrived back in the shop, made his declaration of love for her all the more surreal. I wondered, at times, whether it had all been a case of too much cold and 'flu medication going to his head.

I was tutting at the thoughtlessness of the customer who had simply stacked the titles they had been considering in a precarious pile on a stool, when I heard the shop door open and close, followed by the sound of male voices in conversation and laughter. I went to the top of the stairs and crouched down to look through the banisters, before standing up immediately, appalled to have seen Daniel McAdam chatting to Andrew by the till. A wave of horror and momentary nausea swept over me; my humiliations in front of him had been too frequent and too recent for me to be able to cope with seeing him without at least a week's notice. Still, at least he hadn't spotted me. I decided to stay put until he was gone.

'Ros!' Andrew called. My heart sank and I pretended not to hear. 'Ros! Are you there?' I said nothing, remaining perfectly still, lest I should cause a stair board to creak. Andrew said something to Daniel and then I heard him begin to walk towards the staircase. When he reached the bottom, I shook my head at him, waved my hands and mouthed the words, 'I have gone home.' Andrew climbed the stairs towards me.

'What on earth's going on?' he whispered, with an amused smile.

'I don't want to see him, Andrew,' I replied. 'It's just too embarrassing. I need time to prepare. I really, *really* made a fool of myself in front of him.'

'Don't be silly. Come on down,' he said, gently. 'It'll be fine.' He put a hand on my arm.

I pulled it away. 'No, no, I just can't. Just tell him I've left. OK?'

'What? Down the fire escape?' he laughed.

'Hush, Andrew, he'll hear you. Please.' He saw my distress.

'Look, Ros,' he whispered, 'of course I would do that if I could but I can't.'

'Why not?'

'Because,' he said, looking down, 'he can see your legs from where he is standing by the counter.'

I looked down too. 'Oh.'

'Exactly. So just come down, eh? He just wants to know how George is getting on.'

'OK,' I sighed. 'Just give me two minutes to calm down a bit. Tell him I'm busy shoving the last lot of books on the shelves.'

'OK.'

'And tell him I was standing at the top of the staircase because…'

'Yes?'

'I can't think of why I would be standing at the top of the staircase, not moving and not speaking.'

'Neither can I but I'm sure he won't think it's strange.' I knew he was trying not to laugh. 'Or at least no stranger than anything else you do.'

'Andrew…'

'I'm only teasing, Ros. Now,' he pushed me gently back up the stairs, 'go and take a few deep breaths and then come down and join us.'

I went upstairs, removed the leaning tower of paperbacks from the stool, sat down and proceeded to try and reason myself out of my embarrassment.

I told myself that this man was just a neighbour, not a friend, relative or work colleague, and I saw him very infrequently. His good opinion was unimportant to me. I had apologised for any perceived poor behaviour in his company and that should be the end of it. There was no reason why I should feel awkward about his visit – this was not about me, he had simply come to ask after George. All I had to do was go downstairs and greet him politely and calmly and then answer his questions regarding George. And I would be sure to count to three in my head before saying anything – anything at all – in order to guard against an inadvertent faux pas.

I stood up and walked slowly downstairs, fixing my face into an expression of what I hoped was calm serenity. I reached the bottom of the stairs, only to find that they had adjourned to the kitchen. After pausing for a moment to check my composure in the window, I made my way across the shop to join them. Daniel stood up as I entered. 'Hi Ros,' he said, with that relaxed smile of his. 'How are you? Andrew's just forced a beer on me.' He pointed to the bottle on the table.

'Can I get you a drink from the fridge, Ros?' asked Andrew.

One… two…

'Ros?'

'Three.' My look of calm serenity disintegrated. Good God.

'Three drinks?' asked Andrew.

'I don't know,' I said, staring at the table, wishing I could crawl under it.

'Well, how about we just start with the one glass?' laughed Andrew, grabbing a bottle of wine from the fridge and pouring me a glass. 'And see how we go on from there.'

I sat down, sipped my wine and glanced across at Daniel. He was smiling at me and looked much better than he had the last time I saw him. Probably because he'd had a good eight hours' sleep in a proper bed. I wondered if The Blonde was sharing it.

'I've been away on business, Ros,' he said suddenly. 'Otherwise, I would have popped round to see you for a cup of tea and to find out how George was.'

The reference to a cup of tea caused a rush of mixed recollections and emotions from which I took refuge in my wine.

'Where have you been, Daniel?' asked Andrew.

'Just visiting a few of the European offices. I don't have to travel much but, when I do, I tend to be backwards and forwards for a few weeks.'

I remained silent, feeling that I had nothing trivial to say to him. Instead, my mind flooded with inappropriate enquiries and topics, ranging from whether he truly believed I was self-absorbed, which was, of course, a self-answering question, to whether he was indeed in a sexual relationship with The Blonde. I felt Andrew give me a gentle kick under the table. I realised that I had probably been staring.

'Andrew and I are going to the pub shortly. Would you like to come?' I had no idea where the question had come from. He looked surprised.

'Sounds good,' said Andrew.

Daniel hesitated. 'You know that would have been great but I'm actually out for dinner this evening. But another time we should do that. And perhaps George could come too. How is she?'

Andrew looked at me. 'Ros probably knows that better than I do. George is always outwardly cheerful at work, isn't she Ros?'

I nodded. 'She copes very well,' I said. 'She just wants everything to go as smoothly as possible for Lottie's sake. Her parents are very supportive. But, you know what George is like. She doesn't want to be a burden to anyone and I have no doubt she has her darker moments which she just chooses to keep to herself.'

Daniel sighed. 'I emailed her some weeks ago and I'm going to call her but I just wanted to find out how she was generally before doing that.'

'I'm sure she'd like to hear from you,' I said.

We talked a little longer about George and then about the business and I was grateful that Andrew's presence reminded me to keep all tendency towards impropriety firmly in check. It was about half an hour later that Daniel glanced at his watch.

'Well, I'm now in danger of keeping someone waiting, so I'd better go.' He pushed back his chair and stood up. 'Good to see you again, Andrew,' he said, holding out his hand. 'And you too, Ros.' He put on his long, black coat and walked towards the shop door. 'OK, well, if I don't see you before, have a good Christmas.' We returned the sentiment and I watched as he exited the shop and strode up the hill, in the direction of his dinner date. I wondered whether The Blonde was at that moment checking her watch, entertaining the possibility that Daniel McAdam had changed his mind about her and decided not to come after all. I doubted it. Men didn't change their minds about women like her. And she knew it.

'Come on,' said Andrew, heading back towards the kitchen, 'let's just chuck those bottles in recycling and then head off. I feel in need of a Guinness and God only knows what you're in need of.'

'What?' I said, suddenly listening, 'Why? What have I done?'

He shook his head. 'Jesus, Ros. I know it was tricky for you but spare a thought for him. You sat there like a bloody wet weekend.'

'I invited him to come to the pub.'

'Yes but with a face like you were inviting him to a wake. Would it have hurt you to smile? You know, just the once?'

'Sorry.'

He emptied the dregs of beer down the sink and rinsed the bottles. 'So, come on, what do you think your problem is?'

'What?'

He placed the beer bottles in the recycling box and turned to look at me. 'Well, I know you think you've embarrassed yourself a little in front of him but it's not just that, is it?'

I sighed. 'Isn't it?'

'Well, if it is, it's a bit of an over-reaction.'

I sat down on the nearest chair, leant on the table and put my head in my hands. 'I really don't want to think about it, Andrew. I probably won't see him again anyway.'

Andrew pulled out a chair and sat down next to me. 'No?'

'Oh yes… George…'

He rolled his eyes. 'Christ, you're an eejit.' I was about to object to this unprovoked abuse but he didn't pause for breath. 'Look, just have a think about what makes you anxious when you see him and then get over it, so that we don't have a repeat performance of this evening's shenanigans.'

'What makes me anxious?' I looked at him in disbelief. 'Er… well, let's see. The guy is monied, successful, self-assured and pursued by sophisticated blondes.' I counted off the points on my fingers. 'Now let's just compare and contrast that with his experience of me: a self-absorbed, self-pitying, slightly unhinged, drunken floozy, who spies on his dinner party guests at midnight and takes men she hardly knows into dark alleyways to show them a good time.'

Andrew laughed. 'Ros… oh God, you know what, never mind.' He stood up. 'Go and get your coat, we're going for a drink.'

'And is that the lecture over with?' I asked.

'Yes, that's me done.' He smiled and handed me my coat. 'Now, hurry up. The Guinness is calling me.'

Chapter 26

I had just one half day to complete my Christmas shopping. I had been working pretty much full-time since George's party and things had barely eased up since her return. This was all good news from a business perspective but it had left me a little behind with my Christmas preparations, particularly as I had volunteered to host the staff party and, of course, been volunteered to have my entire immediate family to stay for three days.

To be fair, these were not as significant issues as they might have been. My mother and sister had realistic expectations of my ability to host with any level of sophistication or organisation. Even when I had been living a contented existence in London, they were well-used to my not-so-secret dependency upon *The Secret Chef of Highgate*, who would deliver 'gourmet meals for six to sixty' straight to your door, in foil trays, concealed in unmarked brown paper bags – 'culinary pornography', as Tom used to call it. Consequently, Celia was bringing Boxing Day supper and my mother was arranging almost everything but the turkey for Christmas Day.

The staff party too was ninety-nine per cent covered, thanks to a clandestine collaborative effort between Andrew and myself. My shopping list this particular afternoon, therefore, consisted primarily of gifts, decorations and hors d'oevres. However, as I dithered over the latter in Waitrose with just one day to go before the dinner, I realised that I didn't have enough coordinating dinnerware for five people, having lost several items from each of the two sets I possessed. I checked my watch and called George, whom I knew would either be in the playground or at home.

'Hello?' I could hear adult chatter in the background. Playground.

'Hi George. It's Ros. Can you talk?'

'Hi Ros. Yes, it's fine. I came to school to collect Lottie but she's just been invited to a friend's house for tea. Hang on a minute.' I heard her talking rapidly to another adult. 'OK, Ros. I'm just leaving the playground now. How can I help?'

'Sorry to bother you, George, but I wondered if I could borrow a dinner service from you for tomorrow night. I've now only got four complete, matching place settings. What do you think? I could swing by and pick it all up if you're OK with the idea.'

'Oh Ros, that's no problem and, you know, I'm more than happy to drop it all off tomorrow – I've got your key. It's just so lovely of you to host. I am well aware that it was my fault that a restaurant wasn't booked this year.'

'What? Don't be silly. We just didn't get round to it. Anyway, I wasn't going to make too much of a fuss but I wanted the table to look nice and I'm just picking out a few nibbles to go with the pre-dinner drinks. I might even have a bash at making something! What would you do?'

'Ooh well, now, I tell you one really easy and fun thing; vodka tomatoes.'

'Really?'

'Yes. My friend Gill makes them. You inject vodka and Tabasco sauce into cherry tomatoes. She used a spare syringe left over from when the cat was on insulin.'

'OK...'

'Then you need lemon juice and... ooh, something else which I forget.'

'Sounds perfect.'

'Absolutely. Great fun. I have a little book with loads of things like that in it. Really simple, make ahead stuff. Sherry prawns are another good one.'

'They do sound good.'

'You say you're in Waitrose now? Would you like me to text you a little list of things to get?'

'Are you sure you don't mind? Apologies for being hostess with the leastess.'

'Nonsense. Now, Ros,' I heard a beep as she reached her car and then the door opening and closing as she got in, 'I wonder if this might be a good time to ask you an extremely cheeky question.'

'Fire away.'

'Well, I got a call when I got home at lunchtime from Daniel McAdam.'

'OK...' I experienced a sensation not dissimilar to driving, at speed, over a minor humpback bridge.

'He was so sweet. He is lovely, Ros.'

'Yes.' I stopped pushing my trolley, suddenly equally intrigued and anxious as to where this might be going.

'Well, he said he'd bumped into you and Andrew and that you had suggested that we all get together.' Had I really suggested that? Perhaps I had. 'And dates are just so scarce around Christmas, I wondered Ros if...'

The penny dropped. 'You'd like him to come to dinner tomorrow.'

'Well, I was thinking more of him just popping round to join us for drinks afterwards. What do you think? I mean, Bobby is coming and, if we had one more man, we'd have three boys and three girls and I thought that might be nice for Andrew too.'

'Hmm...'

'I mean, don't worry if you don't think it would work, Ros. I haven't invited him, or even hinted at it. It's your party and your decision. I just thought...' I leaned over my trolley and closed my eyes, trying not to think any of this through.

'Of course, George, that's not a problem at all. And he can eat with us, if he wants. I'm sure it will stretch.'

'Really? Shall I bring some extra food or come earlier to help with the cooking?'

'No, no, it's fine. I'm not going to any trouble – pasta, that kind of thing. There'll be plenty to go round.'

'Oh you are lovely, Ros.' She sounded relieved. 'I would so like to see him but in... in frivolous circumstances. The last time I saw him was, well, rather intense.'

'No, that's all fine. Really. Will you go ahead and invite him then?'

'Well, I wondered if you would do that? I just think he might feel a bit awkward if I invite him to your home.'

I remained bent double, standing up only when an elderly fellow shopper placed her hand on my back in concern. I gave her the thumbs up, to indicate a state of well-being, and she smiled at me cautiously, withdrawing her hand and backing away, as one might in the presence of an unfamiliar dog. 'Of course, you're right, George.

I'll call him tonight. Could you text me his number along with the shopping list?'

'Will do.'

'And thanks for your help, George.'

'Nonsense, it's a pleasure.'

We said our goodbyes and I then wandered the aisles until her shopping list arrived about five minutes later along, of course, with Daniel's number.

As I made my purchases, I took some comfort in the fact that, at such short notice, less than two weeks before Christmas, Daniel probably wouldn't even have to come up with a lie in order to avoid dinner and drinks with the staff of *Chapters*; I was certain he would have a genuine, prior engagement. But I would still have to invite him and I wasn't looking forward to that.

–

Later that evening, I debated whether or not I should have a drink before making the dreaded call. In the end, I concluded that, as I felt unable to speak to him in my current state of high tension, there was little option but to pour myself a large glass of Pinot Grigio. I sat down with a book and had drunk approximately half the contents of the glass before I felt ready to get it over with. I dialled. To my delight, and near euphoria, I got his answerphone. I waited for the beep.

'Hi Daniel. It's Ros, your neighbour. I was speaking to George this afternoon on the phone and she—'

'Hi Ros.'

Oh dear. 'Oh hi, Daniel. I was just leaving a message.'

'Yes, I was in the shower.'

In the shower.

'Ros? Are you still there?'

'Yes. I am. Sorry to get you out of the shower.'

'No, no, I had finished. But can you just hang on a moment while I get my robe?'

I attempted to force the image of a small, white towel, from my mind. There was a clatter as he put the phone down and then, a moment later, he was back.

'So, Ros, how are you and how can I help?'

'Right.' I closed my eyes, forgot about the small towel and focused. 'Well, I was speaking to George this afternoon and she said she had spoken to you and she knew that we had mooted the idea of going for a drink and she wondered if you might like to join us tomorrow evening for *Chapters*' Christmas dinner and drinks. Oh, and it's at my house – which is why I'm doing the ringing.'

'That's a great word, "mooted", isn't it? But I'm a bit confused,' he sounded amused, 'is George inviting me, or are you?'

I hesitated. 'Well, we're both inviting you. George proposed the motion and I'm seconding it.'

He laughed. 'You have a way with words, Ros. Now, this is very kind of you – both – but are you sure I wouldn't be crashing? You know, the odd man out? The guy who doesn't know his Dickens from his Dostoyevsky.'

He couldn't be thinking of actually coming, could he? 'Er, well, no, because Joan is bringing Bobby. There would only be six of us in total, including you, so you would be balancing the boy/girl ratio. It's very low key. I'm going to be injecting cherry tomatoes with vodka – that kind of thing.'

He laughed again and I found myself joining in. I remembered the evening when we had laughed about his beard; it seemed an awfully long time ago. 'Sounds intriguing.'

'But not tempting.'

There was a pause. 'I'm extremely tempted.'

'Is that a yes?'

'That's a yes and a please.'

'Around eight o'clock?'

'See you then. Oh and what's the dress code?'

'You did hear me say that Joan and Bobby were coming?'

'Enough said.'

'Bye then.'

'Bye, Ros.'

I returned to my book and read the same paragraph three times before deciding to give up and see what was on TV. A repeat episode of 'What Not to Wear' made me wonder about what *to* wear the following evening. Up until then, I hadn't given the topic much consideration but now, presumably spurred on by Susannah and Trinny as they harangued some poor woman into exposing her cleavage and revealing her knees, I suddenly felt a need to look my best. I silenced the fashion harpies with the press of a button and went upstairs to consider my sartorial options.

Chapter 27

Less than twenty four hours later, I left Andrew to shut up the shop and hurried home to arrange my vodka tomatoes and sherry prawns on presentation platters and place them on the coffee table in the living room. I then set the dining table, adorning it, in what I hoped was an artistic manner, with yet more foliage from the garden. I stood back, pleased with the result, especially the holly and ivy napkin rings – I just hoped no injuries would be sustained during their removal. I popped as much fizz as I could fit into the fridge to chill and closed the door on Tony and Geraldine, the husband and wife catering team who had already been hard at work in my kitchen for the past two hours. I then ran upstairs to change into the little black dress which I had owned, but ignored, for a number of years, and into which, the lovely local seamstress had breathed new life, by altering it to fit perfectly. Black tights, black heels, lipstick and a quick up do and I was ready to receive.

I went downstairs, selected a Christmas compilation on the iPod in the living room and, wanting to save the first pop of a cork until the others arrived, poured myself a glass of cold Sauvignon Blanc. I lit the candles I had placed around the reception rooms, switched on the fairy lights running up the stairs and around the doorways, and went into the living room to await my guests. I didn't have to wait long. The doorbell rang and I checked my watch, 8.10pm. They were certainly keen.

I walked into the hallway and towards the front door, smiling at the thought of what Joan might be wearing. However, as it turned out, it was Daniel standing on the doorstep, dressed in an undoubtedly expensive dinner suit, white shirt and bow tie, only partially concealed under a heavy, black coat. He was smiling and carrying a bottle of Veuve Clicquot.

'Am I early?' It struck me that his relaxed grin had the completely opposite effect on me.

'Not at all,' I said.

'But I'm not late?'

I shook my head.

'Good,' he said, 'because I know the importance you place upon punctuality.'

I stepped back and he came into the hallway, closing the door behind him.

'Let me take your coat.'

'Thanks.' He placed the champagne on the floor, removed his coat, handed it over and then retrieved the bottle. 'I'll just go and pop this in the fridge for you,' he said, walking past me, towards the kitchen.

'No, don't!' I cried, slinging his coat over the banister and hurrying to place myself between him and the kitchen door. 'You can't go in there. It's out of bounds.' I stood with my back pressed to the door and my arms outstretched across it, barring access.

'OK, OK,' he said, stopping in front of me and laughing. He looked up at the ceiling at then back at me.

I looked up. 'What?'

The doorbell rang. He smiled and handed me the bottle. 'For the fridge. I'll get the door.'

I took a deep breath and turned to open the kitchen door.

'Oh and, Ros,' he said looking at me over his shoulder, as he walked towards the front door.

'Yes?'

The doorbell rang again and he tapped his shoulder. 'Your strap is showing.'

I tutted, quickly tucked in the errant bra strap and hurried into the kitchen. Even with the door closed, I could clearly hear the conversation at the far end of the hallway. Joan and Bobby were the new arrivals – Joan effusively greeting Daniel and Bobby quietly enquiring as to my whereabouts.

'She's in the kitchen but, whatever you do, don't attempt to enter. She's adjusting her underwear and doing appalling things to innocent vegetables with a syringe,' said Daniel.

I filled six champagne flutes, placed them on a tray and, with Tony holding the door open just wide enough to enable me to exit, I slipped back into the hallway. Despite my load, I was immediately greeted with breath-taking hugs and a distinctly European number of kisses, whilst Daniel relieved me of the tray before disaster struck.

I smiled at Joan. She was wearing a heavily fringed and beaded black dress, accessorised with a feather boa and a sparkling headband.

'You're a flapper!' I laughed.

'I am. Do you like it, my darling? Watch this.' She performed a mini Charleston routine down the hallway. I suspected that the glass of champagne I then handed her, following a brief round of applause, might not be her first drink of the evening.

I passed a second glass to Bobby and complimented him on his dinner suit. I looked at Daniel. 'Is the matching attire, purely coincidental?'

'Absolutely,' said Daniel, taking a glass for himself.

'Hmm…' I laughed, 'well, I'm not entirely convinced but never mind. Now look, the kitchen is, for the time being a no-go area, so come and make yourselves comfortable in the lounge. And do try a vodka tomato and a sherry prawn; both George's recipes.'

'I think I spot a common theme,' said Daniel, popping a tomato into his mouth. He coughed.

'Have I been a little too liberal with the Tabasco?' I asked, as Joan thumped him on the back.

'No, but if Joan carries on like that, I'll be in danger of bringing it all back up again,' he said, stepping away from her, in order to avoid the ongoing pounding.

Joan laughed, raucously, and moved in on the sherry prawns. 'Now, I simply must try one of these little things, Rosalind. What did you say they were?'

'Sherry prawns, Joan.'

'Sherry prawns…' She took a bite. 'Absolutely delicious, dear. I shouldn't be at all surprised if these are an aphrodisiac, you know. Here Bobby, have three.' More raucous laughter. I glanced at Daniel, wondering if he would survive the evening but he seemed genuinely amused, and not at all uncomfortable, when Joan flopped down on a sofa and patted the seat as an invitation for him to come and sit next to her. I sat down on the other sofa, next to Bobby, helped myself to a glass of champagne and a tomato, and began to relax, as Bobby ran through the Maldives itinerary for me.

Ten minutes later, I was on my way back to the kitchen to fetch the champagne for top-ups, when the doorbell rang again. I altered course and opened the front door to George and Andrew.

'You've come as a pair!' I exclaimed. 'How nice – saves me answering the door again.'

'Yes,' beamed George, coming in and adding her coat to the pile draped over the banister, 'Andrew is my chauffeur this evening. And,' she said, looking him up and down, 'what a remarkably handsome chauffeur he is. Don't you think so, Ros?'

I looked at him, as he slipped off his Timberland jacket to reveal a tuxedo and bow tie. 'You boys are so naughty!' I said. 'I didn't think men knew how to communicate by phone!'

'What do you mean?' asked George, looking bemused.

'You'll understand when you go in the living room, George. But, anyway, yes,' I smiled at Andrew, 'I have to agree with you. He looks remarkably yummy this evening.'

Andrew tutted and raised his eyes. 'Sorry, but I've had enough of standing here being treated like a piece of meat. Can I have a drink, please?'

'Absolutely,' I said, 'could you get the fizz from the fridge in the kitchen, Andrew – George, you're not allowed in there – and top-up everyone else's glass? There is a glass each for you and George already in the living room.' I grabbed the coats and started up the stairs. 'I'm just going to pop these into the guest room.'

From upstairs, I could hear muffled chatter and laughter from the living room and I was hopeful that there had been no awkwardness between Daniel and George. I was laying the coats out on the double bed, when I heard someone coming up the stairs.

'You left a trail of debris in your wake,' said Andrew, entering the room and adding two scarves and a glove to the large pile of outerwear on the bed.

'Thanks,' I smiled at him. 'Are you OK?'

'Yes, I'm all right.'

'You're doing a grand job.'

'Am I?' He sat down next to the coats.

'Yes.' I bent down and picked up another stray glove. 'It must be difficult sometimes.'

'Sometimes,' he said, sipping the drink he had brought with him, 'but most of the time it's just good to see that she seems to be doing OK.'

'I think she is OK,' I said. 'Or at least as OK as anyone could be in those circumstances.'

There was a pause as we listened to Joan's voice, followed by loud, general laughter, to which we added our own.

'Come on,' I said, 'let's go down and reveal the surprise.'

'Yes,' he said, 'that's the other reason I came up. Geraldine says it's ready when we are.'

'Great, and…' I took his hand, pulled him up and headed towards the door, '…I have party games planned!'

'Oh dear.'

'I knew you'd be pleased.'

—

An hour and a half later, we had finished the main course and were sitting around the dining table playing our second game of the evening. The first, Pass the Parcel, played following the warm seafood salad with baby courgettes, had, I thought proudly, been a great success. It was as a consequence of the parcel passing that we were each now sporting a moustache, George's prize having been 'A moustache for every day of the week', which she had thoughtfully shared out amongst us. Bobby was wearing '*The Spiv*', Joan '*The Waiter*', Daniel '*Grandpa*', George was sporting '*The Detective*', I had been given '*The Dictator*' and Andrew was modelling '*The Sherriff*' which, according to Joan, made him "the very image of the wonderful Freddie Mercury".

We had now added large, red, plastic spectacles to our facial attire, each with a card, bearing the name of a famous person, place or landmark, stuck in a special little holder across the top of the frames. The aim of the game was, of course, to guess what was written on the card by asking questions of the other players. It had been agreed that the last person to successfully guess what was on their card, would complete a circuit of the garden, whilst singing 'Ding Dong Merrily on High.'

I had, after just three questions – *Am I a woman? Am I dead? Was I a little bit annoying?*– identified myself as Princess Diana and Andrew hadn't been far behind – *Am I a man? Am I a politician? Can I see out of both eyes?* – with Gordon Brown. After another five minutes or so, Daniel had guessed that he was The Eiffel Tower and George had discovered that she was The Nile. Bobby was, quite understandably, feeling a little defeated by Idi Amin but Joan was soldiering on determinedly with James Joyce. So far, she had discovered that he was a man, that he was not a 'Bertie ice-cake', a cross-dresser, a fetishist or a vegetarian and that he didn't, as far as we knew, like roller-skating. I began to suspect that Joan was actually rather keen on the idea of running round the garden and, furthermore, as she incorrectly guessed Voldemort, Sir Bruce Forsyth and the Reverend Sun Myung Moon, that she was more drunk than anyone else at the table.

'Oh dear me,' she laughed. 'I am such a dreadful guesser. However,' she wagged an index finger at us, 'I am not giving up. No, I am *not* giving up.'

Of course, we couldn't help but laugh along with her. However, after at least a dozen more wide-of-the-mark guesses, ranging from Peter Sissons to 'the man who invented Fruit Pastilles', I decided it was time to give her a clue.

'Look, Joan,' I said, re-affixing my moustache, which had started to come loose, 'this person is Irish and is also a favourite author and poet of Andrew's'

She rubbed her chin. 'Er...' We waited. 'Er...'

'Come on, Joan. Someone Andrew greatly admires.' I laughed. 'He's declared his deep, deep affection for this person on a number of occasions.'

Andrew sighed. 'I can't deny it, Joan. Deep affection.' He placed his hand on his heart.

'Deep affection...' Joan massaged her temples in a dramatic indication of deep thought. 'Deep affection... Someone Andrew loves... Hmm... now, whom does Andrew love?' she mused quietly. 'Whom does Andrew love...?' Her face suddenly lit up and, with Cassandra-like futility, I realised, too late, what was coming next. 'Andrew loves George!' she cried, banging the table, before immediately recognising her mistake and clasping a hand to her mouth, where it then remained, in an attitude of petrified horror.

I glanced round the table. Andrew was motionless and staring at his empty plate, his features fixed in an expression which I interpreted as suicidal resignation. Bobby's eyes had widened into near-perfect circles, whilst his mouth hung, silently, ajar. Daniel was looking at us all in puzzled amusement and George... well, I simply couldn't bring myself to look at George. Only Frank Sinatra remained unaffected by the crisis, as he continued, unphased, to advise us to have ourselves a merry little Christmas.

The tension near unbearable, I was just about to run screaming from the room, when George spoke.

'Aah, well,' she said, quietly, 'what a simply lovely thing to say. Thank you so much for saying that, Joany. You always know how to make someone feel special.' I looked at her, swaying slightly in her chair and beaming at us all, and I realised that I had been mistaken; Joan was not the most inebriated person at the table. That dubious distinction fell, thank God, to George. 'And I know he does,' she continued, leaning unsteadily towards Andrew and taking his hand. 'I know you all do. You've made that very clear to me, even without Joany declaring it. And I hope you all know just how much I appreciate all your kindnesses and how much I love you all in return.' She used her napkin to wipe away a single tear. 'Thank you,' she whispered.

I experienced a sudden, and overwhelming, sense of euphoria at disaster averted, but managed to resist the urge to stand up and applaud. Instead, I decided to go and ask Geraldine if we could have dessert.

'I won't be a moment,' I said, primarily to Andrew, who had the look of a man being unstrapped from an electric chair.

'Yes, that's right,' he murmured, as I hurried from the room.

Mission accomplished, I returned to the dining room, a few minutes later, to hear a distant, prolonged and utterly tuneless wailing of the word 'Gloria' and to find Andrew, George, Daniel and Joan huddled at the open French windows, peering into the darkness, waiting for Bobby to come back into view as he completed his circuit of the garden. At last, he re-appeared, breathless, and a little muddied, having slipped, he said, on a particularly treacherous patch of wet leaves. Joan, showing a complete disregard for her own cleanliness, welcomed him back inside with an enthusiastic hug and then proceeded to 'get the worst off him' with her feather boa. I smiled. Normal service had been resumed.

—

I waved off Bobby and Joan at around midnight and then returned to the living room with an offer of teas and coffees to my remaining three guests.

'I'd love a coffee, Ros,' said Andrew, 'but you come and sit down and I'll make it. Daniel? George?'

'Coffee for me, please,' said Daniel. 'Black is great.'

'I would love a peppermint tea, Andrew,' said George. 'If you have any, Ros?'

I nodded. 'There's a box behind the spotty caddy, Andrew. I'll have one of those too, please.'

He disappeared off into the kitchen.

'This was such a lovely thing you and Andrew did this evening, Ros.' George smiled across at me. 'Those caterers were superb.'

'The food was good, wasn't it? And Joan... and Bobby...'

'They are such good value,' laughed George. 'What did you make of it all, Daniel?'

'I thoroughly enjoyed myself. Thank you for inviting me.' He smiled and turned to look at me, as I sat down next to him. 'I only hope I'm lucky enough to be on the guest list again next year.'

'Well,' I said, 'even if you're not, you can always peer over the hedge, can't you?'

'Poor Andrew,' said George, suddenly, 'being left all alone in the kitchen. 'I'm going to go and give him a hand.' And she was gone.

There was silence for a moment before Daniel spoke. 'I *have* thoroughly enjoyed myself, you know.'

I smiled. 'So you said.'

'Yes, but I wanted to make sure that you knew that I wasn't just being polite.' He shifted his position slightly so that he was now facing me. 'And while we have a few moments alone, I want to apologise – for the night of George's party.'

'Oh God, no, please,' I groaned. 'Don't bring that up and, besides, you didn't do anything wrong at all. It was me—' I broke off mid-sentence and put my hands up to my face. 'Please, do you mind if we don't talk about it? I cringe even at the thought of it.'

I looked up to see him shaking his head. 'It's my fault you feel like that. I just need to explain something to you.'

'Daniel,' I held up my hand, 'I've already told you that I was just being silly, assuming it was all about me.'

'Tea's up, guys!' announced George, as she held open the door for Andrew with his tray of hot drinks. I looked at her and realised that she had sobered up remarkably quickly since dinner. Quite a talent. Andrew handed round the drinks. I glanced at Daniel; he appeared perfectly at ease. Whatever he had wanted to tell me, clearly wasn't troubling him now.

'So, Ros,' said George, 'Andrew's just been telling me about this wedding the pair of you are off to in January. Sounds like it's going to be quite an event.'

'Yes,' I said, relieved at the interruption and change in topic. 'The bride is a very, er, particular person, isn't she Andrew? I don't think she'll be doing things by halves.'

'And you are both friends of hers?' asked Daniel.

'We are mutual friends of the groom,' explained Andrew. 'I worked with him when I was a lawyer and Ros has known him since university. He introduced Ros and I to each other. And yet, remarkably,' he drank his coffee, 'neither of us hold that against him.'

'Well, I'm jealous,' said George, 'I love a good wedding.'

'Andrew has a spare ticket,' I said, smoothly, 'don't you Andrew? Why don't you take George? Or have you already allocated it?'

He flicked me a look of almost imperceptible shock, whilst placing his half-empty mug on the coffee table. 'It's true. I have an option of a plus one, if you'd like to come along George.' He sounded impressively casual.

'Oh Andrew, I couldn't do that,' said George, sounding, I thought, as if she probably could.

'Why not?' I said. 'It'd be really nice for me to have someone to talk to.'

'Thanks for that, Ros,' said Andrew, dryly. 'Hey, Daniel, why don't you take Ros's spare ticket and make the day bearable for me too?'

'Are you in need of an escort, Ros?' asked Daniel.

'Oh, the four of us!' said George. 'Now *that* would be fun. What's the date?'

'Second weekend in January,' said Andrew.

'Well, Andrew, you have a think about it and, if you truly can't think of anyone else to take, I would love to come.'

I smiled across at Andrew but he was too busy smiling at George to notice.

'Can you make that date, Daniel?' asked George.

'Actually, George, I haven't quite been invited yet,' laughed Daniel. 'Ros may well already have someone else lined up.'

'Oh, I'm sorry, Ros,' said George, with an embarrassed expression. 'I've let myself get carried away with the idea. How rude.'

'No, no, George,' I said. 'Not at all. The thing is, Daniel,' I said, turning to him, 'based on her knowledge of my personal life, George can be pretty certain that I haven't got anyone in mind to take along. Not unless Andrew *finally* comes up trumps with a poorly-groomed gay guy. So, if you would like to come along, you are more than welcome.' Now that the offer had been made, he looked slightly awkward. 'Oh, but not if you have plans with your girlfriend,' I said, hurriedly, guessing at his discomfort. 'A wedding isn't the type of thing you go to without your partner, is it?'

He hesitated. 'No, I'm sure she'd be absolutely fine about it. Can I just check the date and get back to you?'

'Of course,' I said, feeling unaccountably crushed, 'and if you can't make it, that's fine. I will have George – ooh and Andrew, of course – to talk to. Just let me know.'

'Thanks,' he said.

'I didn't know you had a girlfriend, Daniel,' said George, looking a little deflated. 'Have you and Tish reconciled?'

He shifted uncomfortably. 'Er… no, no we haven't.'

'So it's someone new then?' she persisted.

He ran a hand through his hair, which left him looking, I thought, pleasantly dishevelled.

'Er… yes, that's right.' He scratched his nose. 'We, er, met at your party, actually.'

'The blonde woman at the bar,' I said, flatly. Everyone turned to look at me. Daniel, I thought, looked oddly relieved.

'That's right,' he smiled. 'She was at the bar when I was getting you a drink. Sarah Millbank.'

I tried hard to return the smile.

'Oh, Sarah Millbank,' said George. 'Yes, she's a very determined sort of person. Oh, well, that's nice, Daniel.'

He laughed. 'Hang on,' he said, reaching into his pocket and taking out his Blackberry, 'I can check that date now, can't I? I don't know why I didn't do that right away, you know, end all the suspense.'

We waited whilst he tapped at the keys. 'As it happens,' he said, still focused on the small screen, 'I have nothing on that weekend and would love to come,' he looked up at me, 'if the offer still stands.'

'I only invited you thirty seconds ago,' I said. 'I'm not quite that fickle, you know.'

'Then it's a date.'

'OK,' I said.

'Super,' beamed George. 'Who's driving?'

–

When Andrew and George's taxi arrived, I ran upstairs to fetch everyone's coats and, when I returned, we stood for a few moments in the hallway, saying our rapid goodbyes, whilst the driver revved his engine impatiently.

'See you Monday, Ros,' said Andrew, giving me a hug. 'And thanks for tonight.'

'It was fun, wasn't it?' I said.

'Ros, let's try to meet up before I go to Oxford.' George squeezed me like a boa constrictor. For someone so increasingly slight she had, I reflected, incredible upper body strength. When she released me, I saw that she looked a little tearful. 'I have had the best time,' she said, quietly. 'Thank you.'

'An absolute pleasure, George,' I said.

Andrew shook Daniel's hand, George kissed him lightly on both cheeks and then they headed outside and walked towards the taxi, with Andrew taking her hand to keep her steady on the gravel in her high heels.

I left the door open and turned to Daniel, who was putting on his enormous coat.

'That looks warm,' I said quickly, anxious to avoid any silence which I might fill with an inappropriate enquiry or statement. At this point in our relationship, I reasoned, inanity was definitely the safest course, even if I did sound like my mother. 'I just love wool, don't you?'

Perhaps not surprisingly, he chose not to respond to the enquiry and, instead, looked at me and smiled.

'What?' I asked. 'Oh God, have I still got that moustache on?' I felt my upper lip.

'No,' he laughed. 'It fell off when Joan told everyone that Andrew loved George.' I tried not to twitch. 'Don't worry,' he continued, 'you look great.'

'Well, thank you,' I said. 'I do try, you know.'

'OK then,' he said, moving towards the door. 'I guess I will see you the second weekend in January – if not before. Give me a call about transportation nearer the time. I'm happy to drive. Are you and Andrew planning to stay over?'

I nodded. 'Yes – I hadn't really thought of that. Tom gave us a heads-up and we've managed to book rooms at the Hall. But they're both twins so, if they're fully booked, we could share. I mean,' I felt myself reddening, 'I could share with George and you could share with Andrew. But, actually, men don't tend to share... do they? So maybe... hmm, yes, we'd have to think about that.'

He smiled his relaxed, un-relaxing smile. 'We'll work something out,' he said, before changing the subject. 'I heard you say to Bobby that you are here over Christmas?'

'God, yes, with the entire family.' I laughed and shook my head. 'It's going to be chaos. And you're in Edinburgh?'

'Only for New Year. Miles and his girlfriend are with me for Christmas, so we may run into each other.' There was a brief silence, during which I smiled and found myself resisting an unexpected urge to ask whether Sarah Millbank would also be joining him.

'Anyway,' he said finally, opening the door a little further, 'goodnight, Ros. And thanks again.' With one hand on the door, he leaned towards me, placing his left arm around me and twisting slightly, to kiss me on the cheek. I rested my hands his shoulders, as I went to return the kiss. He let go of the door and turned a little further towards me. The simple gesture of farewell was executed in a matter of moments, but I was surprised to find myself noting every stage of its progression. We separated, before he turned again and reached for the door.

'Bye then, Ros,' he said, jovially, his breath forming clouds as he stepped outside and began to walk away.

'Happy Christmas!' I called, noting a slight suggestion of hysteria in my voice.

He laughed and waved again without turning round. 'Happy Christmas!'

I closed the door and leaned back heavily against it, putting a hand to my forehead. 'Damn fizz,' I said to myself, before going back into the living room to collect the mugs and blow out the candles.

Chapter 28

I went to see George, the following Wednesday, after work, to exchange gifts before she headed north with her parents. When I arrived, the latter were playing tennis on the Wii with Lottie but they downed their remotes long enough to say hello and to quietly express their thanks for the help and support given to George over the past few weeks.

'Alistair and I think Lottie and *Chapters* have saved her, you know,' said Ruth, when George went to the kitchen with Lottie.

George's father nodded. 'Those extra hours you gave her helped enormously,' he said.

'And I'm not entirely sure what kind of staff party you threw last week,' smiled Ruth, 'but it was the first time in weeks that we have heard her laugh about anything.'

'We all love George very much,' I said, as George and Lottie re-appeared – Lottie with a flapjack and some milk and George with a bottle of wine and two glasses.

With Lottie eager for the recommencement of the game, it was agreed that it should be relocated to the den, in order to give George and I a chance to talk.

As soon as the game-players disappeared from view, George poured two glasses of wine and we each took a sofa and put our feet up.

'My goodness, what a year, Ros,' sighed George.

'I'm so, so sorry, about the way things have turned out,' I said.

'Well...' She placed her glass on the low table at her side and offered me one of the mince pies her mother and Lottie had made that afternoon. 'These look slightly leathery to me,' she smiled. 'Feeling brave?'

'They look better than anything I could have produced,' I said, taking one and biting into it. 'Delicious,' I mumbled. George laughed. 'No, honestly,' I insisted, 'they are delicious.' She smiled. 'So you're OK?' I asked.

'Yes, I am.' She hesitated. 'The thing is, Ros... it wasn't a surprise.'

'No?'

'Oh, I mean, when he sat down and told me that night that he was going, and why he was going, I was, of course, shocked to the core.' She shivered slightly. 'But, on reflection, I realised that I had been fighting to hold onto him for quite some time. It was quite exhausting, really. So, when he said it was over, I believed him and it was a relief in many ways – you know, because I could finally stop fighting.' She sipped her wine and smiled sadly at me over the top of her glass. 'And, more recently, I've admitted to myself that I was only trying to keep us all together for Lottie... not for me.'

I nodded and waited for her to go on. This was the first time that George had told me how she felt about the break-up, rather than focusing upon how it affected everyone else, and I was anxious not to interrupt. 'I know,' she said, 'that when you found yourself on your own, your devastation was due to the fact that you still loved him and because it was all so inexplicable. But my situation is really quite different, Ros. We were seeing less and less of Mike and I had watched his priorities change over a number of years. Lottie and I were once everything to him…'

She paused, turning her head to look at the photograph of a grinning Mike and Lottie which sat on the table beside her. 'But, gradually, we became something he had to schedule into his life around his job, along with haircuts and dental appointments. It's no surprise India works with him. The office is where he lives, where his heart is.'

My stomach lurched at the sound of India's name. 'You talk about it so calmly, George.'

She smiled. 'As I say, it has been a long time coming, Ros, and, you know, my own feelings couldn't remain unchanged. If I was going to stay strong and sane for Lottie then I had to put myself in a place where his dying interest in us didn't destroy me. I loved him for being Lottie's father and I accepted the lack of time he spent with us and made the best of things, but, eventually, I stopped trying to excuse it to myself and so… well…' Whilst talking, she had continued to gaze at the photograph but she now turned to look at me again and I saw that her eyes were full of tears. 'The only thing that breaks my heart,' her voice caught and she took another sip of wine, 'is the baby.'

'I know, George.'

'He had always been adamant that Lottie was enough. And now…' I moved to sit next to her and took hold of her hand. She shook herself. 'I'm fine, Ros, and the bottom line is that he and I agree that we are better off apart and we both want to make that work as best we can. That is an enormous comfort to me, you know.' She smiled. 'Along with you and Joan and Andrew. Work is key – my mind is occupied and you lovely people are forced to spend time with me and I get paid for it! Of course, you know, I would do it for nothing.'

'George,' I said, 'I don't know what we'd do without you. We were so miserable while you were away. Andrew was...' I attempted to disguise my hesitation by developing a renewed interest in the plate of mince pies. 'I must have another one of those in a moment,' I said, leaning forward.

I sat back to find her looking at me enquiringly.

'We were all just very worried about you.'

'Well, you can stop worrying now,' she smiled. 'I'm well on the road to recovery. How about you?'

'You mean, am I on the road to recovery?'

She nodded.

'Ah George,' I sighed, 'if only I had your disposition, your goodness. As it is...'

'You can't forgive?'

'I can't.' I said simply, with a wry smile. 'Try as I might – and I don't – I can't forgive him. However,' I reached for another mince pie, 'I am starting to forget. Or at least, to remember a lot less often.'

'Well, I'm pleased about that, anyway.'

'Yes. Oh and I forgot to tell you! You'll get to meet him.'

Her eyes widened. 'I will?'

'Yes, at Tom's wedding.'

'My goodness, Ros! Will that be the first time you have seen him since—'

'Yes.' I pulled a face and pretended to nibble my cuticles.

She laughed. 'But seriously, are you OK with that?'

'Well,' I bit into the second mince pie and paused to swallow, 'it will be a case of suck it and see.' She looked concerned and I laughed. 'I'm only teasing you, George. Don't worry. I have no intention of causing a scene. It will be fine. I'm really looking forward to the weekend.'

'Me too,' she smiled. 'I think the four of us will have such fun. And it's so nice to see you getting on so well with Daniel. He's such a lovely man.'

'Yes, he seems very nice.' I said. She sighed and topped up our glasses. 'What?'

'Nothing,' she smiled. 'Everything will, as Willy Wonka once said, come out in the wash. And,' she continued, nudging me, 'Joan tells me that, astrologically speaking, she has very high hopes for us both in the New Year.'

I raised my glass. 'Well, here's to the New Year, then.'

George clinked her glass against mine. 'The New Year,' she laughed.

Chapter 29

'Oh well, isn't that beautiful, Ted? It must have cost you a fortune, Celia,' said my mother, fingering the tube of eau de nil cashmere. 'Yes, lovely. A very lovely… woollen… item… thing.'

'It's a snoop, Nanny,' said Stephen.

'A snood, darling,' said Celia, smiling. 'It's a snood, Mum. You wear it round your neck like a scarf and then you can pull it up over your head like a hood when it gets cold.' She took the snood and demonstrated.

'Well, that's just marvellous,' said my mother, retrieving the snood and adding it to her pile of gifts. 'Whoever would have thought of that? I will have to save that only for very best.'

Celia shot me a glance and we each stifled a laugh.

'Right,' said Dad. 'What's next?'

'I've done all mine, Grandpa,' said Ben, 'and so has Stephen. Can we go and play?'

My father glanced around. 'I think there may be one more here somewhere, boys. Something for Aunty Ros.'

'What are you talking about, Ted?' said my mother. 'Ros has opened her pyjamas, haven't you Ros?'

'Yes, I have,' I smiled, 'and very lovely they are too. I shall be wearing them this very night.'

'No,' my father began to search through the mountain of torn wrapping paper, 'there is another for Rosalind. But anyway,' he smiled at Ben, 'you two go and play with some of your new things and we'll start to tidy up.'

'Will you play on the Xbox with us later, Grandpa?' asked Stephen.

'Only if there's lots of guns and killing.' My father began to laugh.

'Oh Ted!' said my mother. 'You are dreadful. Isn't he girls?' But she joined in the laughter nevertheless. 'Celia, do you want to come and help me in the kitchen, so we can give Ros a chance to tidy up in here?'

'OK. David,' said Celia, 'you couldn't just go and supervise them in the dining room with that science lab thing, could you? I'm just thinking of Ros's carpets.' She followed my mother into the kitchen, as David hoisted himself out of the armchair.

'She's all concern about your carpets,' he said, bending down and placing a hand on my shoulder, 'but what about my skin? Last time they got one of those things, my hands were blistered for weeks.' He sighed. 'I don't know what I see in them all sometimes, you know.' He grinned at my father before disappearing after the boys.

My father smiled after him, before resuming his excavation of the wrapping paper mountain. 'Ah, here it is,' he said at last, proudly producing a poorly-wrapped, oblong package. 'I knew it was here somewhere. Come and sit down.' We got up from the floor and went to sit together on the sofa. He handed me the parcel. 'Happy Christmas, sweetheart.'

I looked at him and smiled. 'What's this? Is it from you?'

'It is.'

'Not from Mum?'

'No. Just from me.'

'How exciting.' I carefully opened the wrapping.

'I thought you might need a new one,' he said.

I placed the red, leather-bound photograph album on the sofa beside me and leant over to hug him.

'Thank you,' I said.

'I've even started it off for you.' He picked up the album and opened it. Occupying the entire first page was a copy of one of the many photographs taken by the waiters at the restaurant on the evening of Dad's 70th birthday party. It was the first one taken – the one before we were all actually 'ready'. Mum and Dad were sitting at the head of the table, Mum settling Stephen on her lap and Dad with an arm around Ben, who was standing to his left. Celia, David and I comprised the second row, with myself in the middle. Celia appeared to be adjusting her dress, looking down and to her left, laughing at something forgotten, whilst David was leaning backward, craning his neck around me to see what was causing her such amusement. Dad's head was turned towards me and we were looking at each other, smiling broadly. He was holding my hand.

'Ah, Ros,' said Dad after a moment. 'Now, this is the kind of memory for us to hold onto, isn't it?'

'Yes, it is,' I said, hugging him again.

'You've done so well. And been so brave. We all think so.'

'I don't know about that, Dad. I'm not quite there yet, you know,' I said, letting him go and wiping my eyes.

My mother appeared in the doorway, wearing her new 'Top Granny' apron and carrying an enormous, metal spoon. 'Ros, do you have a—' She stopped, noticing my tears. 'Oh Ted, what are you doing, upsetting Ros on Christmas Day?'

'I am not upsetting her, Lilian, we are just having a chat.'

'Well, she looks upset to me.'

'I'm fine, Mum,' I said. 'Dad was just reminding me how much I'm loved.'

'Well,' she said, her voice breaking slightly, 'in that case, you carry on, Ted, because you are loved, Rosalind.' She dabbed at her eyes with her apron. 'Very much indeed.'

I got up and walked over to her to give her a hug. 'Good God, don't you start,' I laughed. 'I'm just starting to lose my reputation as The Weeping Aunty with the boys and this is going to set me back several months.' I kissed my mother. 'Anyway,' I said, removing the last tear from my cheek with a dab of my crumpled Kleenex, 'Dad has just given me a wonderful present, which has left me with some de-cluttering to take care of.' I smiled at my father and then headed upstairs into the study, to power-up the shredder.

–

Our walk around Verulamium Park after Christmas lunch left us all, with the exception of Stephen and Ben, with a desire to do nothing but flop by the fire with a piece of Christmas cake and a cup of tea. I went into the kitchen to organise the refreshments, whilst David went in search of something to occupy and, hopefully, to tire the boys.

'I'm not sure that Celia's going to be over the moon about this,' he said, as the three of them walked through the kitchen and towards the back door, Stephen and Ben armed with large, plastic, futuristic-looking weapons. 'Now look,' he said, re-tying Stephen's scarf and turning up the collar of Ben's coat, 'you can use the trees and the fences for target practice but not each other. OK?' They groaned in unison. 'I'm serious,' he said, attempting, and failing, to look stern. 'It's too cold. I see you shooting at each other and you come straight in. Is that clear?'

They nodded meekly and ran outside, quickly disappearing into the depths of the garden.

'What were those things?' I asked, putting a tea-cosy on the pot.

'Water guns,' he sighed. 'They're from my brother. God, you can tell he hasn't got kids. Who gives children water guns in December?'

I laughed. 'Well, it'll keep them occupied for a while and they'll come in soon enough if they get cold.'

'I suppose so,' he smiled. 'And, er, Ros,' he picked up the tray laden with mugs and Christmas cake, 'no need to worry Celia with it, eh?'

I placed a finger to my lips, implying complicit silence, and we rejoined the others in the living room.

—

Mum and Dad were snoozing on the sofa and Celia was just finishing her second cup of tea, when my phone rang and she realised she was sitting on it. She pulled it out from under her, tutting at a comment from David regarding melodious farts, and looked at the screen.

'You've got a text, Ros,' she said, squinting and holding the phone at arm's length. 'Who's Daniel?'

I looked up sharply from the Banksy book on my lap.

'Aah,' said David, noting my reaction. 'Who *is* Daniel, Ros?'

Celia nudged him.

'He's my neighbour,' I said. 'The one who killed Mr Edward.'

'Oh,' said David, 'sorry. Didn't realise the name had unpleasant associations. Thought he might be...' He trailed off, coughed, and turned to look at my curtains. 'These are nice, Ros,' he said, fingering the fabric.

'Oh, for goodness sake, David,' said Celia, 'just shush. Here you go, Ros.' She leant over and handed me the phone.

'Thanks.' I entered the passcode and read the text.

> *It would be much appreciated if you could keep*
> *your young house-guests under control. Sylvia*
> NOT AT ALL *amused. D*

'What is it?' asked Celia.

'Oh, he's just wondering about the Christmas bin collections,' I said. I looked at David and tried to sound casual. 'I wonder how the boys are getting on.'

He shifted his position, his eyes widening slightly.

Celia turned to him. 'What have you done?'

'Nothing,' he said, getting up. 'I haven't done anything. But Ros is right. I'll just go and see how they're getting on in the garden.'

Celia grabbed his belt. 'No, you sit down and relax, darling. I'll go.' She swept from the room.

236

I offered David a sympathetic smile. 'I'll go too. I'm sure it's nothing.'

I went into the hallway, grabbed my coat and then went into the kitchen and put on my wellingtons. Outside, Celia was already half way across the lawn, coatless, and heading for the undergrowth. I hurried after her, catching her up a few moments after she reached Stephen and Ben, both of whom were perched precariously at the top of the small step ladder, usually kept at the side of the shed. They were talking to someone over the hedge, a conversation which Celia now joined. She turned to me, smiling, as I approached.

'Oh Ros,' she said, 'I have just met your neighbours, Daniel and Miles.' She mouthed the word 'phwoar' at me; I tutted and rolled my eyes in return.

'Daniel is my neighbour; Miles is his brother,' I said, matter-of-factly.

'Phwoar,' she mouthed again. I pulled her away from the hedge and peered over the top. Daniel and Miles were standing together, dressed for winter and each holding a glass of brandy.

'Hi Ros,' said Daniel, raising his glass towards me. 'Happy Christmas. We've just been getting to know your nephews. They drew attention to themselves by firing their water guns at us, as I showed Miles the proposed site of the new summerhouse.' He sipped his brandy. 'Impressive range.'

'Sorry,' I said. I looked at Ben and Stephen. Both hung their heads. Stephen bit his lip.

'Sorry, Aunty Ros,' said Ben.

'Sorry, Daniel!' shouted Celia, cheerfully, unseen behind me. I glared at her over my shoulder. She had now been joined by a relieved-looking David. 'Phwoar,' she whispered, giggling.

'That's all right, Celia!' Daniel called back.

'Anyway, boys,' she said, reaching her arm up towards Stephen and helping him down, 'come on inside now and get warm and let's leave Aunty Ros to talk to her neighbours. See you later Ros.' She winked at me. 'Bye, Daniel! Bye, Miles. Lovely to have met you!' she called, before leading all three boys back towards the house.

'Sorry about that,' I said, returning my attention to Daniel. 'Now, what happened with Sylvia?'

'Sylvia?'

'You said Sylvia was cross.'

'Well, she is. Always.' He smiled.

'But not about the water-guns?'

'I doubt it,' he grinned. 'She's in Perthshire, visiting her cousin. But I didn't think you'd come and sort out the ruffians if you thought it was only me they were abusing.'

I shook my head. 'You're dreadful. You know I'm on very thin ice with that woman and she's best buddies with my landlord.'

'I apologise,' he said.

'Hmm...'

'Sincerely.'

'OK,' I smiled.

Someone coughed.

'Oh, hi, Miles,' I said. 'Are you having a good visit?'

'Well, I was until my arse got soaked by a jet of freezing water.' He turned round and bent over to reveal a large wet patch on the seat of his pants.

I laughed. 'I'm sorry,'

'Yes, I can tell,' he said, dryly.

'Well,' I said, 'I'd better head back inside.'

'Really?' said Daniel. 'Because I was just about to invite you in for a drink. You know, while Miles dries his arse – and to show you that there are no hard feelings.'

I hesitated. 'Thanks but I'd better not. If it was just my parents, I would, but Celia and co are only here until tomorrow evening and we don't get together that often.'

'Of course,' he said. 'But why don't you come round when they've gone then? Miles and Lizzie will still be here and they're sick of it being just me.'

'That's quite true, Ros,' said Miles. 'Lizzie in particular is very depressed by the all-male nature of the company.'

I wondered, fleetingly, as to the whereabouts of Sarah Millbank. Probably spending Christmas with her own family.

'They're not going until after dinner, so I wouldn't actually be free until nine-ish.'

'Perfect,' smiled Daniel. 'See you then.' He turned to his brother. 'Come on, Miles,' he said, placing a hand on his sibling's back, 'let's go and get you into some dry pants.'

–

Celia and my mother stopped talking as soon as I entered the kitchen, a fact which I chose to ignore, as I closed the door behind me, kicked off my boots and hung up my coat on one of the hooks on the wall.

I turned to find the pair of them staring at me and grinning inanely.

'What?' I sighed.

'What?' returned my mother.

'Why are you looking at me like you are two years old and I am a glitter ball?'

'Celia says your neighbour is lovely,' said my mother. Celia nodded, still grinning.

'Did she?' I went over to the sink and filled the kettle. 'I'm making myself a fresh cup of tea. Anyone else want one?'

'You told me his brother was gorgeous, Ros,' said Celia. 'But you didn't mention him. My goodness, he's good-looking.'

'Is he?'

'Oh for goodness sake,' she laughed, 'don't tell me you haven't noticed.'

I sighed again and turned to face them. 'OK, if you must know, he had a ridiculous beard for the first few months of our acquaintance so, no, I didn't notice, actually. And then, by the time I did, I had already firmly established myself as an eccentric, self-centred slapper.'

'Rosalind!' My mother looked appalled. 'What a thing to say.'

'Well, I'm sorry but there it is.' I opened the dishwasher in search of clean mugs. 'I just don't want either of you getting your hopes up regarding Daniel. He's not interested and neither am I.'

'Ros,' said Celia, 'we're not trying to match-make. It's just that he's clearly fond of you. He's invited you for drinks tomorrow night, hasn't he?'

I looked up sharply. 'How do you know that?'

'I hid behind the shed for a while.' She smiled, sheepishly.

'Jesus, have you no shame, Ce?'

'Ros, please don't blaspheme,' said my mother. 'Not on Christmas Day, dear.'

'I'm sorry,' I said, putting a teabag into a mug, before turning round to face them, 'but Daniel has just ended a long-term relationship with a perfectly-formed blonde and is now in a new relationship with another perfectly-formed blonde.' Their faces fell. 'Yes. He has a girlfriend, so, please, just forget about it. You're making me feel that you're desperate for me to find a man.'

'We are not at all desperate,' said Celia, coming over and putting an arm around my shoulders. 'Are we, Mum?' My mother raised her eyebrows. '*Are we, Mother?*' said Celia, sternly.

'Oh, of course not,' said my mother, tutting. 'It's just that when Celia comes in from the garden saying that there's a Greek god living over the hedge… well, tell me what mother's ears wouldn't prick up.'

I laughed. 'Well, just remember that he has a trail of Aphrodites in his wake.'

My mother joined us at the sink and cupped my face in her hands. 'No one as beautiful as my Ros,' she said. 'There's no one as beautiful – inside and out.'

'Thanks, Mum,' I said, hugging her.

'Yeah, thanks, Mum,' said Celia.

'Oh and, of course, your bone structure is excellent too, Celia, but you've got David. It's Ros who's all alone and needs the confidence boost, isn't it?'

I laughed and Celia shook her head despairingly. 'Come on, you two,' I said, 'let's go and see if there's anything good on telly.'

Chapter 30

My mother spent the fifteen minutes between Celia's departure and my own pressing me to change out of my jeans and polo-neck into a dress because, she claimed, it was ill-mannered to wear denim to a Christmas drinks party. I quibbled with her use of the word 'party', before appeasing her by putting on a skirt; however, I refused point blank the offer of a necklace and it was actually something of a relief to find myself out of the house and turning into Clarendon Road.

As I reached Daniel's drive, it struck me that this was the first time I had been to his home since that April evening, when I had come to forgive the beardy bloke for murdering my guinea pig. How things had changed. On the upside, I was much better dressed and on the down-side… Interestingly, I found myself unable to pinpoint the downside but an undeniable sense of regret made me certain that there was one.

I rang the bell. Miles answered the door. He was holding his coat.

'Hi,' he said, 'come on in. Daniel is just on the phone. He won't be a moment.'

I looked at the coat. 'Have you just got in?' I asked.

'Er...' He looked a little awkward. 'No, actually, I, or rather we,' he glanced over his shoulder towards the stairs, 'are just on our way out.'

'Oh, right.' It was my turn to feel awkward. I looked down at the bottle of wine in my hand. 'So, this wasn't such a great time for me to call then. I had wondered whether it might be a little late – and whether you might all have somewhere else to go.'

'No, no,' he smiled, 'it's only Lizzie and me who are popping out and only for an hour or so. I'm sorry to be so rude but an old school friend of mine called this afternoon and it's my one chance to see him before he heads back to the States tomorrow, so...'

'Oh, that's fine. Don't worry.'

'Well, actually,' said a heavily accented voice from the top of the stairs, 'I don't think it's fine at all. I was looking forward to some female company this evening.' The owner of the voice, a petite, shapely brunette with a broad smile, came into view.

'Don't worry if you didn't understand a word of that, Ros,' said Miles. 'She's from Glasgow.'

'He's so funny,' she said, punching him on the arm. 'Hello, Ros, I'm Lizzie.' She held out a hand. 'And I'm so sorry that my rude fiancé is dragging me out tonight to some boring, blokey gathering when I had been looking forward to a good old natter. I've heard a lot about you.'

'Ah well, Lizzie,' said Miles, hurriedly handing her a pink, velvet coat and dark green scarf, 'let's be off. We don't want to be late.'

'For what, exactly?' she asked. 'For tales of pervy History teachers and the day you ran the 800m with your willy out? I've heard it all before, Ros,' she said as he pushed her gently out the front door. 'I've heard it all before. Hope you're still here when we get back! Oh, bye Daniel!' she called, as Miles pulled the door closed behind them.

'Hello, Ros.'

I started slightly and turned to find Daniel standing behind me, his hand still raised in farewell to his brother and Lizzie. 'Good God, you made me jump,' I laughed, handing him the bottle of wine. 'My Dad brought it, so it should be good,' I said, taking my coat off and hanging it over the bottom of the stairs.

'Great, thanks.' He held out an arm to direct me into one of the front rooms of the house. 'Come through. I see you met Lizzie.'

'Yes,' I said, sitting down on the nearest sofa. 'She seemed fun. I didn't realise that Miles was engaged.'

'He wasn't, until last night.'

'Really? Ah, how lovely. I would have offered them my congratulations if I'd known.'

'I'm really pleased for him,' he said, opening the doors of a large drinks cabinet. 'She is lovely and keeps him grounded. My parents would have approved. Now, what can I get you? There's red or white wine, gin, whisky, brandy... anything except Malibu, basically.'

'Oh that's a shame.'

'I know, but Miles and I always drink that first.'

'I'll have a white wine,' I said, 'just to be a bother and make you walk all the way to the kitchen.'

'Fizz?'

'Go on then – as it's Christmas.'

While he was gone, I took the opportunity to examine the room in greater detail. Its furnishings and decor differed considerably from those of the open plan area at the back of the house. The furniture was older: some antique in appearance and some simply aged; and the colours of the fabrics and paintings were darker and warmer, reminding me of my parents' home.

But the most striking aspect of the room was undoubtedly the photographs. Miles, Daniel and a couple, whom I assumed to be their parents, were everywhere: building sandcastles on the mantelpiece; playing tennis on the bookcase; embracing on the windowsills; and celebrating birthdays across the walls. In one photograph, the couple appeared to be in their mid-fifties – I couldn't see one in which they looked any older.

'Merry Christmas,' said Daniel, returning and handing me a glass of champagne.

'Merry Christmas.' I clinked my glass against his, as he sat down next to me. 'Great photos.' I gestured toward the beach scene on the mantelpiece. 'That one reminds me of a particularly blustery holiday spent in Woolacombe, when I was about seven or eight.'

He smiled. 'Actually, you're not far off. That's Saunton. I'm nine and Miles is twelve. He buried me like that every single beach day but it was warm, so I rarely objected.'

I laughed. 'You and he seem very close.'

'We are.' He smiled again and then paused, looking up at me before continuing. 'I was sixteen when we lost mum and dad and I don't know what I would have done without him. He put everything on hold for me. Kept me going.'

I swallowed. 'I'm so sorry about your parents.'

'It wasn't easy but, as I say, I was very lucky to have Miles and also to have had sixteen years with wonderful parents. I think it's important to remember that. So, how did your Christmas go?'

I found myself slightly thrown by the rather abrupt change of subject, crashing, as it did, my own embryonic train of thought regarding Daniel's determined focus on the positive; however, I had no desire to force him to continue his reminiscences and, after a momentary pause, I managed an appropriately light response.

'Oh, it was lovely, actually,' I said, sipping my champagne. 'No major arguments or breakages. I class that as a great success. And I don't get to see Celia as much as I'd like, so that's been lovely.'

'She looks very like you.'

'Yes, we get told that a lot.'

'Except the eyes, of course. And you're taller – which comes in handy during those over-the-hedge conversations.'

I laughed. 'So,' I ventured, 'how about you? Has it just been the three of you, or have you seen anyone else?'

'Just the three of us since Christmas Eve.'

'Is Sarah with her parents?'

'Sarah?' He looked momentarily puzzled, before adding, 'Oh, Sarah. Yes, she's away.'

'And when does she get back?'

'Tomorrow, maybe. Shall I top you up?'

'No, no. I had a large glass with dinner so must take it slowly. I'm going to detox from tomorrow. An awful lot of alcohol has been consumed in my house over the past three days. That's what living with my mother does to me.'

He laughed. 'Is it an interesting relationship?'

'She's lovely,' I sighed, 'but, you know, she worries.'

'About what? About you?'

'Yes, you know, what I'm wearing, who I'm seeing… that kind of thing. Although,' I reflected, 'I must admit that,' I glanced down at my skirt, 'she seems to be largely at peace about my wardrobe these days.'

'Quite rightly,' he said. 'But do I take it that the dating issue is still troubling her?'

'God, no,' I said, waving way the question. 'The pressure's been right off since I started seeing Ryan Reynolds.' I paused. 'Actually, Ryan wouldn't be her ideal. A young Alan Rickman would be more her preferred choice. You know, someone with intensity, intellect and slow-motion diction.'

'Andrew, maybe?'

I looked at him in surprise. 'Andrew?'

He was concentrating on his wine. 'I just wondered if she might have had Andrew in mind for you,' he said absently, still staring at his glass. 'He ticks all the boxes and you clearly get on very well.'

'Well,' I said, frowning, 'I don't know whether she has hopes for Andrew and I but she'll be disappointed if she has. He's lovely but, clichéd as it sounds, we're just good friends.'

'I'm sorry,' he said, looking up. 'I was probably being too personal.'

'Not really,' I said, 'it's just that Andrew is… well… it just doesn't really feel fair to discuss him.'

He smiled. 'OK, noted.'

'Good. Now, tell me all about your relationship with Tish. What went wrong there then?'

'I met someone else,' he said, seemingly unperturbed by the fact.

I put my hands over my ears. 'No, don't tell me! I was just teasing you about being too personal about Andrew. I don't really want to know.'

'Don't you?' he said, putting down his glass. 'Are you sure? Because Lizzie insists it's the kind of situation women love.'

'Does it involve an unfaithful man getting his nether regions caught in a mincer?'

'Sadly, no. However, it does feature a baffled bloke and an inscrutable woman.'

'Fortunately,' I said, as he picked up the bottle and poured a little of the contents into my now almost-empty glass, 'I enjoy a good confused male/enigmatic female tale, almost as much as one of agonising castration.' I slipped off my boots and tucked my legs up under me. 'So fire away.'

He nodded solemnly. 'OK, well… things hadn't been going too well with Tish for a while, actually.'

'Charlie…' I murmured.

He looked at me, apparently intrigued. 'You knew about Charlie?'

Oh dear God, I was turning into my grandmother, who had been loved and feared in equal measure for articulating her every thought, on everything from bowls to bowel function.

'Did *you* know about Charlie?' I countered.

'Of course,' he sighed, 'but, you know, I was distracted. I admit it was my fault.'

'Good for you. That's a very responsible attitude. Do continue.'

'Right, well, as I said, I had met someone else.'

I nodded. 'Sarah Millbank.'

'No, not Sarah Millbank. I didn't meet her until George's party.'

'Do you mean to say that you are now being unfaithful to someone with Sarah Millbank?' I asked.

'Ros.'

'Yes?'

'I could tell this story a lot more quickly if you'd stop interrupting, you know.'

'OK. Sorry. So, you had met someone else, but not Sarah Millbank. A different person.'

'Yes, a different person.'

'Who?'

'A work colleague.'

'Is she married?'

'Ros.'

'Sorry.'

He looked at the table. 'I forgot the nibbles. Want some?'

'Always, but I want to hear the end of the story first.'

'I'll be quick,' he said. True to his word, he seemed to return before he had gone, with bowls of nuts and vegetable crisps which he placed on the table in front of us. I smiled at him, aware of an increasing sense of well-being and only the slightest, and easily suppressed, nagging doubt that I was perhaps drinking a little too quickly.

'You know, Daniel,' I said. 'I'm really enjoying this anecdote.'

He laughed. 'Well, I hope you're paying close attention because I shall be seeking your advice at the end of it.'

'Oh, God. What a responsibility. OK. Press on. You have met a woman at work. Are you able to tell me who she is? I promise not to blab.'

He hesitated before, apparently, deciding to accept my assurance of discretion and providing the requested detail. 'Charlotte.'

'Charlotte?'

'Yes, Charlotte.'

'And does Charlotte have a second name?'

He hesitated again.

'Oh for goodness sake, Daniel. I'm not going to tell anyone.'

Again, he relented. 'Green. Charlotte Green.'

I thought for a moment. 'Ooh, that sounds familiar. I think I knew a Charlotte Green once. Maybe it was at school. Anyway,' I shrugged, 'I like her already. How did you meet?'

'She joined the team about a year ago.'

'Are you her boss?'

'God, Ros.'

'Sorry, but I just need all the background details. Context is very important to women.'

He sighed. 'OK, well, no, I'm not her boss.'

'Good. And, obviously, you are attracted to her?'

'She's extremely likable.'

I gave my head a dissatisfied shake. 'Extremely likeable? It's hardly Cathy and Heathcliff, is it, Daniel? And does she find you 'extremely likable'?'

He shrugged his shoulders. 'God knows.'

'Really? You can't tell?'

'I honestly can't,' he insisted.

I tutted. 'Rubbish. You must be able to. Is she single?'

'Yes.'

'Oh, well then, you must be in with a pretty good shot.'

He looked pleased. 'Really?'

'Of course!' I said, flattered that he seemed encouraged by my assurances, as if he genuinely set some store by my opinion. 'My sister told my mother that you looked like a Greek god!'

'You know,' he said, picking up the bowl of nuts and offering them to me, 'I really like Celia.'

I put my glass down on the coffee table and took a handful of nuts. 'I must say, though, Daniel, that I'm slightly surprised that you split up with Tish and her bottom, when you're so uncertain about your chances of success with Charlotte.'

He laughed. 'I know that you hold Tish's bottom in high esteem, Ros, but, for me, it simply wasn't a big enough reason to stay together.'

I stared at him, incredulously. 'What? You thought Tish's bottom wasn't big enough?'

'That's not what...' He sighed. 'How much have you had to drink, Ros? You didn't hit the whisky while I was getting the nuts, did you?'

'No, but Andrew says he's got a sieve and a colander that hold alcohol better than I do.'

'OK. I'll make a note of that for future reference,' he said. He was still smiling but appeared a little subdued.

For the first time in our acquaintance, I felt sorry for him. 'You're not seriously feeling glum about Charlotte are you, Daniel?' I asked, punching him lightly on the shoulder.

The smile broadened reassuringly and he shook his head. 'No, it's just a little hard to know how to play it. It's a bit of a new one on me.'

'Because they usually fall at your feet?'

'No.' He sounded mildly affronted. 'Not at all. I just feel a little differently about the situation – about her.'

'Ah, that's so sweet,' I said, sipping at my champagne. 'Please do accept my apologies for my flippancy. I was judging you by my own shallow standards. But anyway,' I punched him a second time, 'I have no doubt she will come to her senses very soon and drag you into the stationery cupboard.' He rolled his eyes but seemed amused. 'Ooh, unless she's gay!' I added. 'Have you considered that possibility?'

'She's not gay.'

'Insane, maybe?'

'I did wonder – but no.'

'Well then, I think it's just a question of time, Daniel.'

I had addressed this remark to the bowl of crisps but now looked up at him. He was squinting at me, in the manner of someone trying to find their location on a map. 'You think so?'

'I do. However, if she does turn out to be insanely gay, or gaily insane, just be sure to move on quickly, won't you?'

He nodded. 'I'll do my best.'

'Good, because I spent many months wanting someone who didn't want me and I very much regret the time wasted.'

'But you don't want him anymore?'

'No, I don't.' The simple truth of the statement came as a shock. 'No, I don't,' I repeated quietly. 'Ah, but,' I wagged a finger at him, 'I am still a little bit cross with him about it all – or feckin' furious, as Andrew would say – and that's not good, is it?'

'Probably not.' He was looking at me with concern in his Greek god eyes and I found myself wondering what it would be like to be Charlotte, or even just a fill-in Sarah. 'So, when do you think you'll stop being feckin' furious?' he asked.

I ignored the unanswerable question. 'You haven't told me where Sarah Millbank fits into all this.'

He seemed to relax. 'She doesn't really.'

'So she's off the scene then?'

'She was never really on the scene.'

'Well, George will be pleased about that at least.'

He laughed. 'Yes, I got that impression at dinner last week.'

There was a brief pause in the conversation, during which I decided I didn't want to talk anymore about the women in his life.

'Tell me about the summerhouse plan. That sounds a great idea.' I said.

He brightened, seeming to share my enthusiasm for a change of subject. 'Yes, I'm going to put a cinema in it.'

'Ooh, exciting. And when it's all finished, I can make myself some popcorn, climb the ladder and watch movies over the hedge.' I put a hand up to my forehead. 'I was going to request a tour of the site but I suddenly feel a little woozy, truth to tell.'

'How many glasses have you had? No more than two, surely. Come on,' he said, standing up, 'some fresh air will help. You grab your coat and we'll pick up the drawings on our way out. If you wobble, I'll give you a fireman's lift.'

'You should try that on Charlotte,' I said, putting on my boots and standing up.

'Really?'

'God, yes. That would be so manly.' We went into the hall and put on our coats. 'You could stride into her office and say, "Charlotte, I find you extremely likeable" and then chuck her over your shoulder, like a sexy farmer with a sexy bag of spuds.' I paused and held up a finger. 'Only, do be sure to compliment her bottom while it's at eye-level, because if she's ever set eyes on Tish's tush, she might be feeling slightly self-conscious.'

'You know what, Ros,' he laughed, picking up a roll of drawings from the dining table as we headed through the kitchen and towards the French windows. '*You* are extremely likeable.'

'You too,' I said, feeling the compliment. 'However,' I held up the champagne flute, still in my possession, 'that could just be the fizz talking, couldn't it?'

'I suppose it could,' he said. 'Now, come outside and I'll bore you with the details.'

—

It was freezing in the garden and I was glad of my hat and gloves, a Christmas gift from Celia. Daniel illuminated the proposed site of the summerhouse, and the plans, with a torch he produced from his pocket, and proceeded to describe the works, scheduled to begin in late April. I was genuinely interested and, emboldened by the champagne, demanded an invitation to a screening as soon as the work was completed. Daniel, of course, had no option but to grant to the request and then, despite the cold, we sat down on a bench outside, to finish our champagne and peruse the plans in greater detail, so that I could check which way the screen would face and decide whether it would be visible from my garden.

'It's been a funny year,' I said, a little later, as Daniel rolled up the drawings and placed them between us on the bench.

'Has it?'

'Well, it has for me,' I sighed. 'So much seems to have changed but, when I try to think about what exactly, it's all a bit vague. Apart from the fact that some maniacal Percy Thrower-type killed my guinea pig, of course.'

'Hmm... sorry about that,' he said.

'It's OK,' I smiled. 'I never would have met you otherwise.'

He stared straight ahead but nudged me with his elbow. 'That's the nicest thing you've ever said to me, you know.'

'Is it?' I could barely make out his features in the dim light thrown into the garden from the kitchen. 'Actually, it's not even true, is it?' I continued.

'No?'

'No, because I would have met you at George's party, wouldn't I?'

'Oh, yes. But we may not have spoken, I suppose.'

'Maybe that would have been better.' I put my empty glass down on the arm of the bench.

'I don't think so,' he said.

'No, I don't think so, either.'

There followed a comfortable silence, during which I thought about Charlotte, Tish and Sarah and wondered where I fitted in. I suspected I was in my own little category of '*odd neighbour who isn't always annoying – marginally preferable to Sylvia*'. I turned and looked towards the end of the garden.

'What?' he asked.

'I've just had a thought.'

'Yes?'

'Well, I live just over the hedge…'

'That is true.'

'And,' I said, looking at my watch, 'I should be heading home…'

'OK…'

'And the step ladder is still the other side of the hedge…'

'I don't think that's a good idea, at all,' he said.

'Oh, don't be boring. It'll save me a five-minute walk in the dark.'

'I will walk you home.'

'No. Come on. Do you have a ladder?'

He patted his pockets. 'Not on me, no.'

'OK, well, you'll just have to give me a leg-up this side and then I'll clamber down the ladder on the other.'

'That is such a bad idea,' he protested, with an amused smile. He looked down. 'And you're wearing a skirt.'

'Damn. I forgot. Never mind. It'll be fine.' I stood up, taking him by the hand and dragging him after me, until we reached the end of the garden, and the hedge, the latter illuminated by lights in the adjacent borders.

'Ooh…' I said, standing on tip toe, 'it's taller than I remember.'

'Exactly,' he said. 'Come back inside and I'll walk you home.'

'Nope.' I put my hands on his shoulders and lifted my right leg, 'I am determined. Lift me up.'

'OK.' He picked me up and put me over his shoulder, turning so that my head was towards the hedge. 'But hurry up. I can't hold you up there forever.'

'No, no, no,' I laughed. 'I can't scale it from this position, I need a leg-up.'

'Come on, Ros. You're just not trying.' He backed towards the hedge, causing me to shriek and hold out my hands in an attempt to push away from it.

'Shhh, you'll wake Sylvia,' he said, putting me down.

'But Sylvia's in Perthshire.'

'I know.'

We stood there, laughing, unable to speak. Eventually, I said, 'You're right. That wasn't one of my better suggestions.'

'No?' he smiled. 'Because I really came round to the idea.'

'No,' I shook my head, 'I'm afraid the lack of a ladder on this side of the hedge is, in every sense, an insurmountable problem. Hey, but I was right about the fireman's lift, though.'

'Yes?'

'Oh yes, very, er, endearing.' He was smiling at me but appeared distracted by something. 'Have I got twigs in my hair?' I asked.

'No,' he said, 'but you've lost your hat,' I looked down, 'and your hair does need straightening a little.' He gently pushed the stray strands from my face.

I forgot about the hat and looked up at him. Celia was right. He laughed and I put a hand to my mouth. 'I actually said that out loud, didn't I?'

'You did,' he smiled. 'And *that* is definitely the nicest thing you've ever said to me – even if it is the fizz talking.'

I returned the smile.

'Daniel!' A voice called from the other end of the garden.

'It's Miles,' I said.

'I know.' Daniel looked up towards the house and then back at me. He pointed to the hedge. 'Fancy another crack at that sometime?'

'It's definitely on my 'to do' list.'

'Mine too.' He bent down suddenly. 'Here's that hat,' he said, picking it up and handing it to me, before offering me his arm. 'Come on, let's go and say hello to my pesky sibling before I take you home.'

–

I stayed for another half an hour or so, chatting to Lizzie over mugs of tea in the kitchen, whilst Miles and Daniel sat talking in the living room. We had briefly discussed her engagement and she was telling me how she met Miles, when she suddenly changed tack.

'I hear you and Daniel are off to a wedding in a few weeks,' she said.

'Yes, he's gallantly agreed to be my plus one. It's my friend, Tom's wedding.'

She nodded and smiled in an encouraging fashion. I smiled back, feeling as if I was supposed to know what to say next but hadn't learned my lines.

'Yes,' I said, trying to find something to fill the silence, 'and my friend Andrew is coming and also George – Georgina. We all work together.'

'Are you OK with weddings?' she asked. 'Are they something you enjoy?'

'Er… well, if I know a lot of the people going. You know, it's a bit like parties.'

'Well, I'm sure you and Daniel will have a great time. He's such good fun and I know you—'

'Ros,' It was Daniel. He was standing in the doorway, looking at Lizzie. 'Sorry to interrupt, Lizzie, but Ros had said she didn't want to linger too long because her parents are with her.'

'Good God, Daniel,' she said, 'she's a watch-wearing grown-up, you know. Run along and wake up Miles, we're having a lovely natter.'

I put down my mug. 'Actually, Lizzie, much as I would love to stay, he's right. My parents head off early tomorrow and I don't want to keep them up – and they will still be awake, even if they're in bed.'

'Well, I blame Miles, for dragging me out with his Neanderthal chums, instead of letting me stay here and get to know you. Ah well,' she sighed, 'you will just have to come—'

'OK, Ros?' Daniel was back with his coat on.

'Dan,' said Lizzie, raising her eyebrows at him, 'are you about to turn into a pumpkin or something?'

'Well, it was lovely to meet you, Lizzie,' I said, 'even for a short while. And all the best with the wedding preparations and for the big day.'

'Goodness, I'll be seeing you before that, I hope,' she said, giving me a warm hug as I tried to put on my coat.

'Well, I suppose our paths may cross,' I smiled.

'Our paths may cross?' She looked at Daniel and laughed loudly. 'Our paths may cross?'

Miles emerged from the living room. 'Sorry about Lizzie, Ros,' he said. 'She's from Glasgow, you know.'

'You're so funny,' she said, walking over and punching him in the ribs, something for which he was clearly unprepared, judging by the way he coughed and bent double.

I looked at Daniel. 'Time to go,' he said.

We walked to my door, arm in arm, talking mostly about Lizzie and Miles and their forthcoming nuptials and how Daniel would, of course, be best man – his first time, he said.

As we reached the house, I noticed that the kitchen light was still on and I groaned inwardly at the prospect of a grilling from my mother. As it turned out, I didn't have to wait to cross the threshold to enjoy her inquisitive company; she opened the front door before I even had a chance to put my key in the lock.

'Oh hello, Rosalind,' she said to Daniel. 'Your father and I were just thinking about turning in when I heard you on the doorstep.' She continued to address Daniel and I tapped her lightly on the arm.

'Mum,' I said, leaning to my right to force her to make eye contact with me, 'this is Daniel, the Greek god from the bottom of the garden.'

My mother turned pink and laughed nervously. 'Oh, Rosalind, whatever are you talking about? Honestly, Daniel, the things she says. And coming from the mind of such a beautiful, clever girl too.' I rolled my eyes. 'She runs her own bookshop, you know, and, before that, she worked in the City.'

'Good God,' I groaned.

'Hello, Mrs Shaw,' said Daniel, holding out his hand and smiling. 'It's a pleasure to meet you.'

'Oh, call me Lilian, please. Will you come in for a moment, perhaps, Daniel?' she asked.

'That would have been lovely, Lilian; however,' he looked at his watch, 'I'm catching a train to Edinburgh, early tomorrow morning, so I'd better get some sleep.' He turned to me. 'Ros, thank you for coming round. It's been great to see you, as always.'

'Well,' I smiled, 'thank you for inviting me.'

I noticed him take a brief, side-long glance at my mother. I turned to look at her. She was grinning and nodding at each of us in turn. 'You could pull the door to now, if you like, Mum,' I said. 'You're letting all the warmth out of the house.'

'Oh yes, sorry.' She stepped outside, pulling the door closed behind her.

I took out my key, unlocked the door and re-opened it. 'I actually meant with you on the other side of it.'

'Oh, silly me,' she trilled and stepped inside. 'Good-night, Daniel. I hope we meet ag—' I gently closed the door and turned back to Daniel. He was trying hard not to laugh.

'She's lovely,' he said.

'Hmm…'

'Anyway,' he put his hands in his pockets, and addressed the ground, 'I guess I'll see you in a couple of weeks? I'll speak to Andrew before then, about getting there and rooms.'

'OK, great.' I put my hands on his shoulders.

He looked up. 'You're not expecting a leg-up to your bedroom window, are you?'

'Actually, I was just about to bid you goodnight. But you seem a bit tall, all of a sudden.' I looked at my feet. 'I guess I'm in flats.'

'Yes, and Miles bought me lifts for Christmas. Here, I'll come down to your level.' He lowered his head towards me and I kissed his cheek, whilst suddenly realising that I was suppressing a significant urge to throw my arms around his neck and press my lips hard against his: an urge which was accompanied by an image, of startling clarity, in which he was wearing little more than a shocked expression and I was – 'Oh no…' I breathed.

'Are you all right?' he said, his head still lowered towards me, his face just inches from my own.

'No,' I said, hoarsely.

'No?'

'I mean, yes. I'm fine.' I put a hand to my head. 'It's just that my hat is still in your hallway.'

'Oh.' He straightened up and smiled. 'I'll pop it through your door on my way to the station tomorrow morning.'

'OK, well, it can wait… you know, if you're running late.'

'Bye, then, Ros.' He waved as he walked away across the short driveway.

'Bye,' I said, feebly raising a hand, which remained in situ until the sound of his footsteps had faded into silence. Only then, did I allow my arm to fall, my eyes to close and my mind to despair, not for the first time, at Rosalind Shaw's complete lack of insight. Feelings, I told myself, one's own and everyone else's, were supposed to be something one recognised, appreciated and understood – not something you stumbled over, like an unexpected tree root in the dark, or slammed into, like a hastily constructed brick wall across the westbound carriageway of the M4. Why on earth hadn't I seen it before? It all seemed so ridiculously obvious now. All the signs had been there: the desperate need to redeem myself following George's party; the mental turmoil during his visit to the bookshop; my feelings of jealousy towards Charlotte Green... *Oh my God, I had feelings of jealousy towards Charlotte Green!* Good God. No wonder I hadn't spotted The Rat's betrayal coming; I was an emotional half-wit.

Aware that my waiting mother would be thrown into immediate panic by anything less than a cheery 'goodnight', I sensibly refused to darken my mood further by continuing to review the history of my relationship with Daniel McAdam. However, this didn't prevent me from recognising that it was depressingly unlikely that he was, at that moment, on his way home with his head full of warm thoughts regarding Ros, the well-groomed, emotionally-balanced, social sophisticate. At best, he might be intrigued by my rather intense reaction to leaving my hat at his house, or admire my gung-ho attitude to hedge-climbing but, other than that...

Forcing myself to curtail my miserable musings, I turned, unlocked the door and went into the house. My mother was standing, backlit, in the entrance to the kitchen. She came towards me to take my coat and I braced myself for her positivity. 'Oh Ros, darling. What a lovely, lovely young man. He seems perfect.'

I looked at her, as she stood there, beaming; delighted to have discovered, as she thought, that the key to her tragic daughter's happiness lay not over the rainbow but over a five foot beech hedge at the bottom of the garden. 'He is perfect,' I said, before offering her what I hoped was a reassuring smile, and going upstairs to bed.

Chapter 31

Andrew and I re-opened *Chapters* on 3rd January. Neither George nor Joan were due back at work until the following week and, to me, everything seemed oddly incomplete without them. Andrew felt it too.

'It's a bit quiet, isn't it?' he said, as he made us each a coffee and I hung up my coat. 'Not quiet... just...'

'Dull?' I suggested.

'Thanks a lot.' He handed me a mug and sighed. 'I don't know what it is. But I'll be glad when we're all back into the swing of things. So, anyway,' he sat down at the table and pulled out a chair for me to join him, 'from your email, it sounded as if you had a good Christmas and New Year.'

'Yes, I did.' I rubbed my forehead. 'In fact, I'm still not quite over Ant's party.'

'Did you go as a jelly fish again?'

'Yes.'

'How many times is that, now?'

'Three times in...' I thought for a moment, 'thirteen months.' Andrew laughed and shook his head. 'Well, it's easy, OK?' I said, defensively. 'And, when you put the umbrella down, you can spend the rest of the evening looking normal and attracting normal men.'

'And did you?'

I sighed. 'A cowardly lion and Batman, both of whom were OK. But I've decided that I'm off men for a bit.'

'Really? So soon? Am I allowed to ask why?'

I put down my coffee mug, folded my arms in front of me and placed my head on them. 'No. It's too tragic.'

He laughed again. 'What? More tragic than my own tale of woe?'

He had a point. I tilted my head towards him. 'Not quite, but it comes close.'

'Well, I won't make you talk about it, if you don't want to.' He pushed his chair back and stood up.

'Oh, alright then,' I said grumpily. 'If it will stop you banging on about it, I'll tell you.'

He sat back down and looked at me expectantly. 'Well?' he said. 'Spit it out.'

I sat up and took a deep breath. 'I'm really attracted to Daniel.' I quickly put my head back down on my folded arms, hiding my face from Andrew.

'Well, what a shocker,' he said, sounding bored.

I looked up. 'Well, it is quite shocking, actually. I was shocked.'

He shook his head. 'Jesus, Ros, I've said it once and I'll say it again. For someone so bright, you really are incredibly dumb sometimes.'

'I know.'

He stood up for a second time, taking his mug to the sink and beginning to wash it. 'Anyway, moving on. I'm afraid I'm failing to spot the tragic element in all this. He's clearly attracted to you, so what's the problem?'

'He's not attracted to me.'

'Yes, he is.'

'No, he's not.'

'Yes he is and this isn't a panto, Ros, so stop contradicting me. The guy likes you.'

'Then why did he dump his girlfriend for a woman called Charlotte Green who works in his office?'

Andrew put the mug on the draining board and turned to face me. 'Charlotte Green?'

'Yes. Charlotte Green.'

He looked puzzled. 'Charlotte Green reads the news, doesn't she? Are you sure you were really focusing on what he was saying?'

I sighed in exasperation. 'Just how witless do you think I am? I think even I may just about have noticed if the conversation had shifted from unrequited affection to *News at Ten*.'

'Actually, Ros, she's on *Radio 4*. And she's just—'

I cut him off with an angry wave of my arm. 'Oh for goodness sake, Andrew. *News at Ten*, *Radio 4* or *Radio* ruddy *Lollipop*. What does it matter? There's more than one Charlotte Green in the world, you know, and Daniel has worked with this one for a year. She's in his team, she is extremely likeable and he thinks that she's the woman for him.'

He looked at me, doubtfully. 'And he told you that?'

'No, I read it in his bloody tea leaves! Yes, of course he told me. At great length in fact.'

'Well, Ros, I'm sorry because—'

'Oh, it doesn't matter,' I said quietly. 'And I'm the one who should be sorry for shouting and swearing about it. It's just that I really like him. Not just in a 'phwoar' way but in an even-if-he-grew-his-beard-back kind of way.'

'Christ. As deep as all that?' he laughed.

'Oh, please don't tease me, Andrew. I'm a bit down about it, you know. I'm such an idiot. God, I wish we weren't all going to Tom's bloody wedding. Maybe I should just call Daniel and tell him Charlotte can have my invite.'

'Don't be dumb.' He sat back down and put an arm round my shoulders. 'It's going to be fun.' I looked at him, miserably. 'It is going to be fun,' he insisted.

'Well, I'm seriously considering smuggling a hip flask in. You know, just in case it turns out to be less like fun and more like torture.'

He looked at me solemnly. 'I hesitate to remind you what happened last time you drank too much at a social occasion…'

'But you will anyway.'

'Come on,' he said, 'let's go and distract ourselves with some work.'

'Good idea,' I said, forcing a smile, both inside and out, and praying for a busy day.

Chapter 32

When George and Joan did return to work, I decided to confide in neither regarding Daniel. I knew that both would be sympathetic but I couldn't bear the thought of Joan becoming over-excitable, should Daniel decide, as I wondered if he might, to pop into the shop to return my hat or discuss arrangements for the weekend. As for George, well, she had returned from the Christmas break with enough troubles of her own, without me burdening her with the details of my little affair of the heart.

Whilst in Oxford, she had received several phone-calls from Mike, expressing not only his regret over the situation but also his growing doubts regarding divorce. His professed misgivings had culminated in a tearful plea, on New Year's Day, begging George to take him back and suggesting marriage guidance counselling. She had refused, attempting to explain to him that, from her perspective, their marriage had actually deteriorated to the point of quiet crisis some time ago and that, although there might once have been some hope of rescuing the relationship, India Morne and the pregnancy had, for her, represented a final nail in the coffin. Not surprisingly, Mike didn't take this rejection of his olive branch at all well and the divorce was now progressing on less cordial terms. Typically, George's anxiety over all this was not for herself but for Lottie. Astonishingly, she also expressed some concern for India.

'I do feel for her,' she said to Joan and me over dinner at her home one evening after work. The three of us had spent the day working overlapping shifts, whilst Andrew was away, chasing a large collection of books at auction in Somerset. 'It's not an ideal way to enter into motherhood.'

'George,' I said, 'how can you possibly feel sorry for her in any way?'

Joan nodded. 'Such generosity of spirit is another jewel in your crown, my darling,' she said, with a smile. 'However, I fear that I, like Rosalind, would find it difficult to feel any sympathy towards the woman.'

'Well, I don't know her at all,' sighed George, 'and I'm quite sure that Lottie and I are barely a reality for her. However, I do know that she is shortly to have a baby with a man who is, at best, equivocal about being with her. That's a dreadful position to be in and one which I certainly don't envy her. I have a lovely home, a lovely daughter, loving friends and family and I feel better than I have in a long, long time. I regret that my marriage didn't work but I look to the future with optimism.'

'Well, when you put it like that, perhaps even I can summon up a modicum of pity for her,' I said grudgingly. 'But only a modicum.'

George smiled and began to clear away our dinner plates. 'My marriage didn't end because of her, you know, Ros. She was merely the confirmation that it was over.'

We were subdued for a moment before Joan asked brightly, 'So, you two, are you excited about the wedding this weekend?'

'Ah, Joan,' I said, 'I really wish you and Bobby were coming. It would be a repeat of our Christmas fun.'

'I would have loved it, my darling,' said Joan, 'but, don't you worry, Bobby and I will be having *lots* of lovely fun of our own. We are hosting a murder mystery party!'

'How exciting,' said George, with genuine interest. 'Tell us all about it.'

'Well, my character is Lola Von Teeze, a burlesque star, with a murky past and a penchant for dangerous men. Bobby is Lord Walter Claridge, a cross-dressing, but extremely heterosexual, aristocrat – Bobby's wearing fishnets and a lovely blouse and skirt I got in the Peter Jones sale.' She paused to gratefully accept a bowl of the apple crumble now being offered by George. 'All the action takes place in a brothel.'

George and I exchanged glances and coughed simultaneously. 'That sounds very interesting, Joan,' I said, recovering. 'But, you know, I actually looked at a few of those murder mystery games when I was Christmas shopping and I don't think I came across one quite so, er, exciting.'

'Couldn't agree with you more, my darling, which is why,' she leaned across the table and patted my arm, 'I've created my own, you see.' She tipped a little white wine into her empty glass. 'The shop-bought variety had very little genuine intrigue, sexual or otherwise. Now, where's the fun in that?'

George and I coughed a little more, while Joan recalled the original thread of her conversation. 'So,' she said, 'the wedding. Is everything in place for a fabulous weekend?'

'Do you know, Joan, I just cannot wait.' George's face lit up. 'Mike is taking Lottie to see his parents, which will be lovely for her, and I shall be having a delightful time at Shieldhill Hall. I took a peek at it online, Ros,' she said, turning to me, 'and it all looks beautiful. And sharing a room will be such a giggle. We shall be talking until dawn!'

Her evident delight made it easier for me to summon up a degree of enthusiasm for the event. 'Yes,' I smiled, 'sharing a room will be good. But I should warn you that I snore.'

'Oh don't worry about that,' she said, pouring some cream over her own portion of crumble. 'My nickname at school was Trumpet Major.'

'Oh, well that's all right then,' I said. 'Hopefully we'll drown each other out.'

'It will be a glorious symphony of sound,' said Joan. 'Eine kleine Nachtmusik. And will Andrew be sleeping nearby, my darling?'

She was addressing George but managed to throw the briefest of knowing looks in my direction. I looked across at George and thought I detected a flicker of self-consciousness before she spoke. 'I think he's not too far away from us, is he, Ros?' she said.

'No, definitely on the same floor anyway.'

'And your lovely, neighbour?' Joan turned her attention, and her unnervingly penetrating gaze, towards me.

'Er...' I attempted to escape scrutiny of my features by lowering my eyes and focusing on my crumble, 'I think he has managed to book a room. Andrew said there had been a cancellation so, yes, Daniel took that room.'

'And who will be doing the driving?' Joan held onto the topic, as determinedly as a labrador with a chew-toy.

I looked at George and shrugged. 'Did Andrew say he was going to drive?'

She hesitated. 'I think he said Daniel is driving, actually,' she said. 'More boot space. But yes, we should really confirm that and what time we have to set off – that kind of thing.'

There was a pause in the conversation, during which I looked at Joan. She was smiling and looking at George and me in turn. 'Well,' she said, eventually, as George got up to put the kettle on for coffee, 'I think it all sounds like it will be the most marvellous adventure and,' she continued, winking at me in a way that put me in mind of Angela Lansbury in *Bed Knobs and Broomsticks*, 'I shouldn't wonder if there are tales to tell upon your return.' She drained her wine glass for a second time. 'I shall look forward to that.'

Chapter 33

I had just put my small suitcase down in the hallway when the doorbell rang. I retrieved the case, together with my coat and my shoulder bag and opened the front door.

'I warn you, Ros,' said Andrew, standing on the door step, rubbing his hands, 'it is feckin' freezing, so I hope you've got your thermals on.'

'Polo-neck knickers and a big, grey vest,' I said, shutting the door behind me and locking up. We walked to the Audi, in which Daniel and George were waiting. The boot popped open on cue and Andrew placed my suitcase next to the other three and I laid my coat across the top.

'Front or back?' asked Andrew, closing the boot. I looked at him, trying to guess which he would prefer.

'Back?'

He smiled. 'Or front?'

'Back,' I said, beginning to be aware of the cold. He held open the appropriate door for me and I climbed inside.

'Hello, Ros!' beamed George. 'Is it all girls together in the back? Hoorah!'

'Hi Ros,' said Daniel, looking over his shoulder and smiling. It was the first time I had seen him since Boxing Day and I realised, to my horror, that I felt something akin to relief. 'All ready?'

I nodded and smiled at them both. 'Hi, yes. All set.'

'Great,' said Daniel. 'Oh, and while I remember, your hat is on the shelf behind you. Sorry, I didn't manage to get it back to you before now.'

'Not a problem,' I said, immediately conscious that the matter of its return, which had so pre-occupied me, had clearly been of no consequence to him. 'I've got lots of others.'

'OK.' He started the engine. 'Let's go.'

–

Music played throughout the journey, making front-to-rear conversation difficult. We therefore arrived at Shieldhill Hall, an hour and a half before the ceremony was due to take place, with George and I having passed the drive time chatting about friends, work, Lottie, and, quite naturally, weddings past and present. Of course, her wedding, and my own near-miss, were not touched upon but, between us, we had enough tales of events, both perfect and disastrous, to happily pass the time.

On arrival, the four of us checked-in and headed off to our rooms, with an agreement to meet downstairs for drinks half an hour later. Shieldhill was as magnificent a venue as we had expected of Tom and Amy and I knew from my mercenary internet nosings that there wouldn't be much change from £30,000.

George and I were shown to our room by a young man who, we could only assume, had been advised that to smile was a sin punishable by castration. We followed him reverently up a broad, central staircase and then along winding corridors and up a second set of narrower stairs, before finally arriving at a bedroom, tastefully furnished in keeping with the Georgian period of the house. Several small oil paintings hung on the pale green walls; antiquated, hardback volumes of obscure fiction filled a walnut bookcase; and a comfortable-looking, burgundy, velvet armchair was positioned close to the large, sash window, which afforded a view of the surrounding parkland and the entrance to the Hall below. I peered through a white panelled door, into a fair-sized bathroom, in which a free-standing, roll-top bath, with large brass taps, took centre stage.

'Well, this is all rather lovely,' said George, after the undertaker had deposited our bags, accepted his tip and left. She gazed out of the window. 'Recognise anyone?' she asked, pointing outside.

I looked over her shoulder at a group, consisting of three men and three women, now climbing the stone steps up to the Hall. 'No, afraid not. There will be a few of Tom's friends from King's here, whom I might know. And I know his parents, the best man, and one or two of his work colleagues, but, other than that…' I hesitated. 'Oh and my ex, of course. God, I'd almost forgotten about him.'

'That's a good sign, isn't it?' asked George, turning her attention from the gardens to the contents of her suitcase, which she began to hang in the large double wardrobe.

'I suppose it is,' I said, absently, continuing to watch the arrival of the other guests and wondering how it would feel to see him again. What if he were to step out of that dark blue BMW which had just come to a halt on the gravel drive? I held my breath. An elderly couple emerged and I turned away from the window. 'Do you have any preference as to which bed, George?' I asked, picking up my case.

'Not at all,' she smiled.

'OK,' I placed my bag on the bed nearest to me and started to unpack the dress and shoes which, contrary to what I had told Celia at Christmas, I had bought especially for the occasion.

–

By the time George and I returned to the ground floor, Daniel and Andrew were already ensconced in armchairs in one of the smaller, quieter reception rooms adjacent to the bar. The bar itself was, by now, quite crowded, and we were pleased to discover a gin and tonic and glass of white wine waiting for us. We sat down on a sofa opposite the two men.

'You both look stunning, of course,' said Daniel, handing us our drinks.

'Thank you. And you two gentlemen look exception-ally dashing – *of course*,' responded George. 'I think we have the handsomest men in the room, don't you, Ros?'

I looked around. 'Actually, George,' I said, 'I think you'll find that we have the *only* men in the room.' I glanced at the only other occupants, a group of four, elderly women, seated on two sofas, next to a large bay window.

'But still...' insisted George.

'New dress, Ros?' asked Andrew, swinging the conver-sation away from his own appearance.

'Yes, it is actually,' I said. 'What do you think?'

'He thinks you're one of the most beautiful women in the room,' said Daniel.

Andrew stood up. 'The man himself,' he said, reaching over me and shaking a hand just visible above my head. I turned to identify its owner.

'Tom!' I said, getting to my feet and embracing him. 'How are you feeling?'

His hug, usually so reassuringly confident, today felt rather diffident, as if a little drained of its usual energy. We separated and he smiled at me uncertainly. 'Bloody terrified,' he said and we all laughed on cue.

'Well, you *look* wonderful,' I said, taking in the impeccable morning suit which hung so well on his slightly-slimmed frame. 'Been working out?'

'Nervous weight-loss,' he said and we laughed again. He turned to George and smiled.

'Tom,' said Andrew, 'this is my good friend, George.'

'Ah yes,' said Tom, shaking her hand. 'Delighted to meet you. Both Andrew and Ros talk about you in glowing terms.'

'And this,' I said, turning to Daniel, 'is *my* good friend, Daniel.'

'Never heard of you,' said Tom, sniffing and putting his hands in his pockets. I tutted and waited for the second-half of the show. 'Only kidding, Daniel.' He grinned and held out a hand. 'I know *all* about you; everything from killing her pet rat to picking her out of your hedge.' Daniel laughed loudly and I looked at Andrew, who appeared to be suddenly very interested in his shoes. I made a mental note to grill him later as to exactly what he had told Tom. 'Anyway,' said Tom, 'I'd better get going. I was answering a call to pop down and see my mother – she wants reassurance that I am sober and going to go through with it.' There was more laughter, during which he turned to me and took my hand.

'Ros, could I just borrow you for a second – just need a female opinion on something.' He led me to the door of the room, whilst the others sat back down and continued their drinks. 'Ros...' he said, quietly, looking first at me and then back at Andrew, Daniel and George, as if to assure himself we were not being overheard, '...bloody hell that was tactless of me to talk about going through with it.' He ran a hand through his hair. 'The minute I said it I kicked myself. I'm so sorry, Ros, I'm just a jabbering, bag of nerves.'

'Oh for goodness sake, don't be so silly,' I said, hugging him again. 'I'm not in the least offended. I'm sure ninety per cent of grooms, *and* brides, think of legging it at some point.' I sighed. 'Fortunately, hardly any of them actually follow through with it.'

We separated and he touched my cheek with his hand. 'He was, and remains, an idiot. You know that, don't you?'

'Off you go,' I smiled. 'Go and find your mother before she gives you up for lost.'

'OK,' he said, starting to walk away. 'See you later. I'll be the sweaty one at the front.'

I returned to the table and sat back down next to George.

'Everything OK with him?' asked Andrew, handing me my drink.

'Yes,' I said, 'he's just a little on edge. And who can blame him?'

'I know,' said Andrew. 'It's just odd seeing him like that.'

There was a brief silence before Daniel said, 'So, Andrew and I had a quick look at the seating plan before you came to join us but Andrew hasn't had time to fill me in yet.' He smiled. 'George and I need all the background information you can give us – you know, to prevent any clangers.'

'Ooh, yes,' said George, 'whom are we with?'

I looked at Andrew. 'Whom are we with?'

'An ex-colleague from Finlay May. I'm assuming the others are university or school friends.'

'I haven't spotted anyone I recognise yet,' I said, looking round. 'But who's the Finlay May bod? The name might ring a bell.'

'James Jackson?' said Andrew. I shook my head. 'I'm sure you'll have met him – very tall guy.'

I thought for a moment. 'Is he the one who drank his contact lenses?'

Andrew laughed. 'No, that was Jim Hewitt.'

'Oh…' I thought for a moment. 'James Jackson… You don't mean Jamie, do you? Hairy Jamie?'

'Yes,' said Andrew, sipping his Guinness, 'that's right, Hairy Jamie.'

I turned to George. 'Ah well, Hairy Jamie's lovely. You'll like him.' She smiled, a little uncertainly.

'The way you describe Tom's friends,' said Daniel, 'makes me think that maybe there's a circus somewhere missing a few freaks.'

'Yes, well,' said Andrew, gesturing with his pint towards himself and then in my direction, 'as you know, Tom is largely drawn to freaks.' He then embarked upon an entertaining explanation regarding the nature of Jamie's hairiness and how Jim had come to down the lenses.

While he talked, I looked at George. She was listening intently, laughing and occasionally querying a detail. She was looking effortlessly beautiful, with her hair caught up in the same butterfly clip she had worn on the evening of Mike's birthday party. She was, as my mother would have put it, lovely, both inside and out. So lovely, of course, that even noble, upright Andrew, who had been so quietly, but utterly, devastated by the loss of his girlfriend, hadn't been able to help falling for her – a married woman. I knew that he had fought those feelings for a long time; he was still fighting them now, in fact. I turned my attention to him, as he continued the anecdote. He was certainly worthy of her but did she reciprocate his feelings? God, I hoped she did – or would. What if she didn't? What would happen to *Chapters* then?

I sipped my wine and decided not to think about that. I would focus instead on enjoying this weekend, something which was, I told myself, still perfectly possible if I could only stop thinking of Daniel as a missed opportunity. I took some, if slightly cold, comfort from the fact that, even if I had recognised my feelings sooner, it wouldn't have made any difference. Charlotte had been on the scene for some time now and, besides, Daniel had long ago identified me as damaged goods, even without any helpful background information regarding The Rat. I looked at him now, as he checked his watch and pointed at Andrew's Guinness, and I wondered whether I could ever come to think of him in the same way as Tom and Andrew.

Of course, I had never wanted to rip off either of their shirts, so this was a little different, but you never knew. Or perhaps it would just be best to try to avoid seeing Daniel altogether, although with both George, and now Andrew, having a connection to him, that might prove difficult.

He and Andrew did seem to be getting along increasingly well, which wasn't surprising really; they were both kind, good-humoured and intellectual, with neither having any obvious sense of ego. I sighed. How could I have remained embittered for so long with two such shining examples of the male of the species literally on my doorstep?

'Ros?' Andrew was looking at me questioningly and I realised everyone was on their feet.

'Oh, sorry. Are we going?' I stood up but held back slightly to let George walk with Andrew.

'Come on,' said Daniel, suddenly at my side. He held out his arm. 'I know how wobbly you get after the tiniest amount of alcohol.'

I took his arm and looked up at him. He was smiling at me, as if he found me endlessly amusing.

'I know you find me endlessly amusing,' I said.

He laughed. 'Endlessly something.'

I reflected on the comment. 'I like the undefined nature of "something",' I said. 'You know, so that, in my darker moments, I can fill in the blank with "intellectual", "incisive", "insightful" – that kind of thing.'

'You do that,' he said. 'Now, come on. Tom is waiting.'

Chapter 34

Against all expectations, I actually rather enjoyed the ceremony. Amy, of course, looked perfect in an ivory, silk dress, which traced, but didn't hug, her athletic figure. She exuded self-confidence as she entered the room, to the strains of Pachelbel's *Canon in D*, and walked slowly, and unaccompanied, down the aisle created by two blocks of seating, to join Tom, in front of a large, marble fire place at the far end of the room. However, as she made her vows, her voice broke, and she leaned her head against Tom's shoulder, in a gesture of unmistakable, unselfconscious affection and reliance, causing me to chew my lower lip, in an attempt to stifle an unexpected tear. As for Tom, he visibly relaxed and broke into a relieved grin the moment she reached his side, making it apparent that his pre-wedding nerves had had nothing to do with personal doubts and everything to do with an inability to accept that someone as perfect as Amy actually wanted to marry him.

Following the exchange of vows, Amy's sister read a poem by Elizabeth Barrett Browning and this was, in turn, followed by Tom's father singing *Jerusalem*. He had "performed" at Tom's cousin's wedding, which I had attended as Tom's guest, some years earlier, and, from the moment he stood up, my hands began to sweat, as I braced myself for an excruciating three minutes. It wasn't that he was absolutely dreadful, it was simply that he wasn't anywhere near as good as he thought he was and I just couldn't stand the suspense of wondering whether or not he would quite hit the higher notes, or need to swallow in the middle of the longer ones. The situation wasn't helped by Daniel, who nudged me discreetly at the first dodgy note and then began to shift in his seat and clasp a hand to his mouth, as if deep in thought – an obvious indication that he was desperate to laugh.

In order to distract myself, I decided to scan the gathering for familiar faces and it was only at this point that a curiosity as to the whereabouts of The Rat reasserted itself. I looked, as casually as possible, to my left and right but there was no sign of him. I was pleased to discover that I was now neither perturbed by, nor pre-occupied with, the possibility of seeing him again. Nevertheless, I did decide that as soon as possible after the ceremony, I would attempt to locate him on the table plan – although, by now, it had begun to occur to me that perhaps he had decided not to come after all.

I had just spotted Hairy Jamie, and been rewarded with a cheery wink, when Mr Cline senior finished torturing my nerves to polite applause and we found ourselves free to go. Daniel muttered something to me about "whale song", before we exited into the large entrance hall, to be met by numerous, deeply solemn, waiters, proffering glasses of champagne and hors d'oeuvres.

Andrew was, almost immediately, accosted by a tall, slim red-headed woman who reminded him that they used to work together and he and George fell into conversation with her, leaving Daniel and me, for the first time that day, with only each other to talk to. He made some general comments about the venue and the guests, whilst I tried to focus upon the content of his conversation and not upon the depth of his blue eyes and his rather engaging ability to move his right eyebrow independently of the left.

'Sorry, am I boring you, Ros?' he said suddenly.

'Gosh, no, not at all. What makes you say that?'

'Well, you're staring and nodding as if we're on *Question Time* and that's what you do when you're not really listening.'

'Nonsense. When have I ever done that?'

'You did it earlier today, when Andrew was talking about Hairy Jamie. And,' he pursed his lips as if attempting to hide a smile, 'you did it at George's party when you were talking to Mike and that guy who gave you a tour of the garden. Anyway, shall we go and check-out the seating plan?'

'Er...' I had a feeling that his last comment had thrown up a couple of issues rather more pressing than the seating plan. However, as I wasn't immediately certain what these issues were and, consequently, whether or not now was the time or the place to discuss them, I responded with an uncertain nod and we made our way over to the plan displayed outside the double doors of the long gallery, in which dinner was to be served.

Each of the tables had been named with a pun: Suit Table, Comfort Table, Market Table, and so on. I assumed that I had Amy to thank for the fact that I was sitting at Uns Table.

'So,' he said, 'any bells ringing?'

I stared at the chart, searching for The Rat. There he was – on the opposite side of the room to us – on Account Table.

'Well, I've met Nicholas Ward-Parsons, the best man, a few times. And I know Jamie of course, and yes,' I said, pointing at the plan. 'Kirsten Harrison, she was on Tom's course and I was in halls with her. She's very nice and on our table.'

'Anyone else?'

'I'm sure there must be one or two. I think I spotted at least one of Tom's ex-girlfriends during the ceremony but, if it was her, she's changed her hair colour – she used to be a redhead. I think her name was Julia, or Juliet…' I looked over the plan again. 'There she is; Juliet McGee. She's on the table next to us.'

'So, there's no one else then?' I turned back towards him. He was staring intently at the plan.

'No. There's no one else.'

'Excuse me,' said a voice behind me. I turned to face a small, slim woman of about my own age. She had jet black hair, incredibly pale skin and was sporting startlingly red lipstick, on unnaturally plump lips. I knew immediately that I had seen her before. 'Rosalind? It is Rosalind, isn't it?' She spoke in a soft, American drawl.

'Yes, yes it is,' I said, smiling. 'And I know we've met but I'm afraid I am hopeless with names. Are you a friend of Tom's?'

'No, no, I'm Isabel Herrera. I'm actually here with Amy's cousin.' She smiled broadly. 'You know, I saw you standing here and I thought, my gosh it's a small world. I thought, I must go and say hi and tell her how wonderful she looks but, of course, I knew you wouldn't remember me.' She smiled at Daniel. 'I guess things are really back on track for you now.'

I was suddenly gripped by an icy panic. This woman clearly knew something of my past, whilst I, on the other hand, knew nothing about her and had no idea how much she was about to reveal. I ignored the fact that the next obvious step in the conversation was to determine how she knew me.

'Isabel, this is my friend Daniel McAdam.'

'Daniel, hi,' she beamed, shaking his hand. She turned back to me. 'So, yes, our connection is Martin Gardner. He's my ex.'

It all fell horribly into place. Martin Gardner worked with The Rat. She had been a guest at my almost-wedding. I can't have seen her for more than a few moments as I sat, stunned, at the back of the church but who could forget that pallor and those collagen-enhanced lips? I looked at Daniel and then back at The Mouth and resignedly waited for her to tell him all about the wedding that never was: to provide him, at last, with an explanation for that self-pity which he found so distasteful and to provide final confirmation, if it were needed, of my less than impeccable credentials as girlfriend material.

'Let me get you two a refill,' smiled Daniel, taking our glasses and walking away in search of a waiter.

A wholly unexpected sense of self-preservation kicked in. 'Look, Isabel,' I said, quickly, 'my friend doesn't know anything about what happened on my wedding day and I'd prefer not to go into it with him now. Is that OK?'

She slapped her hands to her cheeks with a look of genuine mortification. 'Oh my God! I am so stupid. Oh my God. Of course you don't want some idiot of a woman dragging up something so distressing when you're enjoying yourself at your friend's wedding. I am so, so sorry, Rosalind. I was just completely overwhelmed by a desire to tell you how beautiful you looked and to say good for you for picking yourself up. I just didn't think it through.'

She actually looked as if she might cry. I squeezed her hand. 'Not at all. And thank you. That's a lovely compliment.'

She leaned towards me. 'And I'm glad the fact that the rat is here,' she gestured towards the table plan, 'didn't keep you away.'

Daniel returned with three flutes of champagne. 'Here you go, ladies.'

'Thank you, Daniel,' said Isabel. 'I was just reminding Rosalind about meeting her at a ball a couple of years ago. Martin and I were at her table. We all got incredibly drunk so it's no surprise that she doesn't recall me. I only recall her because I spent most of the evening coveting her dress.'

'Now, when I first met Ros,' said Daniel, drinking his champagne, and putting his free hand in his pocket, 'it was her clothing which struck me too. Let me think… yes, it was a stained bath robe and an enormous towelling turban.'

'He called unexpectedly,' I explained to Isabel.

'And then the next time I met her,' continued Daniel, 'she was wearing antique jeans, a t-shirt which could have given the millennium dome a run for its money in terms of crowd capacity, and sandals like tea trays.' Isabel laughed and I punched him on the arm. 'And then the *next* time I met her, she was wearing a green shirt, jeans and wellingtons and, despite the unfortunate circumstances,' he turned to look at me, 'she was… captivating – chaotic, mildly intoxicated, but captivating.' He turned to Isabel. 'She didn't know it, of course. That's part of her charm.'

Isabel nudged me and spoke in an undertone. 'He's a keeper.' She put a hand on my arm and addressed us both. 'I'm gonna leave you two to chat. Hey, but let's hook-up later though, Rosalind, eh?'

'Yes, absolutely,' I said, before adding, more loudly, as she moved away. 'Lovely to see you again, Isabel.' I turned back to Daniel. 'Thanks for the compliment – if it was a compliment. I know there's more than one way to captivate an audience.'

'No, it was a compliment,' he said. 'You looked good that night. Miles thought so too.'

'Did he? Well, you can tell him that I thought he looked rather nice the evening after in the wine bar.'

'Really?'

'Hmm… yes, just a shame I wasn't in a better mood.' I smiled, ruefully.

'Well, that was our fault, we should have left you alone.'

'Don't be silly, that would have been odd when we found ourselves in the same bar.'

He looked down and hesitated. 'Yes, but we were only in the same bar because we spotted you from outside and Miles suggested a proper introduction.'

'Oh?'

'Yes,' he said. 'So, it was bad timing and insensitivity on our part.'

'Not at all.' I smiled, graciously, realising that I was very much enjoying this conversation. So far, I had discovered that I was captivating in my wellies and that two rather attractive men had deliberately sought out my company in a wine bar. I decided that it was only fair that I should return the compliment. 'Well, I remember thinking that you looked pretty good without your beard at George's party. And, I mean, even with the beard, in your smart suit, you didn't look bad. Of course, in your *Fisherman's Friend* sweater you looked dreadful but—'

He laughed loudly. 'OK, well, thanks for that, Ros.' He continued to laugh.

'Well, I'm just saying that you look very nice.'

'Yes,' he said. 'In fact, I believe the description "Greek god" has been applied to me in the past.'

I sighed. 'Yes. I suppose you don't really need any reassurance about what women think of you.'

'That's not true,' he smiled. 'As you know, I find some women impossible to read.'

'Do you find me impossible to read?' I asked, impulsively, before immediately regretting the question.

He looked serious for a moment. 'The thing is, Ros,' he said, 'I think you find yourself impossible to read.'

I felt myself reddening, confronted with such an accurate assessment. 'Yes,' I admitted. 'Although, I do think I'm getting better at it, actually.'

'OK. And is the current narrative one you wish to share?' he asked.

My attention was caught by a beaming George, making her way through the throng towards us, closely followed by Andrew. 'Well, it's all a bit tragic. Remind me to tell you later.'

'I shall look forward to being brought low,' he said, following my gaze and turning round. 'Hi, George.'

'Hello, you two!' she cried. She was slightly flushed, a sure indication that she was on her second glass of champagne. 'Have you met anyone interesting yet? We have met a couple of Andrew's ex work chums and, let me tell you,' she slipped her arm through his and looked up at him fondly, 'he is so popular with the ladies.' Andrew shook his head and smiled, in an expression of happy disapproval. 'It's true!' protested George. 'And one of them looked daggers at me, which I took as a huge compliment.' Daniel gave me an amused look. 'But I really liked Annie,' continued George. 'She seemed lovely.'

'She is,' said Andrew. 'Have you bumped into anyone you know, Ros?'

'Not really.' I thought it best not to attempt to perpetuate the Isabel lie. 'Shall we join the queue?' I asked, nodding in the direction of the receiving line, in the middle of which, a red-faced Tom was pumping hands and laughing loudly.

'Good idea,' said Andrew and we headed over towards the line. Within a few minutes, having exchanged innocuous pleasantries with two proud mothers, Mr Cline senior and Amy's step-father, we finally reached the bride herself.

'Hello, Amy,' I said, kissing her cheek, 'you look absolutely beautiful.'

'Thank you, Ros,' she smiled. 'I'm glad you could be with us today.'

I introduced Daniel and left her with him, whilst I moved on to Tom. I gave him a hug. 'You look so happy, Tom,' I said. 'I'm really, really pleased for you.'

'I wasn't sure she'd have me, you know, Ros,' he said quietly.

'I realise that,' I said, hugging him again. 'And I under-stand absolutely why you felt that way.'

He broke into a grin and wagged a finger at me. 'Why, you cheeky—' My eyes widened slightly to warn him against profanity. 'You cheeky monkey,' he said, rubbing the top of my head as if I were a naughty toddler.

I laughed and looked back at Amy, who was now looking in dismay at my dishevelled hair. 'Tom, whatever have you done to Ros's hair? What a thing to do.'

'Oops, sorry,' said Tom, with the faux repentant air of a sixteen-year-old school boy, enjoying every second of being admonished by the teacher he fancies.

'Honestly,' continued Amy. 'Poor Ros.'

I laughed. 'It's OK, Amy. I might have deserved it. I was just agreeing with Tom that he'd done much better for himself than any of us would have ever imagined,' I said, smoothing down my hair. Amy smiled indulgently at Tom and he looked as if he were considering rolling over onto his back to have his tummy tickled. I moved on to the chief bridesmaid, resolving to try to get to know Amy better over the coming year.

After shaking the hand of the best man, I waited for Daniel. 'Have a good chat to Nicholas?' I asked, when he joined me at the entrance to the banqueting hall a few moments later.

'I just told him that I would be recording his speech and asking him for tips later.'

'Do you have a date for Miles's wedding yet?'

'Why?' he asked. 'Are you angling for an invite?'

'Oh no,' I said, feeling a little flustered. 'I didn't mean date. I meant *date*. You know, a calendar date.'

He grinned. 'Well, the answer to dates of every variety is no. I think Lizzie is aiming for September but there's still some debate, I believe. Now,' he looked through the heavy wooden doors, into the gallery – an impressively ornate room, hung with multiple oil paintings of aristocracy and illuminated by three, enormous crystal chandeliers, 'shall we go and meet our fellow unstable guests?'

Chapter 35

I decided very quickly that I liked our table. I was seated next to Kirsten Harrison's fiancé, Peter, a photographer from Seattle. Kirsten was as funny and good-natured as I remembered her from halls and Peter was happy to laugh along as we caught up and reminisced. I occasionally glanced across the room at the empty chair in which The Rat should have been sitting but, after a while, it was clear that he wouldn't be making an appearance and I forgot about him and immersed myself in the immediate company.

Daniel introduced me to the woman on his left, Melissa, and to her husband, Colin, who was Tom's cousin. From the accent, I realised that Colin hailed from Tom's mother's side of the family, many of whom still lived in and around Liverpool. Colin entertained us with tales of Tom's boyhood, focusing primarily upon the latter's numerous hospitalisations – the most worrying of which resulted from his repeated attempts to construct an electric chair.

It was too big a reach to try and talk to George and Andrew, or to Hairy Jamie and his wife, but a bit of early shouting established that Jamie was as hairy as ever and was now, to boot, proud father to Hamish, aged eight months.

In between Colin's childhood anecdotes, and the catch-up conversations with Kirsten, Daniel and I talked of family and work. He asked about Celia and growing-up together and then reciprocated with details of his own, seemingly very happy, childhood, spent first in Teddington and then in rural Wiltshire. As he talked, I compared his past with my own, and had no option but to see my harboured, perhaps nurtured, bitterness regarding The Rat as rather embarrassingly self-indulgent. Daniel had clearly been devastated by the death of his parents but neither he nor Miles had chosen to focus upon the unfairness of it all but instead celebrated the time they had enjoyed together as a family. In comparison to the early loss of one's parents, I couldn't help thinking that I had got off rather lightly; a man I had loved, hadn't loved me back. That was painful, and the public nature of the rejection had been undeniably humiliating, but not, I thought, something for me to be ashamed of, or to continue to be angry about. I looked at Daniel now, as he thanked a waitress for refilling his wine glass, and, as much as I was enjoying his company, felt a small ache of regret which I knew better than to dissect.

'What?' He was looking at me enquiringly.

'What?'

'You were staring at me as if I had suddenly re-grown the beard,' he said.

'Was I?' The sound of a spoon being tapped on a wine glass signalled the beginning of the speeches.

'And the answer is 'yes', by the way.' He picked up his wine glass and studied its contents.

'The answer to what?'

He turned to look at me. 'To whether I find you impossible to read.' He returned his gaze to the glass and lowered his voice to a murmur, as Amy's step-father rose to his feet. 'But it's OK, because I haven't forgotten your promise to provide me with a translation later.'

He smiled mischievously and, despite my best efforts, the internal ache intensified. I took a deep breath and nodded towards the top table. 'God, I do hope Tom doesn't put his foot in it with anyone when it's his turn.'

—

As it turned out, Tom's speech went down very well, consisting, as it did, of just the right amount of flattery, sentimentality and leg-pulling. Nick's speech was similarly successful and I noticed that, when dessert was served, Amy had the look of a highly-contented woman who knows that her big day is going very well indeed. She and Tom cut the four-tiered, "Lilac Brocade" wedding cake (we were advised of its official title, with a slight smirk, by Colin), to a volley of camera flashes which would have sent even a mild epileptic running for the Ray-Bans. Yes, it was all absolutely perfect.

After dinner, the guests dispersed to the numerous reception rooms, to bag a sofa or an armchair and relax for the hour or so before the start of the disco. Andrew and Daniel retired to the bar, with Peter and Kirsten, whilst George and I hurried up to our room to change into the dresses we had brought for the evening festivities. On the way upstairs, I asked George about Jamie and his wife, and whether she had enjoyed the meal. She replied positively but I could tell that she was distracted. I had noticed that she had stuck largely to mineral water after the initial reception drinks and I wondered if maybe she wasn't feeling well.

Once inside our room, I put the kettle on and set about making some tea. George, meanwhile, took the dress she was to change into out of the wardrobe and laid it across the burgundy armchair. She then sat on her bed, staring into space.

'Are you feeling OK, George?' I asked, sitting down next to her. 'I have some paracetamol in my bag.'

She looked at me and smiled. 'No, but thank you, Ros,' she said. 'I am absolutely fine. I am having such a lovely time, you know. I just feel so lucky to have you,' she stood up and started to change, 'and Andrew.'

It struck me immediately that Andrew's name seemed to have been added with a certain amount of self-consciousness, but as George's face was now turned away from me, I couldn't be sure. Furthermore, I knew better than to trust my instincts when it came to personal relationships.

'Well,' I said, 'we feel very lucky to have you too.' I got up and pretended to be fully focused on making the tea but my peripheral vision told me that she had stopped getting dressed and had now turned towards me. 'You are very important to me. And to Andrew too.' I added, as I turned to hand her a cup of tea. 'But you don't need me to tell you that.'

'Thank you, Ros,' she said, taking her first sip.

I retrieved my own dress from the wardrobe – the purple one I had worn to George's party – put it on my bed, picked up my make-up case and went into the bathroom, leaving the door open. Then, completely against character and inclination, I forced myself to remain silent, freshening my make-up, whilst listening to the sounds of George putting down her cup of tea, opening her suitcase and removing some of the contents. Eventually, she came to the bathroom door.

'He's important to me too, Ros,' she said quietly. 'He has been for some time, you know.'

It was the most uplifting news I'd had for months. Perhaps for years. However, not wishing to alarm George by weeping with relief and happiness for Andrew, I continued to examine my reflection in the mirror and finished blending the concealer I had dotted around my eyes. Finally, I zipped up the small, red case and uttered the greatest understatement of my life. 'I'm pleased, George,' I said, as I and turned to face her. 'Obviously not quite as pleased as Andrew would be, should you ever decide tell him, but pleased nevertheless.'

She smiled. 'That's good to know,' she said. 'I just hope he still feels the same way when things have settled down for me, Ros.'

'I don't think you need worry,' I said, walking towards her and giving her a hug. 'I don't have him down as the fickle type. But, come on, let's hurry up and get back downstairs before I say anything which will make Andrew want to kill me.'

—

Fifteen minutes later and we were downstairs, searching for Andrew and Daniel. After checking the bar, we found them back in the room in which we had waited before the ceremony, this time occupying the two sofas in front of the large, bay window. Peter and Kirsten were still with them and they shifted along one sofa to make room for me, whilst George sat, a little self-consciously I thought, next to Andrew and Daniel on the opposite sofa. Andrew noticed her hesitancy too and looked at her, and then questioningly at me. I attempted an uncomprehending smile but must have failed to pull it off because Andrew, immediately suspicious, rolled his eyes despairingly, whilst I guiltily looked away and chewed my lower lip. I caught Daniel's eye and saw that he was, true to form, quietly observing these silent exchanges with some amusement. I smiled at him and then laughed. Andrew and George joined in and Kirsten and Peter smiled, in a bemused, but affable, *when-in-Rome*, kind of way.

At some point during the next hour, we answered the call of the ushers and went to applaud Tom and Amy as they danced the first dance to The Ramone's *Baby I Love You*. George then dragged Andrew onto the dance floor, at which point Daniel asked me if I would like a drink and the two of us left George dancing energetically round Andrew and headed for the bar.

On arrival, we ordered our drinks and went to sit in a quietish corner.

'How are your feet doing?' asked Daniel, gesturing towards my silver shoes.

'Hmm...' I said, leaning forward and inspecting my toes, 'so far, so good but I wish I'd brought my Jesus sandals for the disco.' He smiled. 'So, how are you enjoying the event?' I asked.

'Having a great time,' he said. 'And you?'

'Yes. I wasn't sure if I was going to or not because, well, sometimes weddings can go either way, can't they? But, yes, I am.' I looked at him. He was studying me over the top of his glass. 'The best bit is seeing Tom look so happy.'

'Yes, he does seem to have the air of someone who can't quite believe his luck.' He shifted in his seat. 'I have to say, Ros, whilst I'm a fan of that dress you're wearing, it is unnerving me slightly.'

'It is?'

'Yes, because I can't help recalling the last time we had a drink together and you were wearing it. I didn't exactly cover myself in glory.'

'Shut up. You know perfectly well that you were fine and that I was a disaster. Perhaps, I should have burnt it.' I smoothed the fabric across my lap. 'And, now you mention it, it is an interesting choice on my part. I knew a therapist, Tina, who would have had a field day with it.'

'What do you think she would have said?'

'Probably that I'm trying to lay its demons to rest, telling the world that I'm OK with past mistakes – something like that.'

'And would she be right?'

'Maybe. Or maybe it's just a favourite frock and not at all to blame for what I get up to when I'm wearing it,' I smiled.

'OK, well let's just ignore its past and enjoy its present.' He raised his glass. 'Why don't we finish our drinks and then go and whirl it, and you, round the dance floor? I'm not sure I can compete with Andrew's slick moves but I'm pretty sure I can outdo you in those heels.'

Chapter 36

The disco had been set up in the library, with the DJ situated at the door-end of the room, to the left of an enormous fireplace. In the corner farthest from the DJ, a smaller, second bar was in operation and doing brisk business although, of course, thanks to the generosity of our hosts, no money was changing hands. The Lilac Brocade wedding cake had been relocated and was now on display in front of the long row of French doors which ran the full length of one side of the room. It had, I noticed, been given its very own spotlight.

The library afforded a dance floor of impressive size; however, when Daniel and I arrived, the only people on it were the bride and groom and one or two older couples – the latter attempting to execute jive moves to The Black Eyed Peas. The remainder of the fifty or so people in the room, including George and Andrew, were sitting enjoying drinks, at small tables positioned around the edges of the dance floor.

'Oh dear,' said Daniel. 'Fancy being conspicuous?'

Tom turned round and beckoned to us. I grimaced. 'Oh God and now we've been spotted.'

Daniel took my hand. 'Come on,' he said, 'we can do this.' And he led me onto the dance floor.

We opted for a spot not far from Tom and Amy and, just as I had decided that the shoes would have to come off sooner rather than later, the DJ faded out will.i.am and co and made an announcement. 'And now, ladies and gentlemen,' he boomed, in an accent midway between Los Angeles and Reading, 'it's time for our first request of the evening and this one is for mother-of-the-bride, Linda, from her loving husband, Charles.'

I groaned, whilst smiling and applauding politely, as the unmistakable introductory strains of *Lady in Red* filled the room. I smiled at Daniel and started to head towards a vacant table but he took my hand and gently pulled me back. 'That would be incredibly disrespectful to Linda and Charlie's musical taste,' he said.

I laughed. 'I suppose it would.'

He encircled my waist with his arms. Linda and Charles sashayed past us, smiling approvingly at our evident appreciation of Chris de Burgh.

'So,' said Daniel, after a moment, 'would now be a good time for me to remind you that you have a tale of self-discovery to tell?'

'I guess it might take our minds off the horror of the current situation.' I looked around at the sparsely populated dance floor. 'Do you think he's going to torture us with the whole thing?'

'I fear so.'

I looked across at Amy's mother and step-father, now swaying gently on the spot, her head resting on his chest, whilst, nearby, Amy and Tom danced with the grace of Darcey Bussell and Jay Kay respectively. I smiled and looked up at Daniel. He was smiling too. This, I decided, was the moment. I took a deep breath. 'OK, well, there are two key events in this narrative,' I began. 'The first occurred on the day I was supposed to get married.' I looked up at him for a reaction but he merely raised an eyebrow. 'Did you hear me?'

'Yes, you said that the first key event occurred on the day you were supposed to get married.'

'And you aren't shocked by that?'

'I want to pace my anxiety levels because, knowing you, there'll be much worse to come.'

I smiled again. Increasingly, the flight of The Rat was losing its power to chill and terrify and was instead taking on the appearance of an entertainingly scandalous dinner-party anecdote. 'OK, well,' I continued, 'the second key event was the murder of Mr Edward.'

'Er, I hate to quibble over the facts so early on in your story but I think you'll find that that was actually a case of death by misadventure.'

'Objections will be considered only if submitted in writing,' I said.

'Do you have a pen?'

'Shush. The first—'

'Ros?'

I looked up at him and sighed. 'Yes?'

Daniel shook his head. 'Not guilty of the interruption. I didn't say a word. It was him.' He indicated over my right shoulder.

I stopped dancing and turned round.

'Hello, Ros.'

I stood, unmoving, looking up at him; a bewildering variety of thoughts and emotions clamouring for my attention, each demanding priority.

'Hello, Ros,' he said again, swaying slightly as he spoke. I felt Daniel take my hand and I was aware that Tom was now at my side and talking rapidly.

'Marcus,' I said.

He offered me a lopsided smile and nervously ran a hand through his thick, dark hair. Tom was still talking and now placed a hand on Marcus's arm. Marcus shook him off, staggering a little as he did so. 'Sorry, Tom,' he said, regaining his balance, 'but I need to talk to Ros.'

'Talk to me later,' I said, in a surprisingly calm voice which didn't sound like my own.

He shook his head. 'I need it to be now.'

This time, I saw the derailment coming. I was standing outside those church doors again only, *this time*, I knew that no good thing could possibly be waiting on the other side. For the second time in my life, I thought, it's all about to come crashing down. I shrugged internally and my sense of resignation surprised me.

'I need it to be now,' he repeated, more loudly, in the manner of an angel in the school nativity play who wanted to make sure that the mums at the back could hear. 'I need to tell you, Ros, that I love you very much... very much indeed. And I have never stopped loving you – not for one minute. But I did stop being *in* love with you.' I was vaguely aware that the music had been cut and that conversation around the room was being smothered into silence by a Mexican wave of shushing. We were centre stage, spotlights and all. Marcus cleared his throat, in preparation for his next line. 'But I *am* in love with Al and I should have told you that long ago. I haven't been fair to you, or to Al. I am so very sorry, Ros.' He took a wobbling step towards me, holding out his arms, in an appropriately theatrical gesture of supplication – of friendship and reconciliation. 'Please forgive me, Ros.' He squinted at me uncertainly. 'Can you forgive me?'

That, I mused, was a very interesting question. However, there was a rather more pressing matter to resolve first.

'Al?' I queried.

'Alan. Alan Bullen,' he clarified.

'My goodness.' I shook my head and laughed. 'I really wasn't expecting that.'

I turned to Daniel, who was staring, disbelievingly, at Marcus. 'It's fine, Daniel,' I smiled, squeezing his hand reassuringly, before letting it go.

I looked at Marcus, his arms still extended towards me, the asymmetric smile still balancing precariously on his lips. I almost felt sorry for him; he really hadn't thought this through at all.

I clenched my fist, pulled back my arm as far as it would go and swung with all my might at his jaw.

I heard him yell, and saw him stagger backwards towards the Lilac Brocade wedding cake, but I was already well on my way to the door by the time I heard the subsequent crash and the sound of fifty chairs being pushed back as their occupants rose to their feet. Aside from that, I was aware of nothing, other than gentle applause, courtesy of Isabel Herrera, as I made my sweeping exit.

Chapter 37

I sat, huddled in my coat, and assessed the situation, and my options. Focusing, first of all, on the here and now, the first, immediate and unavoidable truth was that I had ruined the wedding and, more specifically, been instrumental in the destruction of a very expensive cake.

What was it that Tom had said all those months ago about Amy not being able to cope with a broken nail on her wedding day? I also seemed to recall actually having made some sort of specific promise to him about not decking anyone at this event. I groaned. I wouldn't blame Tom if he never spoke to me again. In fact, now that he was married, he might have very little choice in the matter. Well, I could, and would, apologise but, somehow, simply saying 'sorry' when you've ruined the most important day in two people's lives didn't quite seem to cut it. I knew, and they knew, that Rosalind Shaw punching her ex-fiancé in the face would be the only thing anyone would really remember about today. I dabbed at my eyes with the lengthy piece of loo roll which I had brought with me from the ladies for that purpose.

And then there was Daniel. Kind, funny, intelligent, achingly gorgeous Daniel. It had all been going so well. We had had a lovely day together, with me looking well-groomed and behaving in a not-at-all-self-pitying fashion.

We had been slow dancing, in a relaxed, humorous manner, and I was about to enlighten him as to my past history and present feelings, in an equally relaxed and humorous manner and then... And then Marcus had turned up and announced that he was in love with my ex-boss and instead of saying, '*Marcus, my darling, thank you for your, eventual, candour but this day belongs to Tom and Amy. It would be neither appropriate, nor indeed possible, for us to attempt to discuss such a sensitive issue this evening,*' instead of saying *that*, I had punched him. Well, nice one, Ros.

I blew my nose and looked around me. I was sitting a little way from the Hall, on a wooden bench which encircled a large oak tree. I had decided to sit on the far side of the tree, with my back to the Hall, just in case anyone thought to look for me out here. Not that they would. I shivered. It must be below freezing. I pulled my coat around me and my hat further down on my head and wondered what to do next. Going back to the reception was out of the question and I didn't want to go to my room because I suspected that George would now be waiting there for me and I was just too mortified to see her.

If only I'd had my car, I could have driven to a B&B. I thought about asking a member of the Hall staff to call me a taxi, but this would have necessitated attempting to negotiate my way to the front desk without being spotted. In any case, I had failed to collect my purse from the room during my flying visit to fetch my coat and hat. I sighed at my characteristic lack of foresight and planning and decided that I would just have to remain outside for a little longer and hope that George wasn't in the room when I finally went back up.

I tucked my knees up onto the bench, pulled my coat down over them and closed my eyes, trying to achieve some kind of calm.

'On balance, I think you should burn the dress.' I started slightly and looked up to see Daniel standing in front of me, dressed for the season, in his long black coat, black leather gloves and a striped scarf. 'May I join you?' I stared at him in silent, stunned surprise. 'I think I'm just going to interpret that open mouth as a yes,' he said, as he sat down next to me.

'I didn't think anyone would look out here,' I mumbled, as if talking to myself, unable to quite accept his presence as a reality.

'Ah, yes, but, when you think about it, some of our most significant encounters have taken place in gardens haven't they?' He smiled down at me. 'So I thought I'd give it a go.'

We sat in silence for a few moments.

'I didn't punch him because of Alan you know,' I said eventually.

'No?'

'And I didn't even punch him because he climbed out of a church window on the day we were supposed to get married and then refused to tell me why he'd done it.' I blew my nose a second time.

'Really?' Daniel looked at me, his expression serious. 'Because some people might view that as sufficient provocation.'

'No.' My abject misery was temporarily supplanted by a renewed, rising anger. 'It was more the outrageous arrogance of deciding to explain himself, at his own convenience, and without any thought whatsoever as to how that might make me, or anyone else, feel. I was just so…' I struggled to find the right word, 'enraged.'

'I could tell.'

I looked at him and relaxed back into despair. 'I was having such a nice time too.'

'Yes.'

'And the irony of it is that I was just about to tell you all about Marcus. I mean, I wasn't going to tell you about him and Alan, because I didn't know that, but I was going to tell you everything else. I hadn't wanted to tell you before because… oh God, it doesn't matter now anyway.'

'I already knew, Ros,' he said quietly.

'What?'

'I already knew about Marcus and the church window.'

'You did?' I thought for a moment. 'Did George tell you?'

'George? No. Mike told me, soon after you started working with George but, of course, I didn't realise who you were until the night of George's party. Oh and you didn't punch Marcus by the way.'

'I didn't?'

'No. You missed. He was just a bit the worse for wear and fell over when he dodged your fist.'

I inspected my right hand and nodded. It hadn't struck me before that it hadn't actually made contact with Marcus's face. 'Still ruined the cake though,' I sighed.

'No, he fell to one side of it. Took out a table of side plates and a floral display but the cake is intact.'

'Oh.'

'So it's not quite as bad as you think.'

'Still pretty bad, though.' I hugged my knees through my coat.

'Here.' He took off his scarf and wrapped it around my neck.

I looked up at him, tearfully. 'Thank you. You are so nice,' I said. 'That was part of the second half of my narrative, actually. Not that there's any point in telling it now.'

'Oh, I don't know,' he said. 'I think I might enjoy the second half even more than the first – and, God knows, that turned out to be value for money.'

I rested my forehead on my knees and sniffed. 'I do actually think I would feel better for telling you, if you don't mind listening. But you must promise not to feel sorry for me because I will be fine, although I think it would be best if I didn't see too much of you in future and, of course, I never want to meet Charlotte.' He coughed loudly and I looked up. 'Are you OK?'

'Yes,' he said, banging his chest, 'it's just the cold air. Sorry, go on, you mentioned Charlotte,' he coughed again.

'Right,' I put my feet back down on the grass and leaned back on the bench, 'well, when I came to see you after you killed Mr Edward...'

'Yes?'

'Well, even though you had that beard, I wanted to buy new shoes.' I looked at him and shrugged.

'Sorry, is that the entire second half of the story? Because I have to confess that I was hoping it would focus a little more upon how nice I am.'

'Don't you see? *You* made me want to buy shoes. Even with the beard.' I sighed. 'Anyway, it doesn't matter. Suffice to say it's a miserable situation.'

He looked at me blankly. 'So far, all you've told me is that I inspired you into a footwear purchase,' he said. 'I fail to see the miserable aspect of that.'

'The miserable aspect,' I said, addressing, and then beginning to shred, the piece of toilet paper in my hands, 'is that I wish I had recognised how I felt sooner. Not, of course, that lack of timing really has anything to do with it because Charlotte—'

He began to laugh.

'What?' I exclaimed, turning to face him. 'Why are you always laughing at me? Even now, when I'm in the depths of despair, you're finding me entertaining.' I pulled off my hat and threw it to the ground in frustration. 'Well, I don't want to be entertaining. And I don't want to be the eccentric, but harmless, neighbour who's OK for a drink when there's no one else around on a Bank Holiday.'

He bent down and retrieved the hat, before placing it gently on my lap. 'You're determined to lose that, aren't you?'

'Oh shut up.' I slumped back, feeling exhausted, defeated and, I realised, on the verge of renewed tears.

'Well, what do you want, then?'

'What?'

'Well, you've told me what you don't want. Now tell me what you do want.' I looked up at him. He appeared to be genuinely interested as to what my response might be.

I decided to opt for the undisguised truth. 'I want to be wanted,' I said, simply. 'By you. The way you want Charlotte Green.' I looked up at him and managed a philosophical smile and shrug, in spite of the tears now trickling down my cheeks. 'Now, come on, admit it, *that* is pitiable, isn't it?'

He gently wiped away a tear with his gloved hand and lowered his face towards mine. 'Ros,' he said, quietly, after a moment.

'Yes?' I said, a trifle hoarsely.

'Charlotte Green reads the news on *Radio 4*.' He leaned forward and kissed me gently on the lips. 'OK?'

Taken by surprise, I blinked up into the now familiar blue eyes. He was looking down at me with an unreadable expression on his face. I tried to recall exactly how much I had had to drink. Had he just kissed me? Yes, he had. And it hadn't felt like he was just trying to cheer me up. I was pretty sure he wouldn't have kissed Sylvia, or any of his other neighbours, like that if they were having a bit of a down day.

He touched my cheek again. 'Ros?'

'You wouldn't kiss Sylvia like that, would you?' I asked.

'Do you articulate absolutely every thought which enters your head?' He smiled and pushed my hair from my face. 'But no, I wouldn't kiss Sylvia like that. Not unless it was her birthday.'

'And do you—'

'Ros.'

'Yes?'

'Stop talking.'

'OK.' He took my face in his hands and kissed me again. This time, there was no doubt that we were well beyond being neighbourly. I closed my eyes, put my arms around him and kissed him for some considerable time, before eventually releasing him and posing the obvious question.

'So, there's no Charlotte Green in your office?'

'No Greens of any description.' He began to unwind his scarf from my neck.

'So,' I said, valiantly resisting an urge to begin a reciprocal assault on his clothing, 'why did you tell me that you had a newsreader on your team?'

He sighed, let the scarf drop and sat back on the bench, gently pulling me towards him and putting his arm around me. 'Look, I accept that it was an unusual approach but I knew that you'd had a…' he hesitated '…a complicated time and also that we'd suffered occasional… well, let's just call them misunderstandings. Anyway, I wasn't certain how you felt and, although I wanted you to understand my position,' he gently kissed the top of my head, 'I didn't want you to feel pursued.' He shrugged. 'And Charlotte Green was the first name that sprang to mind.'

I looked up at him. 'You didn't want me to feel pursued?'

'No, I didn't.'

'But you *were* pursuing me?'

'Yes, I was,' he said. 'Determinedly.'

'For how long?'

'God,' he ran a hand through his hair, 'I don't know. It seems like bloody years but I would probably date it from the fox-hunting incident.'

I smiled. 'I like the idea of being pursued.'

'You do?' He leaned towards me.

'Yes. But not quite as much as I like being caught.'

'Here, let me help you with that.'

It was some time before I felt the need to speak again.

'Daniel,' I said, resting against his chest, as he enveloped me inside his now unbuttoned coat.

'Yes, Ros?'

'Well, I was just thinking and, you know, if you were wondering about us, you know, perhaps...'

'What?'

'Having sex.' I looked up at him. 'With each other.'

'Er...' his hand went to his mouth in an attitude of exaggerated thoughtfulness.

'You're laughing at me again.'

'No, I'm laughing *near* you, Ros,' he said. 'Now, what's the problem?'

'It's not a problem at all, actually,' I said. 'I was just going to say that if you were wondering about us having sex at some point...'

'Well, the idea might have been lurking somewhere in the deep, dark recesses of my mind but, you know, it was definitely forming an orderly queue behind romancing you with intimate dinners and theatre trips.'

'OK, well, it was just to reassure you that although, obviously, I haven't had sex for absolutely ages, I have no qualms at all about having sex with you. I just didn't want you to think you had to be, you know, subtle, about it or anything.'

'Well, that's good to know,' he said, fingering the buttons of my coat. 'Thank you for being so direct.'

'Not at all,' I said, reaching up and kissing him again, 'it's my new policy.'

Chapter 38

'So, let me get this straight, dear,' said Joan, as I handed her a mug of tea and sat down next to her in the *Chapters*' kitchen the following Monday morning. 'You and Daniel are dancing to the lovely Chris de Burgh, when Marcus arrives and announces that he is a Bertie Both-ways...' she paused and glanced at Andrew, as he walked through from the shop, '...and announces that he is *bi-sexual*.' She emphasised the politically correct term, prompting Andrew to salute her with his mug as he joined us at the table.

'Well, what he actually said was that he was in love with Alan, Joan. He didn't, at that moment, spell out the specifics of his sexuality. We discussed that yesterday.'

'I'm so sorry, my dear, yes you did say that.' Joan reached across the table and patted my hand before continuing. 'So, Marcus expresses his love for Alan and then you, Rosalind, my darling, attempt to strike him down with your fist. Regrettably, you miss. However he, in his inebriated state, loses his balance and smashes lots of crockery, whilst you disappear off into the night, like Cinderella from the ball.'

'Well, yes,' I said, 'that's what happened. Although I'm not sure that that analogy—'

'Good,' continued Joan, 'because I do want to get the details absolutely right for Bobby and the ladies. They do so all want to know how the weekend went.' I rolled my eyes at this, prompting a grin from Andrew. 'And then,' Joan was now staring off into the middle distance, 'a little while later, you say, Prince Charming discovers you under an oak tree and takes you off up to his room for...' she hesitated, 'for a *hot drink*, I think you said, my darling, is that right?'

'Well,' I felt myself colouring, 'yes, because it had been very cold in the garden you see.'

'Hmm...' said Joan, sipping her tea. 'Oh but you haven't told me what happened to Marcus after he fell over, my darling.'

'Well, Andrew is probably the best person to fill you in on that because I wasn't there.' I turned to Andrew.

Andrew sighed and put down his coffee. 'OK, well, several people ran over to help Marcus up, while several *other* people held Tom back, in an attempt to stop him finishing with his feet what Ros had tried to start with her fist.'

'Oh my goodness,' said Joan, 'so the groom wasn't happy with Marcus either.'

'That's putting it mildly,' said Andrew. 'Anyway, a few of us managed to calm him down and his wife told him that if he was any kind of a friend he would be focusing more on how Ros was and less upon, er, "kicking the shit out of Marcus", was how she put it.' Andrew picked up his coffee and looked at me over the top of his mug. 'I actually think that probably makes her a rather nice woman, don't you, Ros?'

'Yes,' I said, meekly, 'I think it probably does.'

'And poor, bi-sexual Marcus?' asked Joan. 'How was he?'

'Well, someone took him off and gave him a strong coffee and then a friend drove him to wherever it was he was staying. He was OK. Tom said he'd been in touch yesterday and, obviously, Ros has spoken to him.'

'And have you spoken to Tom also, Rosalind?' Joan was determined to discover every last detail.

'Yes, I apologised to Tom, and to Amy the next morning, before they went away. And then I apologised to Tom's mum, and to Tom's dad, and to Amy's mother and step-father, and to the staff at the Hall.' I sighed. 'Everyone was very generous about it but it was quite exhaustingly humbling.'

'Oh, you poor dear,' said Joan, squeezing my hand, 'and you must have already been quite tired out by that late-night hot drink.'

Andrew laughed explosively and stood up to take his mug to the sink.

'But you haven't asked Andrew about his weekend yet, Joan,' I said, wickedly. 'Careful, or he'll think Bobby and the am-dram ladies don't care.'

'Oh, there's no need for me to bother Andrew for details, my dear,' said Joan, finishing her tea. 'I had a lovely long telephone conversation with George last night, so I'm fully up to date with all that.' I watched Andrew's features freeze, as Joan stood up and walked towards him. 'Yes,' she said, reaching up and patting his cheek, 'apparently there's more than one Prince Charming in town at the moment. Isn't that right, Andrew, dear? Although,' she added, straightening her skirt and heading into the shop, 'I don't think he quite got round to giving George a hot drink.'

Chapter 39

It was three o'clock on a Saturday afternoon, several months after Tom's wedding, when I let myself into Daniel's house, dropped my coat and bag in the hall and, after receiving no response to several loud 'hellos', went in search of an armchair. I enjoyed five minutes of simply sitting with my eyes closed, before getting to my feet, retrieving my handbag, and going to put the kettle on.

Once in the kitchen, I looked out into the garden, noticing several large, green sacks in the middle of the lawn. So that's where he was. I took an additional mug from the cupboard and was just reaching up towards the teabags when his arms encircled me from behind.

'Good God, Daniel,' I said, turning round, 'how is it possible for anyone to creep round in those things?' I pointed to the heavy black wellingtons he wore for gardening.

'Actually, I was hiding in the cupboard with the ironing board,' he said, 'waiting for you to get home.'

'Really?' I looked at him uncertainly.

'No,' he said, 'not really, because that would be incredibly disturbing behaviour. It always panics me that you believe stuff like that.' He smiled and kissed me. I forgot about the tea for a moment.

'Nice jumper,' I said, eventually, tugging at a loose, grey thread, hanging from the gargantuan Aran.

'Ah well, I know what a favourite it is of yours, so I put it on especially for you coming round.'

'That's not true is it?'

'No it's not,' he said. 'Well done for spotting that.'

'So what's my reward?' I asked, ruffling his hair. 'You know, for being so astute.'

'As it happens, I've got something rather impressive to show you.'

'Fnarr...' I laughed. 'I can't wait.'

He tutted. 'Ros, you have a one-track mind, which,' he added, 'is one of your most attractive qualities. However, on this occasion, I do actually have something impressive to show you which is unrelated to sex.'

'Oh,' I tried not to sound disappointed. 'OK, but shall we have a cup of tea first?' I said, reaching again for the teabags. 'It's been quite a day so far.'

'Excellent idea,' he said, sitting at the breakfast table and taking off his boots. 'And, er,' he looked up at me, 'do you want to tell me about your day so far? Or was the conversation one you'd rather keep to yourself?'

I placed two mugs of tea on the table and sat down on his lap. 'Unfortunately for you,' I said, kissing his forehead, 'I want to tell you *all* about it.'

He sighed but I knew that he was pleased. 'OK, fire away. Only,' he twisted in his chair, 'can you get off my knee because you are crushing my dibble.'

'Oo-er.'

'A dibble is actually a gardening implement used for making holes, Ros,' he said sternly, shaking his head.

'I know, but you haven't got one in your pocket and you were deliberately being smutty.'

'God, you *are* very astute, all of a sudden' he said, taking his car keys from his pocket and placing them on the table. 'Twice in under a minute. Now, how was he?'

'Well, better than during the phone calls, thank God. But still, you know, it wasn't the most relaxed lunch I've ever had.'

'I can imagine.'

'He started off by apologising, *again*, for his lack of timing, and sense of occasion, at Tom's wedding and so then I felt that I had to say sorry, *again*, for trying to break his face.'

'Well done.'

'And then...'

'And then?'

'Well, he just repeated what he'd told me over the phone, really. About how much he adored me – still – but that, you know, he's in love with Alan.'

'And you had never once suspected Alan of being gay?'

'Well no. After all, he was married *and*,' I added, as he raised a sceptical eyebrow, 'before you say anything, it's not just a case of me being obtuse – no one at work knew.' I paused. 'Oh, but it turns out that his wife has known for years – living a lie, and all that.'

'Are they still married?'

'Not anymore. The divorce came through two weeks ago. Mind you,' I said, reaching for my bag and taking out a cream-coloured envelope, 'Alan's not going to be single for long. He and Marcus are entering into a civil partnership in July and we're invited.' I handed him the invitation, which he removed from the envelope and perused.

'Well, I'd be delighted to accompany you, if you want to go.'

'I'll need to give it some thought but I probably should really.'

He placed the invitation on the table and put his hand on mine. 'Are you OK?' he asked. 'It can't have been easy.'

'I think it was an awful lot easier for me than for him.' I smiled sadly and picked up my tea. 'You know, I sat there listening to him and could hardly believe that I had been going to marry the man. He… well, all of it, really, seemed so unconnected with me. I found what he told me about gradually coming to terms with his sexuality and his feelings towards Alan interesting – moving even – but only in the same way as I would a well-written magazine article. I didn't feel as if any of the drama really had anything to do with me personally.' I sighed and drank my tea. 'But really, he just wanted forgiveness for legging it without explanation and I gave him that. In fact, I told him that I was grateful to him for opting out that day.' I looked at Daniel. 'Imagine if he hadn't.'

Daniel smiled at me and gently stroked my cheek. 'I bet the pair of you would have had lovely soft furnishings.'

I snatched up the invitation and hit him over the head with it. 'Shut up.'

He laughed. 'OK.'

'So, anyway, where's this impressive thing then?'

'Outside. You'll need your coat.'

—

A few minutes later, we were walking across the lawn towards the end of the garden. Just before we reached the final section, he stopped and turned to me. 'Close your eyes,' he said.

'What?'

'You need to close your eyes. No, actually,' he said, unwinding my scarf, 'I don't trust you. Here, let me blind-fold you.'

'What? This better be very impressive.'

He led me on a little further, until we reached, I guessed, the very end of the garden.

'OK,' he said, untying the scarf, 'you can look now.' He turned me round to face the hedge, which now had a step ladder positioned next to it.

'It's a ladder,' I said.

'It's a short-cut,' he corrected.

'Ah… it's not a ladder, it's a short-cut,' I said. 'And I love it.'

'I knew you would. Want to try it?'

'Naturally.' I climbed to the top of the ladder and peered over into my garden. 'There's another one the other side,' I said.

'I know,' he smiled. 'It's genius, isn't it? A complete solution to the "how on earth do I get over the hedge?" conundrum. So, anyway, continuing over, or coming back down?'

'Both.' I reached over the hedge and rested a hand on the top of the second ladder. 'Ooh, it's a bit wobbly, you know.'

'It'll be fine,' he said, 'I've put some bricks around the bottom of the ladder to steady it.'

'OK, then.' I carefully straddled the hedge, lifting first one leg over, and then the other, and climbing slowly down. 'The bricks are very effective,' I said, before missing the last step and tumbling into the undergrowth.

'Are you OK?' I looked up to see him grinning down at me from the other side of the hedge.

'You're laughing at me,' I said, getting to my feet and climbing back up the ladder.

'Yes, I am,' he smiled. 'But, you know,' he added, more seriously, as I reached the top of the ladder and stood eye to eye with him, 'you are always at your most gorgeous when emerging, dishevelled, from a hedge, Ros.' He extended a hand, pulled me towards him and kissed me in a way which suddenly made me want to be indoors. 'Come on,' he said, eventually, climbing down and helping me back over the hedge.

He took my hand as I stepped down into his garden and we began to make our way back towards the house. We had reached the site of the proposed summerhouse when he stopped abruptly and turned around. 'Actually, Ros,' he said, nodding towards the step ladder and then redirecting his gaze towards me, 'proud as I am of the short-cut, I'm not certain, that it's really ideal,' he said.

'No?'

'I mean, I can't deny that it's great for making you look dishevelled.' He removed a leaf from my hair. 'But what about those occasions when you need to pop round and you're wearing your spike heels and the dress of doom?'

I studied the hedge. 'Well, how about we put a pair of wellies on either side of the hedge and a little satchel for me to put my shoes into?'

'That's not a bad idea,' he said. 'But it doesn't solve the tight dress/short skirt issue – or the problem of wet wellies when it rains.'

'I guess not,' I sighed. 'And, of course, there may be times when I ask you to come round in an emergency and you've just stepped out of the shower and have nothing to wear but a small, white towel and, well, things might, you know, snag a bit.'

He raised an eyebrow. 'A small, white towel?'

I closed my eyes, forming a mental image. 'Very small. Barely a towel at all, really.'

He put his arms around me. 'What if...' he said, 'what if, Ros, you just stayed over this side of the hedge. Mightn't that be a solution to the heels, and the skirt, and the snagging hazard'

I looked at him in surprise. 'What? You mean, live over this side of the hedge?'

'Yes.'

'Your side of the hedge?'

'Yes.'

'With you? All the time?'

'For God's sake, yes, Ros,' he said, running an exasperated hand through his hair. 'With me. All the time. It's no more difficult a concept to grasp than two step ladders, is it?' He suddenly looked concerned and, when he spoke again, his tone was serious. 'Unless that's not something you want?'

I counted to three in my head. 'Of course it is,' I smiled. 'I just wanted to prolong the moment.'

He tutted before returning my smile with one which prompted me to throw my arms around his neck and bury my head in the Aran.

'Ah, but,' he said, after a moment, gently prizing my arms from around his neck and frowning down at me. 'There is, of course, one condition.'

'And that is?'

'I would need you to agree to falling into the hedge every now and then, you know, as a form of foreplay. I couldn't do without that, entirely.'

'Hmm...' I thought for a moment. 'Well, I guess I could agree to that, provided, of course, that you agree to gardening shirtless from May to September.'

'Sounds fair,' he said, putting an arm around me and kissing the top of my head. 'Now, come on inside. I've got something rather impressive to show you.'